ASSUMPTION

The Underground Kings Series

Kenton

Aurora Rose Reynolds

Copyright © 2014 Crystal Aurora Rose Reynolds
Print Edition

Edited by Hot Tree edits Mickey edits, Midian Sosa

Book Cover by Mellissa Gill Designs

Formatted by BB eBooks

All rights reserved. No part of this book may be reproduced or transmitted in any form or by any means, electronic or mechanical, including photocopying, recording, or by any information storage and retrieval system, without permission in writing.

This is a work of fiction. Names, characters, places and incidents are the product of the author's imagination or are used factiously, and any resemblance to any actual persons or living or dead, events or locals are entirely coincidental.

The author acknowledges the trademark status and trademark owners of various products referenced in this work of fiction, which have been used without permission. The publication/ Use of these trademarks is not authorized, associated with, or sponsored by the trademark owner.

All rights reserved.

Table of Contents

Prologue — 1
Chapter 1 Leaving On A Jet Plane — 3
Chapter 2 Word Vomit — 20
Chapter 3 One Tequila, Two Tequila…Floor — 41
Chapter 4 Not My Ass! — 64
Chapter 5 Done, I'll Give Her Crazy — 73
Chapter 6 Annoying Roomies And Bad Guys — 94
Chapter 7 A Whole Lotta Like… — 118
Chapter 8 It's Not Past Tense — 135
Chapter 9 Shit Hits The Fan — 157
Chapter 10 The Slaughterhouse — 169
Chapter 11 Future, Meet Past — 185
Epilogue — 201
Obligation Sneak Peek — 211
Other books by this Author — 212
Acknowledgements — 213
About the Author — 215
All American Root Beer Recipe — 216

Dedication

To the man who showed me what love really is.
I love you, babe.

Prologue

I SEE YOU judging me. I know what you're thinking. She has to be a slut; she works at a strip club and takes off her clothes for money. Yes! I work at a strip club, and you may think I'm a whore for showing off my body, but this is a talent that has been forced down my throat since I was a young child. Look pretty and smile. I put on a show for those who choose to watch. However long I'm on stage, I'm not even me. It's what I imagine an out-of-body experience would be like—a performance, nothing more, nothing less. The people watching make assumptions about who they think I am or cook up a story in their heads of who they want me to be. I'm just another beautiful face.

Beautiful. I hate that fucking word. Who gives a crap if someone is attractive on the outside if they are dying inside? My whole life has been about what I look like. I swear, the only reason my mother kept me was to have a real-life, living, breathing doll she could dress up and control, which is the exact reason why I got as far away from her special brand of crazy as I could as soon as I became eighteen. That's also why I don't date. The first thing guys do is look at me and see a pretty face, a nice body, and an empty space where my brain's supposed to be. They have no interest in getting to know the person I am on the inside. They don't care that I volunteer my spare time, and they couldn't care less that I'm going to school to be an RN. They don't ask about my hopes, my dreams, or about where I see my life in twenty years. They don't care about me at all.

They just want someone pretty to follow them around and tell them how handsome they are, how special they are, while agreeing with everything they say. Fuck that! I did that for too many years. That's why I live inside books. At least there I can choose where I want to be—from the highlands of Scotland to a king's bed in a faraway land—and even if it's pretend, sometimes that's a lot better than reality.

Chapter 1
Leaving On A Jet Plane

I LOOK OUT the plane window, my finger going to the glass, feeling the cold on my fingertips as I look down at the land moving quickly below me. It's funny how, from up here, everything looks so small. I've never traveled in a plane before today. The idea of being trapped inside a tin can while flying at six hundred miles per hour never appealed to me. I take a breath and look at the TV monitor that's in the seat in front of me. The small, animated plane on the screen shows that we're over halfway to Tennessee.

"Are you traveling for business or pleasure?"

I turn my head and look at the guy sitting next to me. He's slightly overweight and balding, but he also has wrinkles around his eyes, giving him the appearance of someone who smiles often.

I debate with myself on whether or not to answer before replying, "Business."

His eyes drop to my mouth then to my chest as I fight the urge to punch him in the throat. I hate when men go from nice to creepy. I shake my head, turning away from him. I don't know why I even try.

I feel a hand on my bare leg and my head swings around quickly. "Touch me again and I will rip off your balls and feed them to you," I tell him in a soft tone, trying not to bring attention to us.

He quickly removes his hand, swallowing hard. "I…I'm sorry."

I shake my head before turning my body away from his. I feel tears stinging my nose, but I fight them back. No way am I going to cry now—not when, just six hours ago, my whole world exploded and I didn't shed one single tear. I lay my forehead to the glass, closing my eyes. I still can't believe how fast my life changed...

I GOT UP yesterday morning and went to the hospital like I always do. I work at one of the busiest ERs in Vegas. I've been working there since I finished school and was required to get my clinical hours for my RN. As soon as I walked into the building, I was loaded down with work. Weekends are always crazy in Sin City, but yesterday seemed worse than normal—two drug overdoses, three stomach pumps, and one gunshot victim. Later, I left the hospital exhausted, only to head to my real job—well, the one that pays me the money I need to live.

"Hey, Angel."

"Hey, Sid." I gave him a half smile as I walked into The Lion's Den, the gentlemen's club I work at.

Do I like working at a strip club? No. Does it pay my bills? Yes. The second I walk in the door at the club, I'm no longer me. My brain shuts off and my body takes over, the same way it used to when I was growing up and my mom forced me into pageants. I'm accustomed to being on display and used for my appearance. I wish life were different, but it is what it is.

Some people complain about being overweight or having acne; I hate being beautiful. I know it sounds stupid. I mean, why would anyone complain about being attractive, right? Here's why: Men see me as an object and women see me as competition. No one is ever willing to give me a chance. They all judge me by what's on the outside, never taking a second to find out even the smallest detail about who I am.

I know I'm a walking cliché. I hate being beautiful, yet I work in a business where I put myself front and center to be viewed and judged.

The difference? For the first time in my life, when I get on stage, it's my choice; no one is forcing me to do it. I get up there to earn the money so I can change my life in order to never be objectified again.

"Tired?" Sid questioned, following me. I have worked for Sid for the last three years. He is a friend of sorts; he's also my boss.

"Yeah. I can't wait until my clinical hours are over and I can start working at the hospital full time instead of having two jobs."

"I don't like that I won't see your face all the time, but I know you need to move on," he conceded.

"Some other girl will come in and you will forget all about me."

"Never, Angel." His eyes moved over my face and he shook his head. "You're working VIP tonight." He followed me down the hall towards the dressing rooms.

"Sure," I agreed, already exhausted. I needed a shower and a bed, but I knew I was going to be there for at least eight hours, so I might as well suck it up.

"The guys coming in are important, so you need to make sure they're happy the whole time they're here."

"I have done this before," I reminded him, stopping outside the dressing room door to frown at him.

"Normally, I wouldn't say anything—you know that. But I gotta go get on a plane, so I won't be here to check on them."

"I'll make sure they're taken care of," I assured him.

"Thanks, Angel." He kissed my forehead like he often did before walking away.

I watched him go for a second before pulling myself together.

"Oh! Look who's here," Tessa said as soon as I entered the dressing room.

I ignored her and tossed my bag into my locker before pulling my scrubs off. Tessa was a bitch; she was just like the girls I used to compete against in pageants. To her, life was a competition, and she was determined to come out the winner, even if she had to throw everyone else under the bus on her way to the top.

"Mick said I could work VIP tonight," she said to one of the other girls in the room.

I ignored her again, knowing better than to tell her that it wasn't happening. I was sure Mick had told her that...after she'd taken him in the backroom and given him something to convince him.

"Pixie said the guys coming in are some big-time land developers, so you know the tips are going to be outrageous. Thank God, because I need to have my tits redone, and that shit is not cheap."

I rolled my eyes and headed for the shower room. I had met a couple of nice girls during my time here, but most were just like Tessa—a whole lot of hair, tits, ass, and not much else.

I stood in front of the mirror and put on a coat of red lipstick before standing back, looking myself over. The VIP dress code was different than the rest of the club. The required outfit consisted of a sheer, black overlay bra, black silk panties, a black garter belt with sheer hose, and black heels. My long, naturally red hair was pulled back on one side by a large flower; the rest was loose and wavy, flowing down my back and over one shoulder. My creamy, white skin, red lips, and smoky eyes made me look almost like a sexy vamp.

"You ready, Angel?" Sid asked, pounding on the door.

"Showtime," I whispered before opening the door.

"You look beautiful. I'm going to take you in there and introduce you before heading out."

"Sure." I followed him down the hall to the club.

The Lion's Den is well known in the area for its exclusivity. The walls are painted a dark brown, and the booths are designed into the walls, making the space feel intimate. The stage is in the center of the room, with a single spotlight shining down on it. Every booth has a girl assigned to it, and VIP has two girls. We aren't allowed to interact with the customers without being asked directly to do so.

The club is less of a strip club and more of a place for men to hang out and drink while having beautiful women tend to them. If they choose to, they can watch the girl in the center of the room put on a show. I have been on stage several times in the three years I've worked here. I haven't told Sid that I don't like it up there, but he normally put me in VIP or assigned me to a booth for the night.

"Why are you so worried about these guys?" I asked Sid.

"They're thinking about opening up a Lion's Den in one of the new casinos they're building."

"That's huge! Congrats, honey." I squeezed his bicep and gave him a smile.

"One day, Angel, I'm gonna take you away from this place. I wanna see that smile every day."

My heart did a little thud. Sid is a very attractive man, but he's not for me. I don't want or need a man. They get you all discombobulated, filling your head with a bunch of lies and then expecting you to follow them around. I did that once. I thought a man was going to save me from the hell I was living in. I gave him my virginity and my heart, and he gave me a child I wasn't allowed to keep and a heart so broken that nothing or no one has put it back together again.

I looked through the two-way mirror at the men around the table in the VIP room.

"All right," Sid said from beside me. "The man in the center at the table is John Barbato. He is the owner of three of the largest clubs in the city. The guy there on his left is Steven Creo. He's some bigwig on Wall Street and has backed more than half the new clubs and casinos opening on The Strip. The guy to the right of John has a location they're interested in purchasing."

"Got it. Who's working with me?" I asked him.

"Tessa. Mick said she would be the best out of the girls we've got on the schedule tonight."

"I'm sure he did," I mumbled, looking back into the room. "What other bouncers are on tonight?" I hated when Mick and Craig worked together. They were both more concerned about hooking up with the girls than what was going on out on the floor.

"Link's here now."

"Good." Link was a good guy and a close friend. He also took his job seriously.

"All right, let me introduce you quickly before I head out."

"Sure." I followed him into the room. The men's heads turned in our direction, and they were smiling.

"Guys, I want you to meet Angel. She's gonna be your girl for the night. You need anything, you ask her and she will make sure you're taken care of," Sid tells them, gesturing to me.

"Nice to meet you," one of the men said, smiling while the others nodded.

"Nice to meet you too." I smiled back.

"Angel will be right back. Give me a minute, guys."

"Sounds good," the one who'd spoken before said.

As Sid and I stepped away, I heard from behind me, "Do you think the curtains match the drapes?" and they all laughed. I hated that saying, and I'd sworn that, once I was free of this lifestyle, I would kick the next man who said it in the nuts.

"Okay, I gotta head out. I won't be back for two weeks," Sid said once we were standing in the hall.

"Have a safe trip."

His eyes searched my face. His mouth opened and closed like he was going to say something, but instead, he shook his head, kissed my cheek, and walked off down the hall, muttering something under his breath.

Tessa came around the corner a couple of seconds later with a smug smile on her face. I hated to admit it, but she was beautiful. Her skin had a natural glow that made her look healthy and youthful. Her hair was black and thick, reaching the top of her ass. Her eyes curved out at the corners, showing off her Asian-American heritage.

"You ready?" she asked, looking at me from head to toe.

I avoided rolling my eyes at her before stepping into the room behind her.

After we took the first orders, we stood back while the men talked. I learned a long time ago to zone myself out. We were there as eye candy and nothing else. There was a knock on the door, and I knew the drinks had arrived. Tessa answered it, opening the door wide, and the man who brought the tray in was someone I had never seen before. He looked to be mid-thirties, and he had long, shaggy, black hair and brown eyes.

When he set the tray down on the table in the corner, he turned and did something odd that had me watching him more closely. His hand went to his back as he looked over at the men, who were still busy talking. When his eyes came to me, he smiled before walking out of the room. I looked at Tessa to see if she had noticed anything strange, but she was busy handing out the drinks and flirting with the men at the table.

We stood to the side again once the men had their drinks. Every once in a while, they would ask me a question about the club, and I told them what I knew. About thirty minutes after they had their first drinks, I called and had more ordered. This time, when the guy came in, he did the same thing—hand at his back, looking at the table. I had no idea who he was, but I planned to find out as soon as the men left.

One of the men received a phone call and stepped out of the room, and when he returned, he had another man with him. They all sat down. This time when they called me over, they wanted a bottle of Chivas Regal Royal Salute Scotch. One glass of the stuff cost close to six hundred dollars, making it over ten thousand dollars for a bottle. I placed the order and waited for it to be delivered.

When the knock sounded on the door, I opened it up, and the same man from earlier came in and set the tray down. I watched to see if he would do the same thing he had done the previous times. Sure enough, his head turned towards the table and his hand lifted behind his back, but this time, he lifted his jacket, pulling out something black.

It took a second for me to realize what it was, and by that time, it was too late. He let off four rounds in rapid succession then turned and fired another round, hitting Tessa. I screamed as he turned the gun on me, and before I could think, I ducked down and ran as fast as I could out of the room. I felt a bullet whiz past me as I turned the corner and another as I entered the main part of the club.

I spotted Mick. Right away, his eyes got wide, and I yelled at the top of my lungs, "HE HAS A GUN!"

Everyone started screaming and running in every direction. I ran into a solid wall, and when I looked up to see that it was Link, he wrapped an arm around my waist, turned, and pushed me behind the bar. I stumbled in my heels, falling to my knees and hitting the ground hard. I crawled under the counter and curled myself into a ball, shaking out of fear for my life. I listened as people screamed but didn't hear any more gunshots. I don't know how long I stayed like that, but it felt like forever until I heard police sirens.

"Autumn," Link called, using my real name, snapping me out of my terrified huddle.

I peeked out from behind my hands as he crouched down in front of me. "Did you get him?"

He shook his head, putting out his hand for me to take. I shook my head no. I was safe; I didn't want to move from that spot.

"Come on, Angel. He's gone."

I shook my head again.

"Nothing is going to happen to you. I promise you're safe."

I swallowed against the lump in my throat, squeezing my eyes closed. "Tessa?" I asked him. His eyes closed and his head dropped forward. "No," I whispered, shaking my head. "No."

"Sorry, Angel," he said quietly.

"Why?"

"Not sure, but the cops are here. I need you to come out of there so you can talk to them," he told me gently, holding out his hand again.

I nodded, reluctantly taking it. Even though I didn't like Tessa, she didn't deserve what had happened to her. None of the people in the room deserved what had happened to them.

"I should have tried to help her."

"Nothing you could have done," Link said, and my eyes went from to the floor to his. He shook his head, wrapped his beefy arm around my shoulders, and walked me over to a barstool.

I sat there until the cops came up a few minutes later and told me that they needed to talk to me at the station.

"Can she get some clothes on?" Link, who had given me the shirt off his back and hadn't left my side, asked one of the detectives.

"Sure," the guy mumbled.

I slid off the barstool and dazedly walked to the dressing room. When I walked in, all the girls were there huddled together and crying. I didn't know what to say to them; most of them had been friends with Tessa. I felt horrible that they had lost their friend, but I was unsure if they would want me to express my condolences.

I walked to my locker and started to pull off my stockings when one of the girls came up to me, wrapping her arms around me. Shocked, I hugged her back, and more of the girls gathered around me. We all stood there silently for a few minutes. Most of the girls were crying while a couple mumbled about how everything would be okay. I wasn't sure anything would ever be okay again; I'd just watched five people die and was lucky to still be alive.

"I have to go with the police," I told the girls when it didn't seem like they were going to let me go.

After a second, they all started breaking away from me one by one, giving me reassuring hugs. "Call me if you want to talk," one of the girls, Elsa, said, handing me a business card with her personal information on it.

I looked at it for a long second before nodding. I had never really been friends with any of them. Maybe that needed to change.

I went to my locker, pulling off my clothes before slipping on a pair of jean shorts, a black tank top, an oversized, grey sweater, and a pair of black flip-flops. I grabbed my bag, shoved everything from my locker into it, and left the room without a backwards glance.

Link was waiting for me outside the dressing room door, his back against the wall, his head tilted back, looking at the ceiling. I've known Link since I started working at The Lion's Den. He's a nice guy, with blond hair cut low to his head, tan skin, blue eyes, and a Southern drawl that made women fall to their knees. He used to flirt with me when I first started, but when I didn't return any of the banter, he laid off and became a friend. He is one of the only people who knows about my past and the things I've gone through.

"You didn't have to wait for me," I told him, pulling my bag across my body.

"I'm not letting you go through this alone." He pulled me into his side.

I could feel tears stinging my eyes, and I fought them back. I wasn't going to cry until this was all over, when I could do it alone while hiding under my covers with my face stuffed into a pillow...like I always did.

"Thank you."

He gave me a squeeze, and I felt his lips at the top of my head.

"I DON'T UNDERSTAND WHY I have to leave the state," I told Link, putting another pair of shoes in my bag. I had no idea how long I would be gone, and Link had made it sound like I wouldn't be able to come back to Vegas for a long while.

"I hate to remind you, but you're the only witness, and from what the cops said, the guy is a killer paid by the Mob to do hits on people."

I sighed, looking around my house. I hated that I was leaving, but I knew it was for the best. I'd been at the police station for over eight hours, going over what had happened. Then I'd sat with a sketch artist. Somehow, the guy who had shot Tessa and those men had avoided every camera in the club. The cops had informed me that I needed to be extra cautious. I was the only witness, and they were concerned that he would come after me.

When Link had found out what they'd said, he'd made a call to one of his friends from back home in Tennessee and asked if he would be willing to let me stay with him until the police caught the guy. The man, Kenton, had agreed, telling Link that I would be safe. I hated that I was leaving my home, but if my only options were either death or moving, the choice was begrudgingly clear.

"I hope they get the guy fast," I mumbled.

"Me too, but until then, you will be far away from here and safe."

"Are you sure it's a good idea to have me stay with this guy? I mean, how well do you really know him?"

"We were best friends growing up. He's a good guy. You'll be safe with him."

I bit the inside of my cheek and nodded before going into the closet to get another suitcase. Might as well pack enough stuff to last me. Once I was all packed and ready to go, we got into Link's SUV and headed for the airport. I was nervous the whole way, feeling like something crazy was about to happen…

"LADIES AND GENTLEMEN, we're about twenty minutes out from our arrival destination. The weather in Nashville is mostly clear and sunny. The temperature is eighty-five degrees. The pilot has now turned on the fasten seatbelt sign. Flight crew, please prepare for landing," I hear through my sleep-ridden state and lift my head from the wall where I was resting it.

The memories of what happened yesterday leave my head as I wipe my mouth with the sleeve of my sweater before looking around to see that everyone is putting their belongings away. I make sure my seatbelt is secure before sitting back. My leg starts quickly bouncing up and down, and I rub the tattoo behind my ear, trying to think about something other than the plane landing.

Once we are on the ground, I wait until everyone is off the plane to make my way out into the terminal. I go to baggage claim and look around, but I have no clue what this guy looks like. All I know is that his name is Kenton and he is supposed to be picking me up.

I don't see anyone who looks like they're searching for someone, so I go to the conveyer belt and spot one of my bags as soon as I get there. I pull it off, stumbling back slightly from the weight as every guy here just watches me without offering to help.

I look around again, wondering if I'm supposed to call someone to tell them that I landed. I pull my phone out, click it off airplane mode, and send a text to Link, letting him know that I have arrived. He sends me a message back, letting me know that Kenton called and told him that he couldn't make it to pick me up and I should just catch a cab to his house. The door would be unlocked, and the address is in the message.

I shake my head, cursing under my breath, and almost miss one of my other bags going around the belt. Luckily, I catch it at the last second. I carry it over to my other bag and turn around just in time to see my last bag about to go through the tunnel. I run as fast as I can in my flip-flops and land halfway on the conveyor belt. My bottom half is being dragged along the floor as I grab the handle of my bag, pulling it back so hard that it flies over me, causing me to land on my back with my hands over my head.

"You must be Autumn," I hear rumbled from above me.

I tilt my head back and look up at the man standing over me. He's upside down, but even from my awkward position, I can tell that he is good-looking. His chuckle makes me grit my teeth. I stand up, putting my bag on its wheels and dusting off my butt before turning back to face him.

"You are?"

He raises a brow at me, shaking his head, looking me over from head to toe. My body heats immediately under his gaze. I take my sweater off, wrapping it around my waist and clearing my throat.

"You are?" I ask him again, getting annoyed that he's obviously finding this so funny, if the smirk on his face is anything to go by.

"Kenton." He smiles. "Those bags yours?" He nods towards my other two bags.

"Yes." I blow some hair out of my face, looking into his amber eyes and wondering why the hell I feel so hot all of a sudden.

He looks away, going over to my bags while I take the time to look him over. He's tall, much taller than my five six. His hair touches the edge of the black T-shirt he has on. He needed a cut a while ago, but judging by the dark scruff along his jaw, I can tell that he doesn't care much about grooming. His shoulders are broad, tapering down to a lean waist. His thighs are thick, encased in a pair of dark jeans that have shredded around the seams, and his wallet is imprinted in the back pocket like he wears them often.

I look at his ass as he leans over. I can't believe I'm checking a man out; I'm not one to be the slightest bit sexually interested in anyone. My eyes travel lower, looking at his feet, which are encased in a very large pair of black boots. I wonder absently if what they say about shoe size is true. I shake my head at my thoughts, dragging my bag with me towards him.

"I thought you couldn't make it," I tell him when I reach his side. My head tilts back to look up into his eyes.

"Yeah, change of plans," he mutters, looking at me.

I wait to see if he's going to say anything else. Apparently, he isn't going to, so I shake my head again and lower my face towards the ground.

"You tired?" His voice is dark and rich, and it does something crazy to my insides. I nod, lifting my head. "Let's roll. You can sleep when we reach the house."

I don't say anything else. Something is wrong with me. *Maybe I'm getting sick,* I think, putting my palm to my forehead. When I don't feel anything, I start to follow him out of the terminal to the car park.

When we reach the parking lot, he stops and pulls a set of keys from his pocket. I hear the beep and look around, expecting him to be driving a large truck, a Hummer, or maybe even a tank. I never expected him to be driving a Dodge Viper. The black-on-black of the car only makes it look hotter. I look at my bags, wondering how we will get them in the car.

"It'll be tight, but they'll fit," he mumbles, pulling my other two bags with him.

I can't help but notice the flex of his muscles as he gets my bags into the car or the fact even his fingers are attractive. It takes some maneuvering, but he does get my bags to fit. I sigh, sitting down on the warm leather once we're done.

"I'm just gonna drop you off at the house. I gotta head out for a bit, but you have free rein. Just make yourself at home. There's food in the fridge and fresh sheets on the bed in the guest room."

"Thank you for doing this," I tell him, looking at his profile. He is seriously good-looking, and the butterflies in my stomach are making me feel anxious about staying with him.

"Don't mention it. So…you and Link?"

It takes a second to decipher his words between the thickness of his accent, his smell, and the nervous energy I'm feeling. Being in his presence, my brain seems to have shut down.

"He's a friend." Shit, maybe I should have said that he was my boyfriend.

I look over at him again; he doesn't seem to be as on edge as I am. He's probably used to women swooning over him. My gut tightens with something, and it takes a second to realize what it is. My body freezes. Jealousy? Really? I must be going into shock or something. I don't get jealous.

"How'd you two meet?"

"We work at the same club," I murmur, squirming in my seat.

"Oh yeah," he mumbles, his knuckles turning white from his grip on the steering wheel. I don't know what that means, but the energy in the car changes, making me want to get away from him.

We drive in silence for the next half hour, the car winding its way through one small town after another until we go up what seems like the side of a mountain. The area is surrounded by forest on either side of the road. We drive for five more minutes before turning onto a dirt road that takes us deeper into the forest. I want to ask if he lives out here and about where he works—and a million other questions—but my mouth has gone dry and the energy in his car hasn't gotten any better, so I decide to keep my mouth shut.

I'm going to be stuck with him for a while, so I figure there will be time for all of that later. I look ahead of us and squint as the image of a large house comes into view. It is a very large brick house. The front has two porches—one on the first floor, one on the second—and both wrap around the front of the house. It's beautiful and expansive.

I look over at Kenton again, gauging if I should ask him if this is his house. His jaw is ticking, and the vein in his neck is pulsing wildly. I have no idea what's set him off, but I figure my best bet is to sit there quietly until he calms down.

We park in front of the house, where there is no real designated parking place. He unfolds himself out of the car without saying anything, and I take it as my cue to follow him. By the time I make it to the back of the car, he has both of my bags out and is back on the driver's side, sliding his seat forward so he can get to the bag in the back seat. Without a word, he carries two of my bags up the front porch and right into the house. I drag my last bag with me, following close behind him.

He sets my bags down at the bottom of the staircase then turns to look at me. "Your room is at the top of the stairs to the right. There's a bathroom across the hall you can use. I have my own." He runs a hand through his hair and looks me over again, anger apparent on his face. "I don't want random men in my house, so if you need to get off, take care of yourself."

I blink at him as he continues.

"The code for the alarm is 4-5-9-3. Don't forget to set it when you're in the house. I don't know when I'll be back, but you'll be safe here." Before I even have a chance to form a complete thought, he is closing the door behind him, shouting, "Set the alarm!" I stand there for a few minutes, just looking at the door. Then I look around for an alarm but don't see one. Tears sting my nose again as I recall the look of disgust on his face when he told me to get myself off. I say a silent, "Fuck you," and look at my bags then the stairs, shaking my head. I can cry once I get settled in the room.

I carry my bags one at a time up the stairs, and by the time I'm done, I'm so exhausted that I lie face-first on the bed, put my head under the pillow, and cry until I fall asleep.

THERE IS A pounding on the door, and I roll, falling off the bed and onto the floor. "You didn't set the alarm," I hear growled.

I stand up, pushing my hair out of my face, and glare at Kenton, who is standing in the doorway with his arms crossed over his chest.

"I looked and didn't see the alarm to set it." I copy his posture, crossing my arms over my chest.

"You should have called and asked me where it is."

I scoff. "With what? Magic? I don't have your number."

"You could have asked Link for it." He shakes his head.

"I'm sorry, but if you wanted me to have your number, I figured you would've given it to me," I retort.

"Did you eat?" he asks, changing the subject suddenly and throwing me off guard.

"Pardon?"

"Did you eat something?"

"No, and I'm not hungry. I'm just really tired," I tell him, rubbing my face. All I want to do is go to sleep and forget about the last forty-eight hours.

"You need to eat something," he chides, uncrossing his arms and placing his hands on his hips.

"Okay, don't get me wrong. I'm really thankful for you looking out for me, but I have been taking care of myself for a very long time. I don't want or need a babysitter."

"Suit yourself." He shrugs then looks me over again, his eyes lingering on my chest.

I glance down and groan. *Seriously?* My boobs are in my bra, hanging over the top of my tank top. I quickly adjust my shirt before narrowing my eyes on him.

He smirks, looking up into my face. "Make sure you set the alarm from now on. The panel is inside the room off the entry, first door to the right."

"Got it." My body is doing that hot thing again, and I wonder why it keeps happening when he's around.

"All right, doll. Get some rest. I'll see you tomorrow." He lets his eyes linger on me for a few more moments and then shakes his head, stepping out of the room.

I go to the side of the bed and turn on the light before walking to the door and shutting it. I lean my head back, closing my eyes and breathing in deeply. I run a finger across the tattoo behind my ear before opening my eyes and looking around. I can do this; I have lived through much worse and come out on top. I just need to get a plan in place.

Chapter 2
Word Vomit

It's been three weeks since I moved to Tennessee. Three weeks of living with Kenton, who I don't see very often, and when I do, he's usually leaving for work or coming in before going to bed. One of the longest talks we've had was the other day when he came in and told me that he had something for me and to meet him out front. I tucked my Kindle away and followed him out of the house, down the front steps, to a small VW Beetle.

"My cousin's wife just got rid of it. You don't have a car, and I know it's not an easy trek to town."

I looked from the car, to him, then back again.

"Here's the key. It has a full tank of gas, new tires, plus a tune-up," he told me, holding out the key between his large fingers. "This is the part where you say, 'Thank you,'" he grumbled, looking at me then at the keys in his hand.

"Um…I… Thank you," I whispered, taking the keys from him with shaky fingers.

He nodded, looking like he was going to say something else, but instead, he left me standing there, looking at the car, dumbfounded by the act of generosity. No one had ever done anything like that for me before.

From that day on, I tried to help where I could. I tried to cook a couple of times, but that was a disaster, so I settled on showing my appreciation in other ways. I kept the house clean, went to the grocery store if I noticed things running low, and even did laundry if I saw it piling up. He told me that I didn't need to do everything I was doing, but I ignored him. I knew he appreciated my help. He was always busy and seemed to be running himself ragged.

When we did have moments to talk, he smiled more and seemed more at ease with me. I lived for the stolen moments I had with him. It was stupid, but I felt like a lost puppy looking for a bone. I hated and loved that he made me feel like that. I had wondered for a long time if I had somehow become asexual. I hadn't been interested in a guy since my first and last boyfriend.

I WALK DOWN the stairs, going into the kitchen to grab some much-needed coffee. I just got off the phone. The hospital I worked at in Vegas has agreed to transfer my hours to a hospital they are affiliated with in Nashville. Then I called the hospital in Nashville, and they want me to start as soon as possible. My shift will be eleven to seven a.m. They told me that, after I'm on staff for a while, I can change up my schedule. It doesn't matter to me what hours I work, just as long as I'm working.

I'm on cloud nine; I can't wait to get back to work. Nursing is something I love doing and am really good at.

I hit the bottom landing of the stairs and go around the corner into the kitchen. Kenton is standing at the stove on the phone. His back is to me, so I take a second to admire him.

Today's jeans are light blue and faded in all the right spots. His red T-shirt fits him snugly, showing off his muscles while enhancing his tan. His head turns towards me; his golden eyes hit mine and then do a head-to-toe sweep.

"You want coffee?" he rumbles out, his deep voice making my girly parts tingle.

I hear him say goodbye to whoever's on the phone before he sets it on the counter. His eyes look me over again and his mouth starts to twitch.

"You want coffee?" he asks again, this time a small smirk playing on his lips.

"I…um… Yes please," I tell him, walking fully into the kitchen.

His house is older, the kitchen showing the wear and tear of having been around for so long. Everything is clean but in major need of updating. The cabinets are a light wood, and the counters are some old laminate that has started chipping around the edges. The fridge, stove, and dishwasher are white and desperately need to be replaced.

He hands me a cup of coffee, and I quickly add milk and sugar before hopping up on the counter, sitting across from him, praying that I don't continue to make a fool out of myself.

"What's your plan for the day?" he asks, looking at me from over the top of his coffee cup.

"I need to go shopping. I left all my work clothes back home and I just got a job in Nashville," I tell him, smiling.

His cup lowers as his hand turns white on the handle. "Like I told you before, I don't want randoms in my house."

My face heats and I take a breath, needing to make sure I understand what he's saying before I flip out and kick him in the balls. "What do you mean by 'randoms'?" I ask, keeping my voice light.

He studies me for a second like he's debating his next words. *Smart man.* "Guys from the strip club."

Apparently he's not that smart. I take another breath as my stomach turns. "Don't worry. I don't bring my work home with me," I tell him, dumping out the almost-full cup of coffee into the sink. I jump off the counter, putting the cup in the dishwasher before grabbing my bag and heading for the door.

I'm used to being judged, but for some reason, it coming from him makes me feel sick. I hate that he somehow has that kind of power over me. I hate that I want him to take a second to get to know me.

I get into the Beetle, telling myself that, as soon as I get back, I'm going to find out the value of the car he got me and give him the money for it.

I quickly ask Siri where I can find a store to buy scrubs, and once I have the directions pulled up, I put the car in drive, do a U-turn in front of the house, and head into town. First, I go to the scrubs shop and spend over five hundred dollars. *Who doesn't need cute scrubs?*

When I'm done with that, I go to a nearby nail salon and get a manicure and pedicure. Then I come across a small soul food restaurant and have barbecue ribs and homemade macaroni and cheese. For dessert, I have made-from-scratch peach cobbler with vanilla ice cream. Now that I can eat whatever I want without worrying about my appearance, I plan on eating everything I've been denied.

When I was growing up and competing in beauty pageants, there wasn't a week that went by that I didn't have a competition. My mom was very strict about what I ate. Everything was premeasured and my calorie intake was no more than what was necessary to survive. I didn't even know what sugar tasted like until I turned sixteen. Then, when I moved to Vegas and my jobs all required me to have a certain image, I stuck with my old habits.

But now? Fuck that! I'm going to eat—and eat *everything*. After eating, I'm not ready to go home, so I go to the movies, buy a ticket, and sit in the dark theater alone, watching as a young woman is attacked by an evil spirit. Well, I think that's what it is… About halfway through, I fall asleep. I wake up to screaming and have no clue what is going on, so I get up and leave.

When I pull up in front of the house, the first thing I notice is Kenton's car parked out front. I really don't want to see him again, but I know I can't avoid going inside forever. I get out of the car, leaving the bags with my new work clothes in the trunk. He doesn't need to know what I'll really be doing. He chose to make assumptions about me, so he can continue to think what he wants.

I'm not going to try to change his mind. Yes, he's good-looking, but I'm starting to see a pattern. He's a dick and judgmental. He's a judgmental dick.

I sigh, walking up the front porch, and as soon as I unlock the door and push it open, the smell of something cooking hits my nose. Even though I ate earlier, my stomach growls. I ignore my stomach and start for the stairs. I have a candy bar in my bag; that can hold me over until tomorrow.

"You're back," I hear from behind me as my foot hits the first step.

"Yep." I look over my shoulder at him. *Why does he have to be so good-looking?*

"I made dinner."

"Good for you," I say sarcastically, going up two more stairs.

"Look, I shouldn't have said what I said earlier." He sighs, and I wonder if he has ever apologized in his life.

"You shouldn't have," I agree, taking a few more steps.

"Will you stop for a second?" He lets out a huff, and I turn to face him, raising an eyebrow. "Come eat so we can talk. You're living here. I think it's only right that we get to know at least a little about each other."

It's on the tip of my tongue to tell him to fuck off, but sadly, my manners are ingrained in me. I turn, walk down the stairs, and follow him into the kitchen.

"Will you get out a couple plates?" he asks, going to the oven. As soon as he has the oven open, the smell of baked chicken hits me, making my stomach growl again. "You really should eat more," he mumbles.

I turn to look at him and feel my temper spike. "I did eat," I tell him, pulling down two plates before getting two sets of silverware out of the drawer and setting them on the counter with a little too much force.

"I mean something besides rabbit food. You need to gain some weight."

I take a breath and blow it out slowly, counting in my head from one to ten. "Okay"—I turn my face to look at him—"I don't know what's wrong with the filter that goes from your brain to your mouth, and honestly, I really don't care." I turn around to face him completely. "I don't appreciate you saying things to me about my job, my free time, or my eating habits. I appreciate what you're doing for me, but it doesn't give you the right to talk shit to me whenever you feel like it."

I inhale deeply before letting out a breath, noticing that his eyes seem to have gone softer. Something about that look makes me feel better, but I finish with, "If you think that's going to be a problem, I can find somewhere else to stay until I can go home."

"You're right. I shouldn't have said that to you." He shakes his head, running a hand through his hair before our eyes meet again. "Let's start over."

"Sure." I nod, my insides twisting under his gaze. Every time he looks at me, I feel like he sees way too much.

He walks towards me, sticking out his hand. "Kenton Mayson."

I put out my hand for him to take. "Autumn Freeman," I tell him, and our eyes lock as his fingers wrap around mine. His touch sends tingles down my spine. I lick my lips, which have suddenly gone dry.

His eyes drop to my mouth before meeting mine again. "Right." His voice seems deeper than before and his eyes seem to have gone darker. "Get the salad, babe." He nods towards the fridge, dropping my hand.

My stomach flips at the word 'babe.' I ignore it and go to the fridge, pulling the salad out as he pulls some potatoes out of the oven, setting one on each plate before adding a golden piece of chicken as well.

"It's a nice night. How 'bout we sit out on the deck?"

"Sure," I agree.

He finishes making our plates, adding butter and sour cream to the potatoes then adding salad to the dishes. "Get the door for me."

I open the sliding glass door in the kitchen that leads to the deck. He sets the plates down on the table before coming back in, opening the fridge, and grabbing a beer.

"You want one?" he asks, holding up the beer.

I shake my head; I've never had beer…or any kind of alcohol for that matter.

"You don't like beer? I got a bottle of wine if you prefer that."

"I've never had it before."

"You've never had a beer?" His voice sounds shocked, and I shake my head no again.

I have worked around alcohol since I was twenty-one, but I have also seen the way it makes people act and have never trusted anyone enough to be that unguarded around them. I watch as he goes to the counter, puts the beer to the edge, and pops the top off.

"Try a sip," he orders.

I reluctantly take it. Why? I don't know. Normally, I would have stood my ground a little more firmly. I put the bottle to my lips and tip it back. The bubbles and cold hit my tongue before the taste. I pull the bottle away, scrunch up my face as the flavor hits me, and hand the bottle back to him.

"Not a beer girl," he assesses with a chuckle.

"It's not bad, but it doesn't taste good either."

"It's kind of an acquired taste. Do you like wine?"

"I've never had it." I shrug, crossing my arms over my chest, feeling like I need to hold myself together.

His eyes drop for a second before meeting mine again. "Most women like wine."

I ignore that comment and watch him go to the fridge to pull out a bottle of wine. He goes to the drawer, pulls out a bottle opener, and starts to screw it into the top of the bottle. His arm muscles flex with every turn, and soon, there's a pop and a hiss.

"I don't have any wine glasses," he says, pulling a coffee cup down. He pours a small amount into the cup, handing it to me.

I take it and put the cup to my face, giving it a sniff before placing it against my lips and tilting it back. This time after the taste hits my mouth, I smile.

"There you go. You like wine," he declares, sounding proud.

I nod and start to wipe my mouth with the sleeve of my sweater. His hand moves towards me, his fingers curve around my jaw, and his thumb runs over my bottom lip, his eyes watching closely. He leans forward, making my stomach drop.

"Let's eat before the food gets too cold," he says.

I nod, taking a step back trying to get myself under control. He fills the coffee cup with wine and waits for me to go outside before following me out onto the deck. I sit down on the iron chair as he sits in a plastic one across from me. I take a second to look around. The whole house is surrounded by trees, and it was built into a kind of valley. There isn't much of a backyard. It all seems to be forest beyond the small area of grass.

"So how long have you lived here?" I take another sip of wine.

"About five years. I had plans to fix it up, but with my schedule, I've only had time to redo my bathroom and bedroom."

"It's a really nice house." I take a bite of the chicken and moan when the taste hits my mouth. His eyes lock on me, making me squirm and lower my head.

"I like it. I really bought it for the view." He takes a bite from his plate.

I nod. I bought my condo for the same reason. "This *is* a nice view."

"Nothing better than coming out here at night with a cold beer and watching the sun set behind the mountain."

"I'll have to try that one day—minus the beer." I lift my coffee cup.

He smiles, and for the first time, I notice a dimple in his right cheek. The sight of that dimple makes my stomach flutter.

"You should smile more," I blurt like the moron he's turned me into.

He smiles bigger, shaking his head while muttering, "*Cute*," under his breath.

The rest of dinner is nice. We laugh and joke, and he tells me about his job and the people he works with. He never asks me about my work again, nor does he give me an in to talk about it.

By the time we are done eating, a chill has filled the air. Kenton goes back inside and gets me a sweater and the bottle of wine, and then he comes back out with a cigar. I drink wine while he lights his cigar, which smells sweet and has me leaning closer to him.

When he's done smoking, I'm completely drunk for the first time in my life, and I'm laughing at everything he says.

"Come on, babe. Time to get you to bed." He pulls me up from the chair, smiling, and I lift my fingers to trace his upturned lips.

"You're really beautiful," I tell him, wrapping my arms around his shoulders.

"You shouldn't call guys beautiful, baby."

I smile before frowning. "My son was beautiful." I am too drunk to notice that his body has gone solid against mine. "Holding him was the only time I've ever been happy…until tonight. I was happy tonight." I sigh, laying my head on his chest. I think I hear him mutter a curse, but my drunken state has me unsure.

"Up you go," he says softly, putting his arm behind my knees and lifting me up.

I bury my face in the crook of his neck, enjoying his smell. I feel him laying me down, and then my shoes are being pulled off.

"Night, beautiful girl."

"Don't call me beautiful," I mumble, cuddling deeper into my covers.

"Night, Autumn."

I feel lips on my forehead and sigh, liking the way his lips feel against my skin.

I WAKE UP to the sun shining brightly through my window. I squeeze my eyes closed and put my hand to my head, which is throbbing. I can't remember much about last night—just drinking wine and laughing a lot. Apparently, I'm not a drinker.

I keep my eyes closed as I get out of bed and stumble across the hall to the bathroom. I turn on the water and jump into the shower, letting the cool water run over me. By the time I'm done, my headache has lessened significantly. I get out and wrap a towel around myself, tucking it under my arms. I open the medicine cabinet and take a couple of pain pills before making it across the hall to get dressed.

When I'm finally downstairs, I feel almost one hundred percent. I pour myself a cup of coffee before heading to Kenton's office. I need to get on the computer and print off the application for the hospital. Even though I got the job already, they still require me to fill it out.

My step falters slightly as I make my way down the hall. I can hear the sound of Kenton's voice. I don't mean to spy, but when I hear him talking about me, I can't help but listen.

"I would never take a stripper home to meet my mom, so your point is moot."

My throat starts to close as I walk closer. I stop in the doorway, taking Kenton in while his face is turned to look out the window. The phone's against his ear and his knuckles are turning white from the grip he has on it.

"Fuck off. She's a stripper," he growls into the phone.

A whimper I can't control climbs up my throat before I can stop it. His head turns my way, our eyes lock, and his get wide.

"Babe," he says then pulls the phone from his ear. "Not you, fucker. I gotta go." He hangs up and looks at me. I want to run so badly, but my feet feel like they are glued to the floor. "Babe," he repeats, looking at me with his eyes wide.

"I'm a lot more than a stripper." I raise my hand before flopping it down at my side when it looks like he's going to say something. "I'm a person with feelings. I have my own hopes and dreams. I don't know how you can judge someone so easily without knowing what they've been through."

His eyes go soft again, but this time, I don't let that stop me. "Honestly, it makes me sad that you're so close-minded, and I'm glad I now see who you really are." Tears clog my throat, forcing me to pause. His eyes have changed again, but I don't know what the look means. "Unlike you, I gave you the benefit of the doubt. The difference is you proved me right more than once," I say softly, leaving him standing.

I go upstairs and change into a pair of jeans and a T-shirt before grabbing my bag. Then I leave. I get into the car and pound the steering wheel a couple of times when I realize I forgot to find out how much the car had cost him. I do not want to feel like he has something over me. I put the keys in the ignition, promising myself that I will look up the Kelley Blue Book value.

I do a U-turn in front of the house and just drive. I have no idea where I'm going, but there is no way I am going to sit around his house all day. I pull out my phone, thankful that I have my headphones already hooked in so I can make a call. I press Link's name as soon as I have his number pulled up on my phone.

"Hey, Angel." My stripper name makes me feel even colder for some reason when he answers.

"Hey. How are things?" I ask him.

"Good. Sid's worried about you. He wants you to call him, but like I told you before, I don't think it's wise to make any phone calls right now."

I need to call Sid, but I feel awkward phoning him for some reason. "Can I come home?" I pull off the road when I reach a small gas station. I put my car in park, leaning my head back, trying to keep the tears at bay.

"What happened?"

"Nothing. I just want my life back," I fib.

"Autumn, you know you can't. Not yet."

"Soon?" I ask on a whisper.

"Angel, I wish I could tell you the cops caught the guy or that they have a lead, but right now, they've got nothing. You're safe there."

That's a joke; I'm in more danger here than I was back home. *Why am I so upset about this?*

"Did you hear me?" Link asks, pulling me from my thoughts.

"Sorry?"

"I asked how you and Kenton are getting along."

"Oh, fine… You know, he goes his way and I go mine," I answer casually.

"What are you leaving out?"

"Guess what? I got a job in Nashville at a hospital," I say, changing the subject. I do not want to talk to Link about Kenton. They were friends long before I was in the picture.

"That's good news, Autumn, but…" He clears his throat, and I can't tell that he's trying not to burst my bubble. "I know you're a long way from here, but that doesn't mean you're one hundred percent safe."

"Only you know where I am, right? So I should be okay."

"Just be careful…and keep Kenton up-to-date about what's going on," he tells me.

"Will do," I say, knowing that I won't be doing anything like that at all.

"Call me if you need anything."

"Okay. Talk to you later," I say softly, hanging up the phone. "May as well go get breakfast," I mutter to myself, putting my car back in drive. I reach a small town after fifteen minutes, pull into the first restaurant I see, get out of my car, and head inside.

The place is small, with a total of five booths and a long counter that stretches the length of the diner, which has short barstools lining the front of it. I walk to a small booth in the back, pushing my bag across the seat before sitting down. The smell of bacon and eggs has my mouth watering.

"What can I getcha, sugar?" asks a pretty, older woman with dark-brown hair that's in a bun at the top of her head as she pulls a pen from behind her ear.

"Coffee, pancakes, bacon, and eggs."

Her head lifts, looking at me. "A woman who's not afraid to eat," she smiles. "Be back with your coffee."

As soon as she leaves, I take out my cell phone and pull up my Kindle app. Any time I need a break from reality, I read. There is nothing better than going on an adventure or imagining two people falling in love.

"What's your name, sugar?" the woman asks, making me jump in my chair.

"Autumn. Thank you," I say when she sets the cup down in front of me.

"I'm Viv. You got man problems?" she asks, sitting down across from me like it's completely normal to sit with someone you don't know and ask them such a personal question.

"Um…"

"Never mind. I see it in your eyes that you do."

"I—" I start to tell her that I don't when she cuts me off again.

"My mamma was able to see things, you know?"

"Sure," I agree, because who am I to judge? For all I know, her mom could have a gift.

"Well, I can see things too," she says. I watch her, wondering where she's going with this. "The guy you like, well… He's kinda an ass, like my old man used to be," she tells me, leaning forward like it's a secret between us.

"Um…"

"Well, you see, he doesn't know what to do with what he's feeling, so he's an ass." She shakes her head. "You hear what I'm sayin'?"

I have no idea what she's saying, but she's dead-on that Kenton is an ass, so I nod my head in agreement.

"Make him grovel. Whatever you do, you make him pay for being an asshole."

"Got it." I smile.

"Now, when you do forgive him"—she shocks me by grabbing my hand—"what you're feeling right now will be worth it in the end."

"Uh, okay," I tell her, patting her hand.

"All right, now you just sit back and I'm going to feed you the best pancakes you've ever eaten in your life. Food makes everything okay." She stands, leaving me wondering what the hell just happened.

Viv comes back a few minutes later with a plate overflowing with pancakes, bacon, and eggs. She sets the plate in front of me before taking a seat across from me again.

"So I take it you're new around these parts?"

"I just moved here," I tell her, my mouth watering from the smell coming from the plate.

"Did you move here to be with the ass?"

I can't help but smile at her name for Kenton. "Um…no, and we're not together. I mean, we have never been together."

"Whatever—tomato, tomatoes." She waves her hand at me, and I can't help but smile at the way she messed up the saying. "You got family 'round here?" she asks, sitting forward in the booth like my answer is really important.

"No." I shake my head, taking a bite of bacon.

"Well, you need to come over and have dinner sometime. *My* ass makes a mean brisket." She smiles, watching me take another bite. "Good, right?" she prompts.

"Very." I nod, covering my mouth.

"You should come over next Sunday. We close the diner early that day and have a big Sunday meal with all the fixings. My daughter and my niece are a little younger than you, but I would guess my nephew is about your age, though he doesn't always show up. I'm sure the girls would like to show you around. One sure way to get your man to mind is to find another man to show him you can have someone else if you want to," she rambles, and I can feel my eyes growing in size, so I cut her off.

"That's very nice, but—"

"No buts. Dinner's at three. We eat early. I'll give you my address. I expect to see you there," she says, standing up, and before I can come up with a good reason not to have Sunday dinner with her, her 'ass,' and their families, she disappears behind the counter and starts taking care of other customers.

I sit there for another hour, eating and reading on my phone. When Viv comes back, she gives me her address, cell phone number, and a very sweet hug. I leave the diner, get in my car, and head back to Kenton's. This time when I get there, his car is gone, and I breathe out a sigh of relief that I don't have to face him for a while.

I WAKE UP to the sound of pounding and the doorbell going off. I roll and look at the clock on my bedside table, seeing that it's after three in the morning. "What the hell?" I mumble sitting up. My brain is still asleep as I stumble through my bedroom door and down the stairs. When I reach the front door, I look out the peephole and see a beautiful woman with dark hair and sun-kissed skin standing outside.

"I know you're in there! Open up!" she yells.

I turn off the alarm and open the door, leaving the night latch in place as I peek out the crack. "Can I help you?"

"Can you help me?" She waves her arms around. "Can *you* help *me*? Yes, bitch, you can help me by telling me what you're doing in my man's house," she says, pushing on the door, the lock keeping her out.

"Your man?" I repeat, putting my weight against the door.

"Yes, *my* man." She shoves the door a little harder and I'm surprised when I hear the sound of wood cracking.

"Look, if you're Kenton's girlfriend, then you need to call him. He's not home," I tell her, not liking the way my chest feels as the word 'girlfriend' leaves my mouth.

"I know he's not home," she says, pressing on the door again.

"You should call him or come see him tomorrow when he is here," I suggest, trying to be reasonable.

"Let me inside." She takes her shoulder and slams it into the door.

She is really crazy. What the hell?

She stumbles back and then runs at the door again like some kind of football player. This time, the door crashes open. I fall on my ass and she flies into the house, falling onto the floor.

"Are you fucking *insane?!*" I ask her, standing and feeling a bruise forming on my hip. I look at the lock on the door, seeing it swinging on the doorjamb.

"You wouldn't let me in." She rolls over, getting on her knees before standing up.

"That's because Kenton's not here, you psycho. Now get out before I call the cops." I walk to the door, opening it wider, signaling for her to leave.

"No, I'm going to wait for Kenton."

"You're on crack if you think I'm letting you stay here to wait for him. Get out!" I point out the door just as lights beam through the house.

I look outside and watch Kenton pull up and park. He sees me standing in the door, and that's when I realize that all I have on is a T-shirt and panties—and it's not even a long shirt. His eyes slide from me to the woman in the house and then narrow.

"Cassie, what the fuck?" he growls at her, walking through the door.

"We need to talk," she cries, taking a step towards him, only to stop when his eyes narrow further.

"You opened the door to her?" he asks, looking at me.

I shake my head no, taking a step back from the look on his face.

His head swings in her direction. "You know what time it is?" he asks.

"Yes. I got home to find all my stuff outside on my front porch."

"You came to my house and forced your way inside when I wasn't home?"

"All my stuff is ruined," she whines on a huff.

"You okay, baby?" he asks as he turns his head my way, his eyes locking on mine.

Heat boils under my skin at the endearment. I want to claw his eyes out.

"'Baby'? Really? You call her 'baby'? You never called *me* that!" Cassie screeches, looking at me.

"I wouldn't get too upset, honey," I tell her softly. "I'm just a stripper and don't mean shit to Kenton." My eyes go from her to him, and seeing his jaw ticking makes me feel better. "Now," I say happily, "if you two don't mind carrying on this love spat without me, I'm going to bed."

I turn and head up the stairs, smiling when I hear Cassie yell, "Stripper?! A fucking *stripper* is living with you?"

I close my bedroom door and crawl into bed. I listen to the rumble of Kenton's voice for a few minutes, and then I hear the door close and the alarm being set. I hold my breath as I listen to feet pound up the stairs. I don't know how I know, but I can feel him standing outside my bedroom door. The hall is silent for a few moments, and then he says my name. I ignore it, pulling the covers over my head.

"I'm sorry," he whispers.

I hear a thump then the sound of feet moving away from the door, and I squeeze my eyes closed, blocking him out. No way am I buying into that again. I run my finger over the tattoo behind my ear, taking comfort in it.

It's the only physical thing I have that connects me to my son. I wasn't allowed pictures or any other reminders from the nine months I carried him or the few hours I spent with him after his birth. Not that I would need them—he was embedded in me, a piece of my soul that was taken from me before I was strong enough to fight for myself or him.

When I was sixteen, I met a guy. His sister used to compete in pageants against me, and he would show up at the competitions and sit in the crowd, looking annoyed about having to be there. He would growl at his mother, telling her how wrong it was what she was doing to his sister. He fascinated me. I wanted someone like him to fight for me or teach me how to fight for myself.

Not long after the first time I saw him, he found me in one of my favorite hiding spots. At first, he was rude and distant, only recognizing me as another snotty pageant girl, but then I told him that I hated it. I explained that I didn't have a choice and what would happen if I didn't perform.

After that, we met often. I trusted him. He told me what I wanted to hear—we could be together, he had an apartment, and he would save me from the life I was living. For a girl who was broken and didn't know any better, he was perfect. It didn't take long for me to fall in love with him and give him the piece of myself that was the only real thing I had to give another person. I thought he loved me too; I thought he was willing to fight for me. He used my weakness to get what he wanted.

In the end, I learned a hard lesson. Not only did he not care about me, but when I ended up pregnant, he turned his back on me, allowing my mother to send me to a home for young girls to give birth to my son before being forced to give him away.

I pull my pillow over my face and cry into the soft material as images of my son flash through my head. I think I memorized everything about him during those few short hours. He was so tiny, weighing only six pounds. His small head was covered in dark hair and his eyes were bluish grey. I remember praying that I would be able to see them one day to know what color they turned out to be.

He had a birthmark on his right thigh. I looked at the small area of discolored skin for a long time while I held him. The shape was unique, just like him. Not long after moving to Vegas, I was walking down the street and looked into a tattoo shop window. I hadn't wanted a tattoo until one of the posters on the wall caught my eye and I saw my son's birthmark. I went inside to find out what it was.

The old guy behind the counter got on his computer and looked it up for me. He told me that the symbol was an Ankh, the origin was Egyptian, and it represented eternal life or the giving of life. I couldn't believe that his birthmark had that kind of meaning behind it.

I knew that my son was the one who'd actually given *me* life; he'd made me fight harder to get out of my mother's grasp. I had hated her before he'd come along, but after she forced me to give him away, I knew the kind of evil she really was and fought until I was finally free.

I MUST HAVE fallen asleep again, but when I wake up, I feel like I have only been asleep for an hour. The sound of the doorbell going off again registers, and I wait to see if I hear Kenton answer it. The house sounds quiet, and I hope the person at the door leaves. When the bell rings again, I let out a frustrated huff.

"Seriously?!" I yell as the pounding starts.

I climb out of bed, stumble out of my room, run down the stairs, and swing the door open without thinking. The alarm starts going off and I run to the keypad, typing in the code quickly before turning and going back to the door.

"Can I help you?" I ask a guy who looks no older than twenty-one. He's tall and lean with tousled, blond hair. He looks like he just came from the beach.

"Holy shit." He looks me over from head to toe, and I groan when I realize I once again forgot to put on pants. "Shit. Please tell me the carpet matches the drapes," he mumbles.

I'm not sure if it's the lack of sleep or the promise I made myself the last time those words were said, but I walk towards him slowly, swaying my hips, my hands going up to his shoulders. His eyes go wide when I touch him, and then I bring my knee up, connecting with his nuts.

He groans, his knees hitting the floor with a loud thud. "What was that for?" he asks me in a breathy, high-pitched voice, holding his junk.

"That was for asking an inappropriate question. Weren't you raised better than that?"

"What the fuck is going on?"

I turn at the sound of Kenton's words. He's standing on the stairs, wearing nothing but a towel. His eyes come to me then lower down my body. I make a mental note that, from now on, I will wear pants at all times. When his eyes stop on my hip, where I have a nice-size bruise from last night's run-in with the lunatic, they narrow.

"How did you get that?" He looks at the guy on the floor then back at me. His jaw goes hard, and I put my hands up in front of me.

"That's from your girlfriend last night."

"He doesn't have a girlfriend," the guy I kneed says, whimpering as he stands.

"Why'd you knee Justin in the nuts?" he asks, walking the rest of the way down the stairs.

I try to take my eyes off him, but they feel glued. His wet hair is dripping onto his body. His abdominal muscles flex with each step. The deep V of his hips disappears beneath the small towel that is also showing off his well-endowed package. He walks past me and goes to the couch in the next room, coming back with a blanket in his hand. I don't even have a chance to think as he wraps the blanket around my waist. I slap his hands away from me, taking a step back to glare at him.

"Oh shit. I'm in love," the guy named Justin declares, smiling at me.

"Why are you here, Justin? I told you I would be at the office late," Kenton growls, taking a step in my direction. I take another step away from him.

"I know, but I needed to talk to you and it couldn't wait."

"You should have called," he scolds.

"I did. You didn't answer."

"Fuck me." Kenton looks at me like he wants to say something, but I shake my head no and take another step towards the stairs.

"You're leaving already?" Justin asks, looking at me with a big, cheesy smile on his face. "We're basically past second base. You touched my junk. It's only fair I get to touch yours."

I can't help but smile at the guy. I see it now. He's not pervy, just strange and kinda cute in a brotherly kind of way. "Sorry. No, I need my beauty sleep, and I work tonight." I shrug, smirking.

"You don't need sleep, my love. You're alread—"

Kenton smacks him in the back of his head before he can finish, and I can't help but smile at him again.

"Nice to meet you, Justin," I tell him, really meaning it.

"You too, Copper." He grins back.

"You know you're still not safe, Autumn. I don't think it's a good idea for you to be working," Kenton says.

I look at him, my eyes narrow, and I growl. "I'm safe and going to work, *ass*, so get over it."

His jaw starts to tick a little faster and his hands ball into fists. "Tell me the name of the place so I can check on you."

"I don't need you to check on me."

"Tell me or I'll have Justin do a run on you and I'll know everything about you down to your last fucking period," he growls, taking a step towards me.

"Ass!" I yell, glaring at him.

"Tell me," he roars, leaning forward, and I can feel the anger rolling off him.

"Vanderbilt," I say, but I pronounce it 'Vander's Belt,' hoping he doesn't catch on that it's the hospital. I don't know why I don't what him to know what I'm really doing. I almost feel like he hasn't earned the right to know.

"We need to talk," he says, his tone softer, but the growl is still there.

"We don't," I assure him, pulling off the blanket and tossing it at him as I walk up the stairs. I hear Justin laugh and Kenton growl something about spankings under his breath before I close the door to my bedroom, smiling.

Chapter 3

One Tequila, Two Tequila...Floor

"SO WHY THE hell did you want to move to Tennessee?" Tara asks. I've been working at the hospital for about two weeks now, and I've been Tara's shadow since the day I started in the ER. Tennessee is nothing like Vegas. Not only are the people different, but the ER here is much calmer. I look at Tara and smile when she raises an eyebrow at me. One thing I learned quickly is that people here have no problem getting in your business or asking personal questions.

"I just needed a change." I shrug, putting away another patient folder.

"I can understand that. I need a change, like a nice sandy beach and a hot guy to wait on me hand and foot." She smiles, her head tilting back like she's imagining herself on a beach right now.

"Autumn, Tara," a deep voice says.

Tara and I look up and smile at the same time.

"How are you ladies this evening?" Dr. D, or Derik, asks. He's a very, very attractive black man; sadly, he is also very, very gay and has an even hotter boyfriend.

"Good," Tara and I say in unison. We laugh, pointing at each other and calling out, "Jinx!"

I've found myself laughing a lot more often since I started working here. In general, I find myself a lot happier period. All of my coworkers are very nice and easy to get along with. So far, I haven't met anyone who is petty or mean.

The one thing that hasn't changed is my relationship with Kenton. I can't get over the amount of anger I feel towards him. Maybe it's stupid and immature on my part, but he hurt my feelings when he said all that to whomever he was talking to on the phone. Worse, I'd thought he'd been starting to like me.

"What are you girls doing this weekend?"

"I need to sleep," I say, closing my eyes for a second. "My body hasn't adjusted to this schedule yet. I swear, if it weren't for coffee, I would be lying facedown on this desk right now." Plus, if I slept, I could continue to avoid Kenton.

He's left me a note daily and somehow got my cell number, so he's started texting me. He never says much. Mostly, he asks how I am, if I need anything, and if I am settling in at my job. I never answer him. I can tell that he is becoming frustrated. I have no idea how to face him, so I do the easiest thing and avoid him like the plague.

"Sleep is overrated. You two should come out with me and Stan this weekend. There's a club that just opened up downtown. We could go out, have a couple drinks, and dance. Wouldn't that be fun?" Derik asks.

I look at Tara, who nods her head, and I quickly agree. I need to start acting my age. I should be having fun and going out, and now that I have a few people I trust, I have a reason to do that.

"Sure, but I won't be staying out late. I have dinner plans with a friend on Sunday in the early afternoon," I tell them. I've had dinner with Viv and her family the last two Sundays, and now, she expects me to be there. Her daughter is really sweet. Plus, her niece is supposed to be coming this weekend and Viv really wants me to meet her.

"That's fine. Two drinks tops." Derik smiles and the desk phone rings.

Tara picks it up and stands suddenly. "Got it," she says, looking at Derik. "When?" she asks and listens for a few more seconds before hanging up the phone. She leaves from behind the desk and I follow her. "The ambulance is in route. Male, thirty-four, gunshot wound to the right shoulder. He's conscious and may need a transfusion. We need to get everything set up. The ambulance is five minutes out," Tara says, and all three of us run down the hall to prepare the trauma bay before the patient arrives.

The ambulance pulls in and what I least expect happens. The guy is conscious, laughing, and joking with the EMTs like this is a routine occurrence for him. He hasn't lost enough blood to need a transfusion, and it doesn't appear that the bullet hit any arteries; it was a clean in-and-out shot. All he'll require is a few stitches and an overnight stay in the hospital.

"Are you sure you two don't want to give me a sponge bath?" Finn, our bullet wound patient asks.

I laugh, shaking my head at him, but Tara doesn't seem so sure about turning him down. His tall, lean body, boy-next-door good looks, and easy smile definitely make him swoon-worthy.

"Not tonight, handsome," Tara tells him, batting her lashes.

His hand goes over his heart as he flops back down in the bed and winces. "You wound me, Blondie."

"I'm sure your ego will be okay." She smiles.

Tara is really beautiful. She has that whole Southern belle look going for her—long, blond hair, big, blue eyes, and a cute personality. Actually, looking between the two of them, I see Ken and Barbie.

"You need to be careful with that shoulder," I scold Finn as he winces again when he sits up.

"I could go home with you and you could look after me." He grins, making me roll my eyes.

"Sorry, but I promised my roommate I wouldn't take my work home with me." I start laughing, thinking about Kenton and what he would do if I showed up with a guy who had a gunshot wound.

"Your roommate sucks," Finn mutters.

"Tell me about it," I reply with a smile.

A second later, my body goes solid when the voice behind me hits my ears. "What the fuck is going on, Autumn?"

I close my eyes slowly, hoping that I'm wrong. When I turn my head, four large guys are standing near the door and none other than Kenton is standing in the middle of them.

"Autumn?" one of the guys says. My eyes go to him and he smiles. "Shit, boss. This is the Autumn who works at 'Vander's Belt'?" He laughs loudly, his eyes going back and forth between Kenton and me.

My eyes shift back to Kenton, seeing his jaw tick. "Um…" I mumble, taking a step back.

"Vanderbilt," Kenton pronounces, his voice a low rumble. The anger in the one spoken word rolls against my skin, creating goose bumps. "Do not fucking move," he demands when I start to take another step back.

My body freezes in place as I watch him move towards me, his eyes locked on mine. I feel stuck in place under his glare.

When he's within touching distance, his hand wraps around my bicep and his mouth comes to my ear. "No more fucking ignoring me," he growls.

If the wetness in my panties is anything to go by, I like his aggression. I look at Dr. D, who is looking at Kenton with his mouth hanging open, and when his eyes come to mine, he bites his lip. Apparently, he is not going to be any help.

Kenton drags me out of the room and down the hall. He stops at the first door we pass, and his hand that's not holding me goes to the handle. Finding it unlocked, he leans into the room before tugging me in with him.

"What are you doing?" I ask when I get over the shock of seeing him here.

"You said you worked at a fucking strip club," he says, letting me go.

"I never said that." I shake my head, crossing my arms over my chest, watching him pace back and forth in front of me like a caged beast.

"You're a nurse?" He stops across the room, watching me. His eyes travel from the top of my head to my sneaker-covered feet.

"I am, but it changes nothing," I hiss, leaning forward.

He storms towards me and I retreat until my back hits the wall. Before I can register the move, his mouth is on mine, his hand twists in the hair at the back of my head, and I gasp. He takes the opportunity to lick into my mouth. I try to fight him; I try to pull my mouth away, but his grip on my hair tightens. When he bites my tongue, I lose it.

I kiss him back, and all the anger I feel towards him goes into that kiss. I bite his lips, bottom then top, and claw my nails through his hair. He growls down my throat, his big body pressing me harder into the wall. We each fight for dominance, but he wins, pinning me in place, his body overtaking mine.

When he pulls his mouth from mine we're breathing heavily, both still holding each other close. I can feel every hard inch of him pressed to every soft inch of me. He places his forehead to mine and it takes a few seconds to come back to myself. My eyes open, meeting his.

"This changes nothing," I tell him quietly, my lips still tingling from his kiss.

"You're right." He takes a breath, his lips moving closer to mine. "*You* fucking changed everything."

"Back up." I push against his chest only to have him press harder into me.

"You don't get to push me away. You don't get to lie to me, even if it's by omission."

"I never lied to you," I mumble, looking away from him.

"'Vander's Belt'—that's not a fucking lie?" His hand comes up to my cheek, forcing my eyes back to him.

Okay, so I might have fibbed, but it wasn't a lie. "You're an asshole," I tell him, still pushing against his chest.

"Call me what you want, but I know you feel this thing between us too. Don't fucking lie to yourself."

"The only thing I feel towards you is anger," I growl.

Then his mouth comes back down on mine, stealing my breath. This kiss is more punishing than the previous one; and I whimper when he pulls away. My hands, which were trying to push him away, are now wrapped into his T-shirt.

His mouth goes to my ear. "If I stuck my hand between your legs, your pussy would be wet and wanting."

I squeeze my eyes closed, trying to get rid of that image. My eyes fly open when his hand cups me over the thin material of my scrubs.

"So hot." His fingers press harder, and I stand on my tiptoes, trying to get away from what he's making me feel.

Part of me wants to jump up, wrap my legs around his hips, and grind myself into him. The other part of me wants to kick him in the nuts and scream in his face for having the power he has.

Kenton

I LOOK DOWN into her big, blue eyes and groan. Fuck me. She is the most beautiful thing I've ever looked at. She's perfect, and I don't just mean on the outside; I mean on the inside too. She's sweet in a way that is hard to believe, especially coming from her lifestyle.

I tried to keep my distance after I picked her up at the airport and got reminded of what she did for a living, but when she was around, I couldn't help but want to soak up a little bit of her time. She's not what I expected. She's not what I wanted, but fuck me if she's not what I need.

From the moment I saw her, I wanted her. I walked into the airport knowing that she wasn't expecting me. I'd messaged Link earlier in the day telling him to let her know I wouldn't be picking her up. I'd had a lead on a case and thought I wouldn't make it in time, and I didn't want her waiting for me.

When I spotted her long, red hair in the crowd, I watched her run for one of her bags. I couldn't help but laugh when she fell forward and landed on the belt before being dragged with it. She didn't give up though. She pulled it off the conveyor belt over her head, falling backwards with the weight of it. She was cute.

When we got into the car and I sat down next to her, the doors closed and her smell suffocated me. Her long-ass legs in her shorts made it hard to concentrate on the road, and then I asked her about how she knew Link. I may get around, but I didn't like the idea of her being with someone who was a friend for some reason, and then she reminded me that she worked at a strip club, throwing all ideas of getting to know her out the window.

I look over her face again and shake my head. I have fucked up with her in ways that even thinking about them makes me sick. I don't have an issue with strippers in general, but I know what happens at strip clubs. I do understand that not all women are the same and there are dancers who work in clubs to make money and nothing more, but I also know that there are some who go home with men at the end of the night or are willing to go a little further in order to make a little extra cash.

"Step back," she says, and I shake my head, pressing deeper into her.

She smells like flowers or something sweet. I have wanted to be this close to her for a long time. Now that I've got her where I want her, I'm not backing off.

"Why are you doing this?" she asks softly, squeezing her eyes closed.

"I want you. I want to get to know you."

"No," she breathes, shaking her head.

"Yes." I press her harder into the wall.

"The things I know about you, I don't like."

I know she's just being honest, but it doesn't mean that it makes my chest ache any less. I don't know her well, but the parts of her she has let me see have been sweet, feisty, and so fucking cute that I have had to stop myself from kissing her when she laughs or does something that makes me smile.

The look in her eyes when she walked into my office when I was talking to Nico on the phone still haunts me. I know that my cousin was trying to make me see that I was interested in her, but I didn't need his help with that. I knew I wanted her; I just didn't know how I could deal with my jealousy. The thought of men looking at her or touching her makes me feel homicidal.

When she spoke, her words tore me open. I knew that, regardless of my own fears, I needed to find a way to deal with it or I'd lose her before I ever even got to have her. Then I went to Nico's house and saw him with Sophie and how close they had gotten. The way she looked at him like he had the power to turn on the sun had me feeling jealous. I wanted that for myself.

Nico was right in telling me to get my head out of my ass. He told me that if I wanted something, I had to take it; I couldn't ever let anyone or anything hold me back. I want Autumn more than I've wanted anything before. I wanted her even before I knew she was a nurse. I would be proud to take her home to meet my family. My parents and sister would love her.

"Give me a chance."

"I can't. You've already said so many cruel things to me. I can't willingly open myself up for more of that from you."

"You know the night I made you dinner, when you told me it was the first time you had been happy in a long time? You weren't the only one who felt that," I gently confess to her.

"I was drunk. Isn't everyone happy when they're drunk?"

I laugh and her eyes meet mine. "Don't lie to yourself."

"I'm not. You're lying to yourself. I'm a stripper, remember? I may not be one now, but I was. I can't change that." She shakes her head, causing her hair to slide against my skin.

How many nights have I lay in bed thinking about her hair spread out around her while she sleeps or hanging over me as she rides me to completion?

"I shouldn't have said what I said. I should've been man enough to admit what I was feeling for you. I said some fucked-up shit in order to cover up how I really felt."

"I don't know," she says, confusion lacing her voice.

"We'll take it slow. I just need you to stop avoiding me. I need to be able to talk to you, to see your face," I practically beg, pushing her hair out of her face.

"Friends?" she suggests with a tilt of her head.

"More than friends, baby, but we can start out as friends." I lift her chin to look into her eyes.

Autumn

OUR EYES MEET and I shake my head. Friends? Can I be friends with him? Probably…and it would *probably* be the stupidest thing I've ever done.

His hand runs along the underside of my jaw, his thumb touching my bottom lip.

"I don't know," I repeat, closing my eyes. "Why?" I don't know if I'm asking him or myself, but I just don't know why I feel this pull towards him.

"What's the worst that could happen?" he asks, leaning into me.

Heartbreak is the first thing that comes to mind.

"Autumn?"

I jump at the sound of Derik's voice and lean around Kenton's wide frame so I can see the door. My eyes meet Derik's, and then his go to Kenton before settling back on me.

"Sorry, but I gotta go and can't leave Tara on the floor alone," Derik says.

"I'm coming right now," I tell him, trying to duck away from Kenton, whose hold on my hip tightens.

"I'll see you Saturday night," Derik says, closing the door.

"What's Saturday night?" Kenton asks, and I feel his fingers dig into my skin.

"We're going out," I tell him, trying to step away again.

"A date?" The word 'date' spits out of his mouth like it tastes bad.

"We're going to a club or something." I shrug, attempting to move again.

"What club?"

"I have to work. I don't have time to play Twenty Questions with you right now," I state, finally wiggling out of his embrace.

"You'll have dinner with me on Sunday," he says rather than asks.

"I have plans."

"With who?" he growls, his jaw grinding.

"Viv," I tell him exasperatedly.

"Viv?" He raises an eyebrow at me.

"Yes, Viv. Now I really need to go." I put my hand on the doorknob to open it.

"Don't think we're done talking," he says close to my ear, startling me.

I look over my shoulder and our eyes meet. I nervously lick my bottom lip and his eyes drop to my mouth. He leans in, and I'm frozen in place. His mouth softly brushes mine and he leans back, looking at me again.

"See you at home, baby," he whispers, making it sound almost like a threat. He smiles, showing off the small dimple that fascinates me.

I inhale a deep breath and nod. My insides are going crazy, my heart beating double-time.

I walk down the hall towards the nurses' station, trying to ignore the fact I can hear his boots behind me. I spot Tara, and her eyes go big when she looks over my shoulder. When they come back to me, she smiles an odd smile and I shake my head in a slight move, letting her know to hush.

As soon as I make it to the desk, a bell goes off and I practically yell that I'll go check on the patient. Tara doesn't say anything. She just nods, and I make my way quickly down the hall to the patient's room. I take my time in the room, making sure everything's taken care of before going back to the nurses' station. I walk around the corner and see that the area's empty except for Tara. I let out a breath I didn't realize I was holding.

"Who the hell is Mr. Tall, Dark, and Handsome, and where the hell did he take you?" Tara asks as soon as I take a seat. I try to think of a way I can avoid answering that question before looking at her. "Please tell me you are sleeping with him regularly."

"Oh God." I cover my face with my hands.

"What? Oh no… Please tell me he isn't one of those guys who look all hot and yummy, but then you get to the package and get a surprise…and it's *not* a good one." She sits back in her chair, shaking her head in disappointment.

"He's just a guy who's been letting me stay with him," I tell her, hoping she'll drop it.

"So, you're not together?" Her eyebrows come together in confusion. "I would've sworn he was your man with the show he put on earlier."

"Nope." I shake my head frantically.

"Sooo…you live together, but you're not together?"

"Yes."

"How the hell can you live with someone who looks like that and not jump their bones?" she asks, dumbfounded.

"He's an ass. Trust me—it's not as hard as you think it is."

"I can see that." She nods in understanding, her eyes searching my face. "You know he wants you, right?"

"No, he doesn't."

"Oh hell yeah, he does. You should have seen the way he was looking at you and then the way he was watching your ass when you guys were walking down the hall. He wants you, girl, and he doesn't look like he is the kind of guy you can put off for very long. Not only that, but why in the world would you want to put him off in the first place? If I were you, I would be waiting for him naked on my hands and knees when he got home and walked through the front door."

"Can we not talk about this?" I ask pleadingly. The images that are now in my head of Kenton and me have started a small throbbing in my core.

"Are we still going out Saturday?" she asks, reading my face.

"Yes," I respond immediately.

"Good. I need to get out."

"Me too," I say softly before getting back to work. The rest of the night I spend quietly trying to think of a way to avoid going home.

"OH MY GOD, you have to try this," Tara says, shoving a drink in my face.

We got to the club about ten minutes ago, and after making it inside, we fought our way to the bar for a drink and to wait for Derik and his boyfriend to show up.

"What is it?" I ask, leaning away from her before taking the drink from her hand.

"An All-American Root Beer. It's so good. You can't even taste the Jack," she promises.

I put the straw to my lips before taking a small sip. She's right; it's sweet and I can't taste any kind of alcohol. "It's really good!" I shout close to her ear.

She takes the drink back from me, lifting it up to the bartender while holding up two fingers. He nods in understanding as Tara sits back down next to me.

"So, how have you and Mr. Hot Guy been?"

I bite my lip and think about that question. How are Kenton and me? Well, I'm still trying to avoid him, and he seems more determined than before to *not* let me avoid him. Before, he would leave me notes or texts, but now, I have to deal with him face to face.

Like last night. I went downstairs to get something to eat, and when I walked into the kitchen, he was there. I couldn't exactly leave without making it obvious that I was dodging him, so I went about making myself a sandwich. The only problem was that, every time I turned around, his body would rub against me or his mouth would come close to my ear when he spoke. No matter what I did, he was there in my space. By the time I left the kitchen, I was a huge mess and had to take another shower. I still can't figure out why he affects me the way he does.

"Earth to Autumn." Tara snaps her fingers in front of my face.

"Sorry," I apologize, shaking the thoughts away.

"So are you going to answer me?"

"We're fine."

"Just fine?" She raises an eyebrow.

"I don't know, honestly," I tell her with a shrug as the bartender puts two drinks in front of us. I slide my money across the bar before Tara has a chance to pay for them.

"Well, he looked pissed tonight when I picked you up."

I take a drink and smile around my straw. He was pissed. I had spent most of the day in bed. Then I'd gone down to the kitchen around five and made a frozen pizza. Kenton wasn't around, so I went back upstairs after eating. I read for a while then sent an e-mail to Sid, who I couldn't bring myself to call. Around eight, I started getting ready to go out, knowing that Tara would be there to pick me up at nine thirty.

When I walked out of my room a little after nine, Kenton was at the top of the stairs, his foot on the top landing. His head turned, our eyes locked, and my body started to vibrate from the look in his eyes. I wouldn't even call it hunger; it was more than that. His eyes took me in and his jaw started ticking.

I knew what he saw; I had on a black, strapless dress that formed to my body like a second skin. Black pumps wrapped around my ankles, lifting me up on four-inch spiked heels. My hair was up on top of my head with little pieces out framing my face. I had on minimal makeup but dark-red lipstick.

"H—" I started to greet him when he looked up at me again, but he opened the door to his room and slammed it closed behind him. I stood there for a second, and then I flipped off his closed door and made my way downstairs. When Tara arrived at the house ten minutes later, Kenton came barreling downstairs like a caveman.

Before I could get out the door and close it behind me, he pulled me inside by my hand, shut the door, and then kissed me. It was not a sweet kiss; it was rough, aggressive, and it left me panting. When his mouth left mine, his eyes were heated and still glued to my lips.

"It didn't come off," he mumbled. I had no clue what he was talking about as his thumb swiped my bottom lip. "*Fuck!*" His eyes came to mine, and I was frozen in place; all I could do was stare at him. "Why won't your goddamn lipstick come off?"

"It's smudge-proof," I whispered, shaking my head out of my daze. I took a step back, and his eyes narrowed.

"I don't like it," he growled.

"What?"

"Your hair, those heels, and that mouth." He shook his head then ran a hand though his already messy hair. "I don't like it."

My eyes narrowed and I opened the door. "Too fucking bad," I snapped over my shoulder as I went down the porch steps. I opened the door to Tara's car, getting in quickly and slamming it closed only to look up as he roared loud as fuck as I put on my seatbelt.

"So, what did you do to piss him off?" Tara asks, bringing me out of my thoughts once again.

"I have no clue. That man is confusing. One minute, he's kissing me, and the next, he's complaining about my lipstick."

"What's wrong with your lipstick?" Derik asks, joining us at the bar.

"No clue," I repeat, giving him and Stan a hug.

"Good, 'cause you look hot and your lipstick is hotter," Stan says, leaning across the bar to call the bartender over. I give him a small smile before going back to my drink.

"So how's Mr. Rough and Rugged?" Derik asks, taking the beer Stan is handing him.

"Who?" I ask.

"You know, the guy from the emergency room," he clarifies.

"That's who doesn't like her lipstick," Tara adds out of nowhere.

"I'm sure he doesn't," Stan says with a knowing smile.

"What's wrong with my lipstick?" I run my fingers over my lips, wishing now that I hadn't worn it.

"Girl, you are not stupid. I don't have a penis, but even I know that, when a man sees a woman who looks like you wearing red lipstick that makes her lips look even fuller, all he can think about is shoving something between them."

"You did not just say that." I frown at her.

"It's the truth, girly," Derik says.

Images of some of the women I have seen in Vegas, the ones who sell themselves, flash through my head, all of them with their bright-red lips and bedroom eyes.

"I need to go to the bathroom." I stand and don't even wait for Tara when she calls for me. I run into the bathroom and franticly wipe at my lips, trying to get the color off.

"Autumn, stop it. What are you doing?"

Tears spring to my eyes and I bite the inside of my cheek, trying to fight them off. I wipe my mouth again and again, but the color won't come off no matter what I do. *Stupid smudge-proof lipstick*!

"Autumn, please stop," Tara says more quietly this time, her hands going to mine at my lips.

"I just want it off."

"You know men will think the same thing whether you're wearing lipstick or not. Some guys are assholes. You're beautiful and sweet. Please don't let something as stupid as lipstick fuck with our night out."

I take a second and let her words sink in, and I let out a long breath. "Thank you," I tell her, pulling the tissue away from my mouth.

"We're friends, and that's what friends do."

It feels good to be friends with a woman, someone who knows what I'm going though, someone I can talk to about the stupid things like I've seen women on TV talk to each other about.

"Now, are you ready to finish our drinks?" she asks, making me smile.

"Yes," I say immediately. I look in the mirror, quickly making sure I look okay before following her out of the bathroom.

When we reach the bar, Derik and Stan have disappeared.

"Do you see them anywhere?" Tara asks, stretching to try to see over the crowd on the dance floor.

"No." I look around, but there are so many people here that I can't even move without bumping into someone. "Oh wait, I think I see them." I grab Tara's hand and start to lead her through the crowd to where I think I spotted Stan and Derik.

I look back over my shoulder when she stops dead in her tracks, causing me to teeter in my heels. I start to ask her what's wrong, when she yells at the top of her lungs, "I love this fucking song!" I bite the inside of my cheek to keep from laughing at her. The song is 'Sexy and I Know It,' and as much as people like the song, I really doubt anyone actually *loves* it.

When she starts dancing, I can't hold it in and start to laugh. Her long, blond hair is flying all over. Her face is a mask of concentration and her hands almost look like she's doing the hand jive.

"Dance with me!" She throws her hands in the air and spins around, closing her eyes.

I look around, seeing that everyone around me is dancing; no one is even watching what Tara's doing. I start to move my hips a little, but apparently that's not enough for Tara, who grabs both of my hands and starts spinning me around with her.

"Tara, stop!" I yell as we fly around in circles. My feet are barely keeping me upright.

"Stop being a party pooper and dance, bitch!" she yells back at me. Without warning, she lets my hands go and starts wiggling all over the place.

I laugh but join her wiggling, and then I bump my hip with hers when the song changes to Ke$ha's 'Your Love is My Drug.' We start jumping around, throwing our hands in the air, and spinning in circles.

I'm laughing so hard and having so much fun that I don't even realize that I'm in the middle of a giant crowd of people and they've all stopped to watch us. When the song ends, we both stop immediately and look around.

"Rock on!" Tara yells, making me lower my head and whisper a quiet, "*Oh my God,*" to myself. "You only live once. Fuck it," Tara says, shrugging before grabbing my hand and pulling me with her to the bar.

"Hey, there's Derik." I point to the other side of the bar, where Derik and Stan are sitting, both of them with large smiles on their faces.

"You two looked—"

"Crazy, I know," I cut him off, taking the bottle of water from his hand and drinking it in large gulps.

"I was gonna say *hot*, girl," Derik corrects with a laugh. "Happiness is a good look on you, kid," he tells me, pulling me into his side.

I take a breath, realizing that I *am* happy—really fricking happy.

"You want another drink?" Tara asks, calling the bartender over.

"I don't know." I look around at all the people who are having a good time and then out on the dance floor at all the people still dancing and laughing. *Screw it. I want to live a little.* "What are we drinking?"

"How about tequila?"

"Never had it." I shrug, watching as the bartender makes his way towards us.

"Seriously?" Tara asks, looking at me with wide eyes.

"Seriously," I repeat.

"Okay, you have to have a shot."

"Why?"

"You are not an adult until you've had tequila," she tells me, her voice all serious.

"Is this a rule?" I ask with a smile as she gives the bartender our order.

"One of many." She looks at me and smiles. "Body shots are another, but we'll get to that another time."

"I'm never doing body shots." I roll my eyes at her.

"A couple shots of tequila and you will do a whole lot you never thought you would." She hands me a little glass of clear liquid and a wedge of lime. "Lick your hand," she instructs. I do, and she picks up a saltshaker, dumping some onto my hand. "Lick it, shoot it, suck it." She nods, and I shake my head but follow her directions.

The salt is grainy on my tongue as I close my eyes and shoot back the tequila. The cool liquid burns down my throat, making me gasp for air. My hand is suddenly shoved towards my face and I cram the whole piece of lime in my mouth, pressing it up against the roof of my mouth, and then I chew on it to try to get rid of some of the heat.

I open my eyes when I hear laughing, and I pull the lime out of my mouth and look around. "What's wrong?"

"You're not supposed to eat the whole lime." Tara laughs and Stan shakes his head, smiling. "Watch me, and then you're going to do it again."

"Okay." I watch as she does exactly what I did, but in the end, she just puts the fleshy part of the lime into her mouth.

"Voila," she says, taking a bow. "Now, it's your turn."

"Okay, but this is the last one," I tell her, taking the salt from her hand while she gets the tequila from the bartender. I do the shot just like she did, the burn filling my chest as I shove the lime between my lips. "Holy cow," I breathe out.

"Now, let's dance!" she shouts, and before I can tell her yes or no, she's dragging me out onto the dance floor.

"OH GOD, KILL me now," I moan, covering my face. My head feels like it's going to explode, my stomach feels like a million bubbles have taken up home in it, and my body feels like it's been run over by a sixteen-wheeler.

"Go back to sleep," a male voice that sounds like Kenton's says and my body goes rigid.

Praying I'm wrong, I peek out from between my fingers. Nope, not wrong. *What the hell happened last night?*

"What are you doing here?" I ask, not sure I want to know, seeing how I'm wearing nothing but a sheet, his body is naked at least from the waist up, and his arm is draped across my stomach, his frame plastered to the length of mine.

"Sleep." He squeezes my waist and my stomach slightly contracts.

I try to remember last night, but my brain is coming up with nothing. My whole night is blank after my second shot of tequila.

"Stop thinking and sleep."

"I have to get up," I tell him, trying to lift his giant arm. My body feels so weak that I stop trying after a couple of seconds.

"You were up all night. You just went to bed two hours ago. You need to sleep. I need to sleep, so stop moving around."

My eyes widen when I realize that his very evident erection is pressed up against my leg. "I can't remember anything," I tell him, covering my face.

"Seeing how you drank a shit-ton of tequila last night, that's not surprising," he mumbles sleepily.

"Please don't say that word." I shake my head. Just the thought of that drink alone has my body ready to revolt. "How did I get home?"

"I'll tell you every embarrassing detail from the time you texted me until now when we wake up later."

"Oh God, I texted you?" I groan.

"You did. Now, go to sleep."

"I feel sick."

"You have nothing left if your stomach," he says on a sigh.

"What do you mean?"

"You were sick all night."

"This just keeps getting better and better," I whisper.

"Sleep, babe," he says quietly as I feel his lips against the bare skin of my shoulder; the touch has my pulse picking up.

"Why am I naked?" I ask, concentrating on the feeling between my legs. I sigh in relief when I don't feel any tenderness or anything that would lead me to believe I did anything stupider than drink too much and send drunken texts.

"You were sick and I put you in the shower last night. I tried to give you a shirt, but you wouldn't take it."

"Oh," I say, squeezing my eyes closed.

"Don't worry. I didn't see anything. *Much*," he says quietly, and I can hear a smile in his voice.

"I'm never drinking again."

"Why?" he asks, sounding surprised. "You had a good time. You just don't know your limit. I will be having a talk with Tara. No way should she have given you shots of tequila on your first night out drinking."

"You are not talking with Tara." I shake my head, imagining him talking to her. I can see it now—it would be a lot of yelling and none of it nice.

"We'll talk about it later. Right now, we're going to sleep, and then later, we're going to my Aunt Viv's house for dinner."

"Your aunt?" I shake my head in disbelief.

"Yep, my aunt."

"How in the hell does this stuff happen to me?" I question as my stomach gurgles loudly.

"You'll be okay. You had some Tums a little while ago." He squeezes my side, and I'm pretty sure my life is like a really bad Lifetime movie.

"You can go to your room," I tell him after a few minutes.

"No, I'm comfortable."

"I'm not," I whine.

"Go to sleep, Autumn."

"I can't."

"You can." He squeezes me again. "Close your eyes and go to sleep or I will give you something that will put you to sleep."

"You didn't just say that."

"Sleep," he growls.

"Can you at least move your arm so I can move?" I pull the sheet up higher on my chest, lifting my head slightly to see if I can spot a shirt anywhere near me.

"Jesus, you're a pain in my ass." He flings his arm behind him and pulls a piece of fabric from behind his back.

"Why do you have this?" I ask when I see that it's a shirt.

"I just told you. I tried to put it on you last night, but you refused."

"Oh," I whisper, slipping the shirt on over my head and then shimmying it down under the sheet.

"Now, lay your ass down and go to sleep." He tugs me back onto the bed, not giving me a choice.

I turn my back to him and try to scoot away, but it feels like it takes all of my energy to move an inch. I close my eyes as he pulls me into him. My ass curves into his hips, his arm wraps around my waist, and his bicep slides under my head like a pillow. I try not to think about how it makes me feel to be so close to him. I try to tell myself that I don't feel incredibly safe and comfortable. Before I can convince myself that I hate how I feel, I fall asleep.

I WAKE UP slowly and take notice that I don't feel the warmth of Kenton behind me, and I open my eyes, wondering if I dreamt the whole thing. I lift my head slightly and look at the clock. "Shit," I whisper, seeing that it's eleven already. I take a deep breath and smell Kenton's cologne. I lift some of my hair to my nose. The smell is so strong that my stomach flips over.

I take my time sitting up on the side of the bed, and I see that a glass full of water, two Tylenols, and a few Tums have been set on the nightstand. I don't want to think that it's sweet that he thought about how I would feel when I woke up and made sure to leave them where I would find them before I got out of bed, but I can't stop thinking about it as I take the pills.

I get out of bed and look down at myself, noticing that I'm not wearing one of my shirts, but a shirt I'm sure belongs to him. I walk to the dresser and get a pair of panties and a bra before going to the closet and grabbing a pair of shorts, a tank top, and an oversized sweater. I open my bedroom door, looking both ways before running across the hall to the bathroom.

Once inside, I quietly shut the door and turn to look in the mirror. I cover my mouth with my hand when I see myself. My hair is sticking out all over my head. My eye makeup is smeared around my eyes and down my cheeks, and my freckles stand out due to how pale I look.

"Kill me now," I whisper to my refection as I grab a couple of makeup remover cloths from the drawer and wipe my face. When I'm done, I start the shower and step inside. I look down when I feel something soggy under my feet. My dress from last night is on the shower floor, sopping wet, so I pick it up and ring it out before tossing it over the shower rail.

I don't know what happened last night, and I can't help but be thankful I don't remember anything. I can only imagine the kind of fool I made out of myself while drunk. I get out of the shower and quickly get dressed before french braiding my hair and putting on some mascara, blush, and lip gloss.

As I'm picking up my clothes from the floor, my eye catches my cell phone sitting on the back of the toilet. I pick it up, looking at the black screen, afraid to click it on. I say a silent prayer that I didn't actually text Kenton last night and that he was just joking when he told me what I'd done. I press the round button before sliding my finger across the screen.

The picture that is now my background has me almost dropping the phone into the toilet. I'm lying across the bar at the club we were at with my dress up around my waist. A guy has his back to the camera and his upper body is bent over me, his face near my stomach.

"Please, no," I whisper, and my shaky fingers press the icon for my text messages. As soon as the screen changes, texts between Kenton and me pop up. "No, no, no..." I chant, reading the messages.

Me: *Why do you hav to so hot?*
Kenton: *Where are you?*
Me: *da clubs lol*
Kenton: *What club?*
Me: *I wants to kis you all ovr*
Kenton: *Dammit, tell me where you are.*
Me: *I asj Tara shesnice.*
Kenton: *I'm on my way.*
Me: *howz that*
Me: *Yoi kisz god*

Kenton: *Go to the bar and ask for water.*

Me: *Tequeda is like watber*

Kenton: *Baby, I need you to find somewhere to sit down until I get there.*

Me: *Sitty with a nicews guy*

Kenton: *Where's Tara?*

Me: *herre*

Kenton: *Parking now.*

I close my eyes and bite the inside of my cheek hard, trying not to cry from embarrassment. I'm never drinking again.

Chapter 4

Not My Ass!

AFTER I READ the text messages in the bathroom, I try to sneak back into my bedroom, planning to hide out until it's time to go to Viv's house for dinner. Unfortunately, as soon as I make it back into my room, Kenton knocks on the door.

I think about not answering, but I don't want to be mean after he so obviously took care of me the night before. As soon as I tell him to come in, he pushes the door open, carrying a cup of coffee in one hand and a bagel in the other. I don't know how to react to him being sweet. Since the day I met him, things have been a roller coaster, and I'm not someone who likes amusement parks.

"I want you to try to eat something," he says, walking around the bed.

"Thanks, and thank you for taking care of me last night," I tell him, taking the coffee from his hand as he sets the bagel down on the bedside table.

"How's your head?"

"Better. Thanks for the Tylenol."

"You're welcome."

The small smile he gives me has my eyes dropping to his mouth. I take in his face, the scruff along his jaw, and the way his hair hangs, touching the collar of his shirt.

"You need to shave," I blurt and look away, but my eyes go back to him when his laugh hits my ears.

"You think so?" he asks, rubbing his hand along his jaw. I want to lean forward and touch his face to see what it feels like against my skin.

"You might like it," he mumbles, his eyes dropping to my thighs.

I don't know if he's thinking what I am, but the thought of the rough scruff on his jaw running along the inside of my thighs has my hands shaking.

"Eat. We'll head out in a couple of hours. I got some stuff to take care of before then, but come find me in the office," he says, his voice sounding deeper than before.

I nod, not able to say anything. I have a feeling that any words that might come out of my mouth right now would be incoherent anyways.

He looks at me again then stands, shaking his head. I watch him as he walks to the bedroom door, stops at the threshold to look at me over his shoulder before tapping the doorjamb twice, and then leaves the room. I let out a long breath, wondering what the hell I'm going to do. I'm drawn to him. He scares the shit out of me. I'm never like this and don't know what to do with the jumbled mess my emotions are in.

"YOU OKAY?" KENTON asks, and I look from the house in front of us over to him and nod before I start to open the door to his car. "Wait here while I come around," he says, unfolding his large body from behind the driver's seat.

I watch him walk around to the passenger's side of the car. Watching him move is fascinating to me. He reminds me of a lion or a bear, his movements fluid, even with his large mass.

He opens my door and I get out, running my sweaty palms down the front of my shorts as I stand. As soon as I clear the door of the car, his hand goes to the small of my back and he leads me up the front porch. He doesn't even knock or ring the bell; he just opens the screen door and walks us into the house.

My feet stop inside the front door. I didn't tell Viv that Kenton was going to be bringing me, and I don't want her to think that I'm rude, even if they are family.

"What's wrong?" he asks, his eyebrows coming together.

"I feel bad. I should have called and told Viv what was going on. I don't like springing this on her," I tell him, fidgeting with the ends of my sweater.

"I called her this morning and told her I was coming," he assures me.

"Oh."

"It's all good. Come on." He grabs my hand, pulling me along with him.

When we clear the front hall, we walk into the large living room, where more than a dozen people turn to look at us.

"Crap," I whisper and then glare at Kenton when he starts to laugh.

"Autumn, you're here! And look! You brought the ass," Viv says, walking towards us.

I feel my eyes go wide at the word 'ass' and start shaking my head at her.

"Oh, honey, trust me. I know this one's an ass." She pats Kenton's cheek, smiling up at him.

"Thanks, Aunt Viv." He laughs, kissing her cheek.

When she comes to me, her hands go to my face, her eyes look me over, and she smiles, shaking her head. I have the urge to bite my lip. I know what she's thinking, and she is oh-so wrong.

"Is Mom here?" Kenton asks her, and I look over at him, feeling suddenly like I might be sick.

"Yep. She's outside with your uncle."

"I'm gonna go get my mom, baby. I'll be right back," he tells me and starts to move away.

"No! I mean...don't do that. I...um, I need to go back to the house," I say quickly, trying to plan my escape. "You guys have a nice dinner and I'll just reschedule."

"Oh, nonsense," Viv says, waving her hand around.

No way do I want to meet Kenton's mom, and there is nothing anyone can say that will convince me differently, I think, feeling the panic rise.

"Honey, I'm so glad you're here," a woman says, walking into the room.

I take her in. Her dark hair is shorter than Kenton's. She's petite; I would guess close to five one. She's wearing a long, flowing dress and a blue jean vest with a wide belt wrapped around her waist. My eyes close and my head falls forward. Now I have no way to get out of this without looking like an ass.

"I thought Aunt Viv filled you in on what was goin' on," Kenton says as he picks the woman up off the floor, giving her a hug.

"She did. Well, kinda. She said you were bringing someone to dinner, and I told her if it was Cassie, I was not going to be happy," she says, and Kenton chuckles as he sets her on her feet.

"I didn't come with him," I blurt like an idiot, causing the woman's eyes to come to me. "I mean…we drove together, but we didn't come together." I lower my head and shake it back and forth. "I mean, we're not together. Viv asked me to dinner a few weeks ago, and I've been coming every Sunday since." *Shut up! Shut up, you idiot,* I tell myself. Sadly, I don't even listen to my own warnings. "Kenton and I just live together. That's all."

Viv gives my arm a squeeze and Kenton's mom looks like her eyes are going to pop out of her head. When I look at Kenton, his eyes are soft as he smiles and shakes his head.

"Mom, this is Autumn. Autumn, this is my mom, Nancy."

"Hi. It's nice to meet you," I tell her, sticking out my hand. *Nope, this isn't awkward at all.*

"You too, honey." She pulls me in for a hug then looks over at Viv and smiles. Viv smiles back, and I can see the wheels in her head are turning.

"I'm gonna grab a beer and go outside with Uncle Maz."

"Sure, honey. Go on," Kenton's mom says.

I want to grab him and have him take me with him. His eyes come to me and light up, and something about the look has me taking a step back.

"I'll be outside, baby," he conveys sweetly, taking a step towards me, and before I can step back again or duck, his hand slides around my waist and his mouth lands on mine in a kiss that forces all the oxygen out of my lungs. When his mouth leaves mine, my fingers go to my lips. "Okay, ladies. Take care of my girl," he says, pulling his eyes from me. His hands give my waist a slight squeeze, and then he turns around and walks towards the kitchen before I can ask him what the hell that was.

"So, it's a small world, huh?" Viv snarks, looking over at Nancy then back at me. "I didn't know your ass was my nephew."

"He's not my ass. I mean…sorry. Your son's not an ass or anything like that," I say, looking at Nancy, feeling my pulse race, and wishing I could teleport out of the room.

"Honey, I know my son, and I know he can be a little rough around the edges, so please don't feel bad for calling him an ass." She smiles with a twinkle in her eyes. "So, how long have you been seeing each other?"

"Oh, no, we're not." I shake my head frantically, looking between the two of them.

"Really?" She tilts her head to the side, studying me.

"No, we're not together," I insist and then glance at Viv, who is wearing a very large smile.

"That's interesting. Don't you think that's interesting, Nancy?"

"Very," Nancy says with a smile.

I look at the two women and can tell that they are both up to something. Between them and Kenton, I don't know what I'm going to do.

"So, Viv said you used to be a dancer. Is that right?" Nancy asks while we're sitting at the dinner table a short time later.

I start to choke on my sip of tea. Kenton pats my back, and I wipe my eyes with my napkin, trying to figure a way out of this.

"She was, and in Vegas no less," Viv confirms. "Maybe we could have her teach us some moves."

"Oh, God," I breathe into my napkin, feeling my face heat up.

"There is nothing to be embarrassed about, child. Hell, if I looked like you, I would never wear clothes," Nancy says, and I hear a few chuckles.

"This is not really happening," I chant to myself, looking over at Kenton, whose whole body is shaking with the force of his silent laugher. "This is not funny," I hiss.

"It's pretty damn funny." He pulls me to him by the back of my neck, putting his lips to my forehead.

"Stop," I tell him quietly, pushing at his chest, not wanting to cause a scene in front of his family.

He smiles again and shakes his head. I pull away and look around the table at everyone watching us. My eyes land on Kenton's dad's. When his go soft and he smiles, my anxiety eases somewhat.

I found out earlier that not only is Viv sweet, but Kenton's mom is really funny and his dad is like a giant teddy bear who often shakes his head when his wife says something a little crazy, pulls his daughter Toni into his side to kiss her hair when she's close, and pats his son on the back when he approves of something he says. I smile back at him before lowering my eyes to my plate.

The rest of dinner is a blur, and before I know it, I'm saying goodbye to everyone and getting into Kenton's car.

"Did you have a good time?" Kenton asks.

I roll my head in his direction and glare. "Did I have a good time? Really?"

He starts to chuckle as he starts the car. I roll my eyes, laying my head back against the head rest.

"My aunt loves you, and my mom already adores you," he says softly as I feel his hand on the bare skin of my thigh.

I pick up his hand, putting it back on his side of the console as he pulls out of the driveway. "Your whole family is very sweet," I tell him, watching as the corner of his mouth lifts up.

"I thought for sure we were making progress," he says, taking his eyes off the road to look at me with his lips twitching.

"You thought wrong." I turn my head away from him, watching out the car window as the scenery quickly flies by.

"You work tonight?"

"Yep," I answer shortly.

"What time?"

"I gotta be there by eleven." I roll my head on the headrest in his direction.

"You gonna take a nap?" he asks, his long fingers tapping on the steering wheel.

"Probably." I shrug. "I haven't really been able to get used to this schedule."

"Can you get on a different shift?" He sounds concerned.

"If a spot opens up, I can ask to transfer," I say, shifting against the leather of his seat.

"You gonna do that?"

"Maybe. The thing is…I really need to think about what I'm going to do. I love Vegas and everything, but this is the first place I have felt at home. I love the people and the lifestyle here. I feel a lot more relaxed than I used to, and I think I might see if I can find an apartment and move here permanently." I don't know why I just said all that out loud. Up until now, it was just a thought rolling around in my head.

"You have a place to stay as long as you want."

"Thanks," I whisper, my heart squeezing.

"You can't move out for a while though," he says, and his jaw starts ticking. "I talked to Link, and the cops are still tracking the guy."

"I know. He told me," I say, feeling a chill slide down my spine.

"Nothing's going to happen to you."

"The whole thing doesn't even feel real." I shake my head. Every time I think about what happened, I can't believe how lucky I was.

"It's very real. Five people were murdered. Don't ever forget that," he growls, his knuckles turning white on the steering wheel.

"I will never forget it," I whisper softly, my hand moving to his jaw, wanting to comfort him, but right when I'm about to touch him, I start to pull away, realizing what I'm doing. Before I have a chance to move away completely, his hand catches mine, pulling my fingers up to his mouth, where he places a gentle kiss.

"Stop fighting this," he says gently. He drops my hand to his thigh, where he covers it with his own. The harnessing warmth of his thigh under my palm has my breaths increasing. "Stop fighting us."

"There's no us," I tell him, shaking my head, trying to pull my hand away.

"You're so fucking stubborn." He tightens his hold on me.

"And you're an ass," I growl, and the car jerks to the right, onto the side of the road.

My body goes forward when he slams on the brakes. His hand goes to my seatbelt, and as soon as he presses the button, he pulls me over and onto his lap. One hand goes to my waist and the other to the back of my head and into my hair, forcing my head to the side.

"Stop," I hiss, trying to wiggle free.

"No. Every time I knock one brick out of place, you put ten more in its place," he seethes.

"Let me go."

"If I have to keep kissing you to prove there is something between us, then fuck it." His hand in my hair fists tighter as he pulls my head back, holding me immobile. "I told you before not to fucking lie to me."

"Please." I don't know if I'm asking him to kiss me or stop what he's doing, but the second the word leaves my mouth, his comes down on mine, possessing me with his kiss. I let go, completely drowning in him and his taste. My hands go to his long hair, gripping it between my fingers.

I whimper into his mouth as his other hand skims the underside of my breast. I've never wanted anyone like I want him. He makes me feel again—something I haven't done in a long time. Something about him makes me want to open up, but the part of me that clicked into place to protect myself when they took my son was so strong I didn't know if anyone would be able to get to the real me again.

"Every time I get my mouth on you, you melt," he says against my lips when he pulls his away from mine. "I know you've been hurt." I close my eyes, turning my face away from him. "I know you don't want to hear it, but I won't stop until I have you."

I shake my head. He turns my face back towards him, placing a soft kiss on my forehead then my lips before lifting me off him, setting me back in my seat, pulling my seatbelt around me, and buckling me in place. We drive in silence for a long time. I don't know what he's thinking, but all I can think about is what would happen if I gave him a chance. Then I wonder if Link told him what happened to me.

"Have you talked to Link about me?" I ask, looking over at him. I don't like the idea of him learning things about my history from someone else.

"To be honest with you, he offered to tell me about you." He looks over at me, his hand coming to my thigh and giving it a squeeze before his eyes go back to the road. "I want you to be the one to tell me. I want you to trust me with whatever it is that has forced you to put up those barriers around yourself."

I let out a long breath, one I didn't know I was holding.

"I want you to come to me, Autumn," he says softly.

Those words make my heart break a little. I wasn't sure I would ever be able to go to anyone ever again. I close my eyes and fight back the tears that've started stinging my nose. When we get to the house, he says a quiet goodbye, telling me that he has some business to take care of. I nod, go into the house, and straight up to my room, where I crawl into bed, pulling the pillow over my head so I can cry.

Chapter 5

Done, I'll Give Her Crazy

(Oops, did I do *that*?)

"WE HAVE A Life Flight coming in," Tara says, coming into the room where I've been taking care of a patient. I automatically stop what I'm doing and follow her. "Derik has already started getting things ready. The victim is a young male suffering head trauma," she says as we hurry into the emergency room.

As soon as the helicopter lands on the roof, Tara and Derik are out of the room, meeting it, while I stay behind and make sure we have enough supplies and everything is in order. When they arrive at the room, my world feels like it closes in around me. A little boy no older than ten is strapped to the gurney. His neck is in a brace, his face is cut and swollen, and his head is bandaged, blood seeping through the white gauze they've used to protect the wound. All I can see is my son. He would be about as old as the boy is. My brain tries to tell my body to move, but I can't. I'm glued to the floor.

"Autumn, I need you to come over here and help me transfer him," I hear Derik say, but all I can do is stare.

"Autumn!" Tara shouts, and my eyes go to her as she shakes her head and then nods towards the young boy, asking me a silent question. I shake my head in response.

"Autumn, I need you to pull it together. We need to help this little guy get better," Derik says gently.

My eyes go to him and I swallow the bile in the back of my throat, turning my emotions off before I start to work on autopilot. For the next twenty minutes, we do everything we can to help save the boy before he is taken into emergency surgery.

"What happened in there?" Tara asks, sitting down next to me on the bench outside of the emergency room.

I shake my head before looking over at her. "I have a son." I close my eyes before opening them again. "I *had* a son," I whisper, correcting myself bitterly. "I put him up for adoption when he was just hours old." I look down at the floor, seeing small drops of blood on the tops of my shoes. "He would be about the age of that little boy. I'm so sorry I freaked. I…" I take a breath, closing my eyes. "I've never even thought about something like this happening." I feel an arm go around my back and Tara's head lean against my shoulder.

"I'm sorry," she whispers.

I nod as tears fill my eyes. I never once thought I would have to help a child. *I'm so stupid.* "All I could think about when I saw that boy was my son lying there."

"Honey," she moans painfully, making me bite the inside of me cheek. Taking comfort from people is something new to me. Hell, having someone care enough about me *to* comfort me is something new to me.

"I think I need to leave for the night," I tell her when I feel tears begin to fall from my eyes. "I'll see if I can get someone to come in. I just don't think I'm going to be a lot of help right now." I breathe through my tears.

"Rach needs hours. She'll come in. I'll give her a call now," Tara says softly.

"Thank you," I whisper, wiping my face. I never cry in front of people. I was never allowed to show emotion like that. One of my mother's favorite sayings was, "*If you want to cry, I will give you something to cry about,*" and she often kept her word.

"Go home and sleep, girl, and I'll see you tomorrow," Tara assures me, rubbing my back.

I stand, giving her a quick hug before I make my way to the front desk. I grab my bag and head out to the parking lot. Once I have my car door unlocked, I toss my bag into the passenger's seat, get behind the wheel, and shut the door. I lean my head back and close my eyes.

All I keep seeing over and over is the little boy, his face bruised and battered from the car accident he was in. I can't even imagine what his parents are feeling right now. I turn the car on, more tears filling my eyes.

I don't even know how I make it back to Kenton's. Once I let myself into the house, I quickly set the alarm before heading upstairs. When I reach the top landing, Kenton's standing in his bedroom door. His shirt is off and the pajama pants he's wearing are barely hanging on his hips. I look at the hand he has resting against his thigh, seeing that he's holding a gun.

I look up at his face again. This time when our eyes meet, his are concerned. Something inside me snaps and I run to him, seeing surprise on his face right before I shove mine into his chest and my arms wrap around his waist as I sob loudly.

"Baby?" he whispers, pulling me harder against him. I'm grateful that he doesn't say anything else for a long time; he just stands there holding me in his arms, offering me comfort. "Come on. Let's lay down." He pulls me with him to the bed, sets me on the edge, and then lays his gun on the nightstand before going to the dresser. I watch as he pulls out a shirt before coming back to me.

I take the shirt from him as he turns around, giving me a little privacy to change. I pull off my scrub top quickly, tug his shirt on, and then kick off my shoes along with my pants. I scoot up the bed as he turns back around. He climbs into bed and his big body wraps around me, holding me against his chest.

"Talk to me," he says as his hand slides through my hair.

I take a breath, my heart beating out of my chest because of what I'm going to tell him. "When I was sixteen, I got pregnant," I whisper, feeling his muscles tighten. "When my mom found out, she sent me away to a home for girls who were expecting." Tears begin to fill my eyes again, so I squeeze them tightly, trying to fight them off. "The day I had my son, I got to spend two hours with him before they took him away from me." I feel a knot form in my throat, making it hard to breathe. "I never wanted to give him up."

"Fuck," Kenton rumbles, pulling me closer to him. Feeling the strength in his arms gives me the courage to continue.

"A little boy was Life-Flighted in tonight." I close my eyes, seeing the child in my head. "When I saw him, all I could think about was my son, who would be close in age to him." I open my eyes and tilt my head back to look up at Kenton. I can barely make out his image with the moonlight shining through the window. "Sometimes when I'm out and I see a little boy, I wonder if it could be him. Logically, I know it's not, but my heart still hasn't accepted that he's lost to me after all these years and I will never see him again."

"I can't imagine that's something easy to accept," he says softly, running a hand down my back. "Why didn't your boyfriend help you find a way to keep your son?"

"He didn't want me or a child. When I told him I was pregnant, he told me he didn't want to have a kid and he was breaking up with me." I cry a little harder, reliving the devastation I felt back then. "He was happy when my mom contacted him, telling him that she was forcing me to put the baby up for adoption and he needed to sign the papers."

"That's fucked up, baby."

"I know," I whisper.

There is nothing else to say. Kenton now knows some of my past—really, the worst of it—and I wonder what he's thinking about as he holds me until I cry myself to sleep.

I WAKE UP feeling cocooned in warmth. It takes a few seconds for last night to come back to me and to remember that I willingly climbed into bed with Kenton. I can only imagine what he thinks of me now. I try to lift my head, hoping I can sneak away from him, but his giant hand is wrapped around my hair, holding me in place. Between that and his leg over mine, I can't move at all.

"You're not sneaking out on me." His voice is gravelly with sleep, and I close my eyes, trying to think of what I need to say.

"I'm sorry about laying all that stuff on you last night." I hide my face in his chest.

"I'm glad you came to me. I'm sorry about your son. I can't even imagine what you're going through." He takes a breath, pulling me closer to him. "If you want, I can find him for you."

"What?" I ask, caught off guard.

"It's what I do, baby," he says completely seriously, and my heart does a double thump at the sweet offer.

"It was a closed adoption," I whisper, tears filling my eyes again.

"Doesn't matter." He shrugs.

"What do you mean?"

"I have ways of finding people. You say the word and I'll find your boy for you."

The building tears begin to fall as I think about finding my son. Then I wonder what I would even do with the information. Would it hurt more knowing where he is? Could I even handle it?

"I don't know," I mumble. "I would like to know if he's happy, but I don't know if I could handle seeing him or knowing where he is."

"I get that." He gives me a gentle squeeze. "You don't need to decide right now. The offer has no time limit on it."

"Thank you." I unconsciously rub my face against his chest, breathing in his unique smell. His warmth and smell have me wanting to get even closer to him.

His hand in my hair pulls my head back as the leg he has over mine moves to between my legs. His eyes search my face for a long moment before his face lowers and his mouth gently touches mine.

"I can't get enough of your mouth," he says against my lips, kissing me again. The hand I'm resting between us starts to inch towards his torso, but I stop myself. "Touch me," he says, grabbing my hand and pulling it to his chest.

His skin is so warm, and the light scattering of hair he has on his chest prickles against my fingers. His hand on top of mine moves to my hip then down the curve of my ass, pulling my hips closer to his. I can feel his erection hard and long between us. I start to breathe heavily; I feel like I can't get enough oxygen into my lungs. My hand on his chest travels up to his hair at the back of his head, running it through my fingers as his mouth travels from mine, down my cheek, and then across my neck, the scruff on his jaw scraping against my sensitive skin.

"Jesus, you smell good," he rumbles against my throat as his tongue touches me there. I tilt my head farther back, pressing my thighs together, trying to alleviate the ache that is building between my legs. "Shit," he groans.

My eyes open and I look at his face, wondering why he's stopping, and then I hear his phone ringing.

"DON'T LOSE THAT look," he orders as he quickly twists his upper body away from mine before turning back over, holding his phone in his hand. His eyebrows go together and he shakes his head, sliding his finger across the screen. "This better be fucking good," he growls, looking at me. His eyes narrow on me when I hear Justin's voice say something about pulling the stick out of his ass, making me smile. "Do not fucking encourage him," he says, shaking his head when I laugh harder after hearing Justin yell through the speaker that Kenton stole me away from him and he's going to find a way to win me back.

"Did you call for a fucking reason, or are you just callin' to piss me off?"

I can't hear Justin's response, but I can tell that Kenton doesn't like it by the look that comes over his face as he listens.

"Fuck," he clips, dropping his head. "Yeah, I'll be there soon." He pulls the phone away from his ear before dropping it to the bed next to my head. "I gotta head out."

"Okay." I bite my lip, wondering what I'm supposed to do. This whole thing feels surreal to me. I don't know if I want to kiss him again or run away and pretend like nothing happened.

"You gonna be okay?"

His question hits my chest and I feel my face go soft at his concern for me. "I'll be okay," I assure him quietly.

"You workin' tonight?"

"Yeah. I feel bad about what happened last night and leaving early. I don't want them to think I'm flighty. I really like working there," I say, absently rubbing the sheet between my fingers.

"Did you talk to Tara last night?" I nod yes and his fingers run over my cheek. "You're good then. That bitch is crazy. She would never let them think less of you."

"Don't call her a bitch," I say defensively.

"I mean 'bitch' in the nicest way possible." He smiles, dropping his face towards mine.

As soon as our lips touch, his hand goes to the back of my head, holding me to him while controlling the kiss. When he pulls his mouth from mine, I can't help the whimper that escapes.

"When's your next day off?" he asks through heavily panted breaths.

"The day after tomorrow," I reply just as breathlessly.

"I'm taking you out."

"Like a date?"

"Exactly like a date."

"Um…" I say, not knowing how to respond.

"It's not up for debate. We're going out."

"Excuse me?" I narrow my eyes. "You need to ask me if I would like to go out with you." No way am I going to let him boss me around.

He rolls until I'm on my back and one of his legs is between mine. His hands capture mine, bringing them above my head. Then he bends his head and whispers into my ear, "Autumn, will you have dinner with me?"

"Maybe." I smile when he growls against the skin of my neck.

"Please?" he asks, his tongue snaking out to touch my sensitive flesh.

My body arches back. Having him cover me is doing crazy things to my body. I don't know if I want to pull him closer or push him away only to climb on top of him. My hands run down his back, feeling his smooth skin under my fingers.

"So, what do you say?" he asks, his hand running down my bare thigh.

"What?"

I feel the vibration of his laughter before he pulls away so I can see his face. "What's your answer? Am I taking you willingly, or do I need to force you?"

My eyes drop to his mouth and he smiles. "I guess I could suffer through a date with you. Who am I to pass up free food?" I ask with a straight face.

His hands go to my sides and he starts to tickle me. I have never been tickled before and it catches me off guard, making me scream in horror.

When he realizes that I'm not shrieking playfully, his body stills and he looks down at me in question. Tears fill my eyes again and I don't even know what to say.

"It's okay," he says gently, removing his hands from my sides and sliding them into my hair. "We can talk about what just happened another time."

No way am I going to tell him about my childhood. Instead of saying that, I just nod. His eyes search my face, and I know he doesn't like what he sees when his jaw starts ticking.

"I gotta go or I would make you talk to me."

"Go. It's not a big deal." I push his chest and he shakes his head.

"Fuck me." He drops his head before lifting it again, his eyes looking me over. "Just like that, you replace those fucking barriers."

"You need to go," I say, really wanting to be away from him and how exposed I feel.

"Swear to Christ, if I didn't know that the reward would be worth it, I wouldn't waste my fucking time with this bullshit."

His words are like a slap in the face and I flinch, closing my eyes for a second before opening them back up. "Get off me," I say softly, and he presses me harder into the bed.

"Shit, I di—"

I cut him off, shoving at his chest and yelling at the top of my lungs, "Get the fuck off me right now!" I wiggle around, trying to break free. Not being strong enough to get him off me has tears of frustration forming in my eyes. "Please get off me," I whisper, closing my eyes. My body loses its fight, knowing that it's pointless; he has all the power.

"This isn't over," he says quietly, kissing my forehead.

I don't say anything; I just wait until I feel him get up. As soon as his weight is off me, I jump out of bed and look around for my stuff from the night before. I quickly grab it and open his bedroom door. Then I shut it behind me and run down the hall to my room, slamming and locking my door behind me.

I drop the clothes in my hands to the floor before I go to the closet, pull out a bag, and start to pack. I need to get out of here. My heart is wide open with him. Somehow, he has maneuvered through my defenses and now has the power to hurt me, and he isn't someone I trust with that power.

He has proven on more than one occasion that he can be an ass. How can I possibly put myself out there to be hurt by him again? I hear him coming down the hall and brace myself. When his fist pounds on the door, I close my eyes before yelling, "Go away!"

"You even think about leaving me, Autumn, and I will hunt your ass down and spank the shit out of you." He pauses and his voice gentles. "I don't have time to talk to you right now, but we will be talking about what happened."

What is happening to me? The sound of his voice has me dropping my bag onto my closet floor.

"I'll text you later, baby," he says softly.

I walk to the bed and lie down, pulling some of my hair to my face to smell it. Just like the last time I slept with him, his scent is clinging to my hair. I need to get it together; I need to stop running from him. I have a feeling that, if I do get away from him, it would be the biggest mistake of my life, and I have made enough mistakes to last a lifetime.

I stand and go to the window to make sure he's gone before I go downstairs. I need my phone out of my bag, and I left my purse in my car last night when I came home. I pull on a pair of shorts and leave my room. I turn off the alarm before opening the front door. The second I hit the front porch, a silver convertible pulls up. I squint my eyes, trying to see who it is, and when I recognize the driver, I run to my car, open my door, quickly grab my bag, and run back to the front porch.

"Do you ever wear clothes?" Kenton's ex, Cassie, yells.

I want to tell her no, but instead, I run into the house, dropping my bag next to the door. I almost have the door closed when it's pushed open and Cassie grabs a handful of my hair.

I have never been in a fight in my life. I have been beaten many times, but I've never fought back, knowing that the consequences would be a lot worse if I did. My body freezes, and then my adrenaline surges. I turn around and smack her across her face. Her hand goes to her cheek, and her eyes widened then narrow.

"You bitch," she says, smacking me back a lot harder than I hit her.

"I'm a bitch?" I shake my head in disbelief. "Get out of this house right now," I say with a scary calmness, holding my stinging cheek. *I'm too old for this crap.*

"How does it feel knowing you're sleeping in a bed I picked out…that I fucked him in?"

Okay, so that didn't feel good, but I keep my face neutral, not wanting to give her the satisfaction of knowing that her words affected me. "Get the fuck out," I tell her, leaning forward and pointing at the door.

"You're sleeping in my bed with my man and you want me to get out?" She lets out a laugh then looks me over.

"He's not yours," I hiss.

"He will always want me!" she shrieks. "Why do you think he hasn't changed the bed or redecorated?"

Wow, this chick is crazy, but her telling me about her and Kenton in that bed over and over again is grating my nerves. I turn and run up the stairs as fast as I can. I hear her following me, but I'm on a mission.

I run to Kenton's room, locking the door behind me. My eyes land on the bed, which is still messy from this morning. I look around and see that he has a large sliding glass door in his room that leads out onto the upper balcony. Cassie starts pounding on the door, and I quickly look at it before running to the bed to toss the covers, sheets, and pillows onto the floor.

The bed is queen-sized, so even with the weight of the mattress, I'm still able to pull it off the bed, pushing it to the side. I see that the side rails hook into the headboard and the slats are what keeps the mattress up, so I toss the slats aside then pull up on the side pieces. The bed falls apart, the footboard falling to the floor and the headboard hitting the wall.

I go to the foot of the bed and pick up the wooden piece, carrying it over to the balcony. I open the sliding glass door and haul the footboard over to the railing. Seeing Cassie's car parked right under me, I say, "Fuck it," and toss it over. It lands in her back seat, making me smile. I do the same with the two side rails; these miss and land near her car on the ground.

Cassie has no idea what's going on; she is still pounding on the bedroom door. I go to the headboard, and with this piece being much heavier, I scoot it across the hardwood floors and out onto the balcony. I lift it over the railing, where it teeters before falling over the other side; the loud crunching sound of glass and metal soothes my temper.

I hear Cassie yell something as she leaves the door. I quickly get the mattress, pushing it out onto the balcony before tossing it over the edge too. With my adrenaline pumping like never before, I look down and watch as it floats like a feather in slow motion, landing with a little bounce on the hood of her car.

Cassie starts screaming at the top of her lungs then pulls her phone out of her pocket.

"Shit," I whisper. I know she's calling the cops. I start wondering where I should hide when the house phone starts ringing. I see the phone on the nightstand light up, and I debate if I should answer it or not when it stops ringing only to start up again. My gut clenches, and I know without a doubt that it's Kenton calling.

"What in God's name is going on?" I hear from outside, and I close my eyes.

Are you kidding me? Why me? Why does this stuff always happen to me? I walk to the balcony door and look out over the railing, seeing Nancy and Viv. Both are standing near Cassie, who is still on the phone. Viv looks up and I start to duck, but I'm too late; our eyes meet and she smiles.

I run to the phone when it starts ringing again. I don't really want to talk to Kenton, but right now, he's the lesser of two evils. "Hello," I answer, trying to make myself sound like I didn't just toss his bed outside and that his mom and aunt aren't downstairs probably wondering how to get me out of his house before I go crazy on him as well.

"Babe," he answers back, the one word said in a tone sounding slightly humorous and slightly pissed.

"How's it going?" I ask, looking around his room, taking it in for the first time. If Cassie did help decorate, she did a crap job. There are two nightstands, one on each side of where the bed used to be. Both are older; the matte black paint is chipping away. The dresser in the corner of the room is in pretty much the same shape.

There is nothing else in the room—no rugs, no curtains; the room is bare except for the furniture. It's a great room. The beige paint on the walls looks new, with beautiful, dark wood floors throughout, large windows that look out over the forest, and the sliding glass door that leads to a large balcony I can imagine having my coffee out on in the mornings. The urge to make over his room hits me when I hear his voice growl down the line.

"Are you listening to me?"

"Um..."

"I asked if you really just tossed my bed over the balcony and onto

Cassie's car," he says in the same amused-slash-angry tone.

"Oh, I…" I try to come up with some other reason why I would have done what I just did without making it seem like I may be insane.

"Do not fucking lie," he says, cutting me off before I can even think of something to say.

"I wasn't going to lie," I snap, knowing that I was perhaps going to fib a little about what happened, but I wasn't going to lie.

"Autumn," he rumbles out.

"Okay, yes," I huff out, annoyed. "I tossed your bed onto her car. Well, really, I tossed her bed *in*to her car, so I was just helping her move it out." I press my lips together knowing how stupid that sounds.

"You were helping her move it out," he repeats, and I can't figure out if he's growling or laughing. "What the hell happened?"

"I went to my car 'cause I left my bag in the passenger's seat last night and I needed my phone. When I was outside, she pulled up. I tried to get into the house and lock the door, but she grabbed my hair. I may have smacked her, and then she may have smacked me back. She started telling me about you and her in your bed, and I may or may not have gotten pissed, ran up to your room, and threw your bed over the balcony onto her car. Oh, and your mom and aunt might be outside right now." I whisper the last part, out of breath.

"You were jealous," he says, sounding slightly surprised.

"No, I was pissed," I correct.

"If you weren't jealous, why would you care what she said to you?"

Okay, I'm not going to answer that question. "I'll buy you a new bed," I tell him, hoping to end this conversation.

"This isn't about the bed, Autumn. This isn't even about Cassie. This is about you realizing what you're feeling and accepting it."

I feel myself heat up. I know what I'm feeling. I just don't know if I can trust him with these feelings.

"Autumn, are you in there?" I hear from outside the bedroom door, and my head drops to look at my feet.

"Your mom's outside the door," I whisper into the phone, looking around the room for somewhere to hide.

"So answer the door," he tells me with an implied, *Duh.*

"I can't answer the door. She was outside with Cassie," I hiss, going over to one of the other doors in the room. As soon as I swing it open, I see that it's a large bathroom with a Jacuzzi tub and walk-in shower.

"What are you doing?"

"Looking for somewhere to hide," I tell him without thinking, walking to the only other door in the room, and as soon as it opens, I see that it's a large, very organized closet.

"You're looking for somewhere to hide?" he repeats, laughing.

"Autumn, I know you're in there. Open the door."

I close my eyes and lean my head back. I have no idea what I'm going to do, but it's time to face the music. I take a breath and walk to the door. I click open the lock, pull the door in a crack, and peek out.

"Hey. Is everything okay?" I ask, seeing not only Nancy, but also Viv standing outside the bedroom.

Nancy smiles and Viv's mouth twitches. "Looks like there was a little bit of an accident," Nancy says, and Kenton starts laughing.

"I'm hanging up," I tell him, annoyed that he is finding this situation so hilarious.

"I'm on my way home," he warns me, and I hear the line go dead.

"Oh, great," I sigh, pulling the phone from my ear. I start to toss it on the bed when I remember that the bed is no longer there, so I squeeze it in my hand.

"Did Cassie hit you?" Nancy asks, her eyes zeroing in on my cheek.

My hand naturally lifts to my cheek and I swallow. "Um…the thing is…she pulled my hair, so then I smacked her, and she smacked me back." Yes, the chick is crazy, but I'm at fault as well.

"Are you okay?" Viv pulls me into a hug, and I feel Nancy put her arms around us both.

We stand there for a few moments. I didn't think they would be offering me comfort after what I just did.

"Oh, isn't this just fucking sweet? Seriously, she hit me and trashed my car and you're fucking coddling her?" Cassie yells.

I pull back from Nancy and Viv before facing her. Her face is red with rage, but there is no mark on her cheek from where I smacked her.

"The cops are on the way. I hope you know you're going to jail for what you did."

Shit, she's right; I'm probably going to jail for what I did. Then I'm probably going to lose my job when I have to tell them why I can't show up to work tonight.

"Why are you here, Cassie?" Nancy asks her.

"I needed to talk to Kenton." She shrugs, glaring at me again.

"You know he's at work, so why are you really here?" Viv asks, stepping in front of me.

"Well, if you really must know, I wanted to tell him about the woman he has living with him. Did you know she's a stripper and was letting random men do body shots off her at a club downtown?"

My stomach drops at her evil tone. I have no idea how she could possible know about that.

"It's all over YouTube." She smirks, reading my face. "Yep, your whore face is all over the Internet."

I feel bile crawling up my throat as I look over at Nancy and Viv. I honestly don't care that people are going to see me acting stupid and drunk, but I do care that the guy in Vegas could somehow see it and know where I'm now staying. I hate the idea of bringing danger to not only Kenton, but everyone else around me—people I really care for and consider friends for the first time in my life.

"Did you do it? Did you post that video?" I ask, ready to push her ass down the stairs.

"Cassie, why the fuck do you keep showing up at my house?" Kenton asks, walking up the stairs. Butterflies erupt in my stomach when our eyes meet, and then his eyes go from soft to hard when they lock on my cheek. "She fucking hit you?" he growls. He must have forgotten that I already told him about our little exchange. His head swings to Cassie, the look on his face forcing her to take a step back. "You hit her?" he asks.

"Don't you fucking dare, Kenton Mayson. She is not the fucking victim in this situation. She hit me then trashed my car."

"You came to my house and hit my woman, and now you want to point fucking fingers? I told you to never show your face here again. I told you we have not one fucking thing to talk about."

I suddenly feel faint. *His 'woman'?* I didn't think I was his, but he just said that I am, and he said it in front of his mom and aunt. I'm not going to explore why that made me feel all squishy and warm inside.

"Now, for the last fucking time, get the fuck out of my house."

"Wait! She can't leave!" I shout, grabbing Kenton's arm.

"I'm out of here," Cassie hisses and hurries down the stairs. I start to run after her, but an arm wraps around my waist and my back hits the solid wall of Kenton's chest.

"Let her go, baby." His lips brush my ear as he speaks.

I shake my head and he squeezes me tighter. "No, she can't leave! She said there was a YouTube video of me from the bar the other night. I don't know who put it up, but maybe she does."

His body goes tight behind me and he lifts me, swinging me behind his back before running down the stairs. I look at Viv and Nancy before following behind him.

The second I reach the front door and swing it open, I see Kenton pacing back and forth, talking on the phone to someone. Cassie is next to her car trying to lift the mattress off of it. Just as I take a step out onto the front porch, two police cars pull up the driveway. Kenton's head swings my way, and he lifts his hand and motions for me to come over.

I look at the cop cars then at Cassie, who is glaring at me while trying to lift the headboard. If things were not so messed up, I'd be laughing at her. I walk to Kenton. His voice is a low rumble when he tells the person on the phone to track the video and have it removed. When he hangs up, his hand goes to the bottom of my shirt and he pulls me until I'm forced to step closer to him.

"Justin's on it. He should have the video down in a couple of hours."

When his arms wrap around me, mine automatically do the same, and I lay my head against his chest. "Don't worry, baby. Everything will be okay," he says right before I feel his lips at the top of my head.

I close my eyes, soaking in the feeling only he gives me, but the moment is broken when I hear someone clear their throat. I open my eyes and turn my head. A cop is standing there, his mouth curved into a slight smile. I don't know what he could possibly be smiling about, but his eyes go from me, to Kenton, then over to Cassie, and he shakes his head.

"Looks like you got a little bit of a situation on your hands here, Mayson," he says, tilting his head towards Cassie and her car, where there is another cop talking to her. "Wanna tell me what happened?"

"Cut the shit, Ford. You know that woman is crazy as hell," Kenton says, and I bite the inside of my cheek, wondering if it's wise to talk to a cop like that.

"You were warned about her. Everyone told you to be careful when you got with her, but you are so fucking stubborn you had to find out that shit for yourself. Seems to me you have been taught a valuable lesson," Officer Ford says as I try to pull away from Kenton, who only holds me tighter. "So what happened?" he asks again.

"Cassie showed up here not long after I left to head to the office. She pushed her way inside."

"So how did the bed end up in her car?" he asks, looking at me.

"I may have lost my temper," I whisper.

Officer Ford smiles then shakes his head before looking at Kenton.

"I want her arrested!" Cassie screeches, and I look in her direction, seeing her pointing at me. "I want to press charges."

"Shit, this is going to be a lot of paperwork," Officer Ford grumbles, shaking his head.

"She pushed her way into my house and attacked my woman. If she presses charges, I will do the same," Kenton says only loud enough for me and Ford to hear. "I will pay for the damage to her car, but I want her gone and to understand that, if she comes back, I will no longer be nice about keeping her away."

I don't know what he means by that, but it doesn't sound good. Officer Ford nods and walks over to where Cassie and the other officer are talking. I watch as he says something to Cassie. Her eyes narrow before getting big, and she turns her head to glare at us.

"Go wait inside with my aunt and mom, baby, while I take care of this," Kenton says, and I wonder if he saw the look Cassie just shot at both of us.

"I'm sorry about this," I tell him. "Maybe I should find somewhere els—"

"You even think about running out on me now and I swear to Christ I will blister your ass," he says, cutting me off.

"Your family," I say softly, reminding him that we're not the only ones he needs to worry about.

"My family is safe and so are you."

I don't know if that's true, but I do feel safer with him than I would anywhere else. Plus, I have a feeling that, if I did leave, he would do exactly as he threatened. What I don't understand is why that thought alone has a dull ache beginning to throb between my legs.

"She's agreed to not press charges if you agree to pay for the damage to her car," Officer Ford says, walking back up to us.

I look over at Cassie and then at the car. I have some money saved up and can afford to have it fixed. I don't want Kenton paying for the damage when this was all my fault to begin with.

"I'll pay for it," I tell Ford.

"You're not paying," Kenton says, shaking his head. I narrow my eyes and try to step away from him so I can fully have it out with him. "She's my ex. If she hadn't shown up, this wouldn't have happened." Well, he has a point, but if I hadn't thrown the bed over the balcony into her car, we wouldn't even be having this conversation. "Go wait inside with my mom and aunt while I get this sorted," he says again, his arms releasing me.

His tone and bossy attitude have me wanting to punch him in the stomach. My hands ball into fists at my sides, and his eyes drop to them before meeting mine again as a smirk appears on his face.

"You gonna hit me?"

I shrug then look at Officer Ford. "Would you arrest me?"

He smiles and shakes his head. I look back over at Kenton and grin.

"Jesus, you're cute when you're pissed," he says, catching me off guard. Something about that statement only serves to make me madder. "Now, stop fucking around and go wait inside."

Without thinking, I kick him in the shin, turn around, and run as fast as I can up the stairs and onto the porch—right into his mom.

Crap.

"Child, I'm starting to wonder if you need anger management," Nancy says, grabbing my hand, pulling me inside the house, and closing the door behind us.

"I'm not normally like this," I mumble, lowering my head when I see Viv smile.

"I don't know what is going on with you and my son, but you're good for him. He needs someone to put him in his place and keep him on his toes. His life is so serious and revolves around people listening to him and doing exactly what he says when he says it. I don't know about you, but that would get old." She shakes her head, smiling.

I don't want to get their hopes up about Kenton and me, so I decide to change the subject and avoid the topic, even though I have a feeling that I'm not going to be able to avoid it much longer.

"So, what brings you guys to the neighborhood?" I ask casually, leaning back on my heels. I bite my lip when Viv starts to laugh, looking over at Nancy.

"Well, Kenton called and said you needed company."

A light bulb goes off in my head and I know exactly what happened. He thought I was going to run off, so he sent for backup. The door opens and Kenton walks in. I'm surprised by the smile that lights up his face when our eyes meet.

"Tow truck's on the way," he says, walking towards me. I look around, trying to find an escape route. He looks at his mom and gives her a grin. "Can you start some coffee while I talk to Autumn?" he asks her.

She looks at me and her eyes sparkle when I start shaking my head at her. "Sure, honey," she tells him, turning towards the kitchen. "Viv, let's go make coffee," Nancy says with a smile.

Viv's eyes come to me and she smiles, shaking her head.

"No!" I semi shout. "You should really spend some time with your son. I can totally make the coffee," I tell them, starting to head towards the kitchen. I feel myself being tugged back by the hem of my shirt. When I look over my shoulder at Kenton, I glare.

"We need to talk," he informs me.

"We'll be in the kitchen," Nancy says, Viv following close behind her.

I close my eyes, letting my head drop forward.

"Thanks, Mom," Kenton says as I turn around to face him and my shirt twists around my stomach. His eyes drop to my mouth and he takes a step towards me. I try to take a step back, but his hand, which is still wrapped around my shirt, prevents me from going far. "You kicked me," he says quietly, his mouth brushing mine, leaving me paralyzed.

"Sorry," I say, getting lost in his eyes.

"Are you really sorry?"

"No," I whisper, watching his eyes grow dark.

"I didn't think so." His tongue touches my bottom lip, making me gasp as his teeth give my bottom lip a punishing nip and tug. My hands lift to his hair, pulling it at the roots, as his hands slide down my sides and over my ass, where he gives me a squeeze.

The feeling of his hands on me has me jumping up without thinking and wrapping my legs around his waist. He groans, pulling my hips tighter against him. My back hits the wall and I whimper. His mouth leaves mine and travels to my ear, nipping it before his lips make their way down my neck, licking and biting along the way. When his mouth comes back to mine, my hips grind against him, trying to get some friction.

"Coffee's ready—oh! Crap. Sorry," I hear Viv say.

My eyes open, my teeth release his bottom lip, and I look over his shoulder, seeing Viv heading back into the kitchen.

His hand cups my cheek, pulling my attention back to him. "I hate that she hit you." His words and the look in his eyes as he studies my cheek make my heart start to pound harder.

"I'm okay. I'm sorry about your bed," I tell him. Now that I'm not in the moment anymore, I feel bad for having lost my temper.

"I needed a new one anyways." He smiles, and my fingers go to his cheek, pressing into his dimple. "We good now?" he asks, and I know he's talking about this morning.

I FIGHT MYSELF on what to say. I need to be honest with him. He scares me, but not exploring this thing with him scares me more. I look over his shoulder before my eyes search his face.

"I know you didn't mean it like you said it. You're the first person in a very long time I find myself opening up to." I cover his mouth with my hand when it looks like he's going to speak. "You're also the first guy since my first that I have been interested in. I feel vulnerable when I'm with you, and I hate that your words have the power to crush me, but they do," I confess softly.

His hand comes to mine, pulling it from his mouth, and he kisses my palm before placing it against his chest. "I say shit I don't mean sometimes. It's no excuse and I'll work on it, but you need to work on opening up to me." His eyes search my face before his lips brush mine again. "You're so fucking fearless that I forget how fragile you are." The words gently spoken against my lips cause my eyes to slide closed.

"I'm not fearless," I tell him, resting my forehead against his. "I'm afraid all the damn time."

"Nah." He shakes his head. "You're a fucking warrior."

Chapter 6
Annoying Roomies And Bad Guys

WHEN I PULL up to the house, it's just after seven in the morning. Yesterday, after the tow truck showed up and Kenton left to go back to work, Viv, Nancy, and I sat around the kitchen drinking coffee and chatting for a few hours. When Nancy asked about the video Cassie had been talking about, I cringed but told her and Viv what had happened and the real reason I was in Tennessee. Nancy was visibly upset about it, and I immediately told her that I would leave if she felt uncomfortable with me being here with her son.

The second the words left my mouth, she grabbed my face between her hands and I watched as tears slid down her cheeks. My heart broke when she looked into my eyes and spoke. "This is exactly where you're supposed to be. This is the safest place for you. This is where my son wants you. This is where we want you, so this is where you will stay."

I started crying and buried my face in her chest, taking something from her I never received from my own mother—comfort. I hated crying, but something about crying while she held me healed a small piece of me. That lost, lonely little girl who was never allowed to show emotion was finally able to cry until she couldn't cry anymore.

I shake my head, clearing the memory, and slide my key into the door. All I want to do is take a shower and go to sleep. I'm exhausted from being up early and not having a nap before going to work. As soon as I can, I'm going to have them change my schedule. There is just no way I will be able to keep this up.

I make my way upstairs and head right to the bathroom. I take a quick shower and wrap a towel under my arms, not even bothering with brushing my hair. I pick my clothes up off the floor and head to my room without turning on the light. I toss my stuff in the direction of my closet before pulling off the towel and begin climbing into bed.

"How was work?"

I scream when I hear Kenton's voice. I jump off the bed and run to the closet, going inside and shutting the door.

"Why are you in the closet?" Kenton asks, and I can tell that he's laughing.

"Why are you in my bed?" I ask through the closed closet door while trying to find something to put on in the dark.

"Someone threw my bed outside."

"*Shit!*" I whisper, closing my eyes. "I'll sleep on the couch downstairs," I tell him, pulling a hoodie on over my head.

When I open the closet door, I find a shirtless Kenton sitting on the side of the bed, wearing a pair of cut-off sweats that have seen better days. Somehow, I find the strength to pull my eyes from him and walk to my dresser, pulling out a pair of cotton Victoria's Secret panties and slipping them on under the hoodie.

"Where is your sexy underwear?"

"What?" I ask, my face heating up from the look in his eyes.

"You know. Silk thongs, lacy shit—where are they?"

"I don't wear those unless I have to. I would rather be comfortable," I explain. I know that a lot of women go gaga over sexy panties, but I couldn't care less. I hate the feeling of something crawling up my ass all day.

"I have to tell you. I have seen you in those things three times now, and all three times, that damn underwear has done more for me than any skimpy shit I've ever seen."

"Can we never talk about you and what you've seen other women wear please?"

He smirks, his eyes running down my legs. "Come to bed."

"No." I shake my head, looking at the door.

"You try to sleep on the couch and I'm dragging your ass back up here to bed," he threatens.

"I don't think that's a good idea."

"Afraid you won't be able to keep your hands off me?" He smiles.

"You wish." I roll my eyes, knowing that is the exact reason why I don't want to get into bed with him.

"Come on, babe. I can tell you're tired."

I look at the bed then him. I am really tired. I open my dresser, pull out a pair of shorts, put them on, and walk over to the opposite side of the bed before getting in. I hear his laugh as he lies back down, shutting off the light. I put my back to him and close my eyes.

I'm just about asleep when I feel him put his hand around my waist, and he pulls me across the bed to him so his body curves around mine and his hand can wrap in my hair.

"What are you doing?" I ask him sleepily.

"Sleeping," he says softly, kissing the back of my head.

I know I should get up and leave or at least put up a little bit of a fight about cuddling with him for the third night in a row, but I can't. I feel too warm, too comfortable, and way too exhausted to fight what I'm feeling. I feel him kiss me again and his hand go a little tighter, and I'm pretty sure I hear him whisper, "She's getting it," as I fall asleep.

I WAKE UP in complete darkness. My first thought is how great I feel. I have forgotten what it feels like to wake up after a good night's sleep. It takes a second to realize that it's pitch black in the room. I sit up quickly and look at the clock on the bedside table, and my heart starts beating out of my chest when I see that it's four o'clock. *I missed work!*

I jump out of bed and run to the door, swinging it open only to be bombarded with bright daylight. I look over my shoulder into the room and see that there are now dark, wooden blinds on the windows, whereas before there were only sheer curtains. My heart, which was already beating hard, starts to beat harder. Kenton put in blinds while I was at work, knowing how little sleep I've been getting. That was sweet. Really sweet.

I go to the bathroom, quickly taking care of business, and then head down to the kitchen. As soon as I make it around the corner, I'm surprised to see Kenton there, wearing the same cut-off sweats he had on last night and a pair of sneakers. His head is back, his throat working vigorously while he downs a bottle of water. The ends of his hair are dripping with sweat along with his bare chest.

I stand there captivated by him; I can't pull my eyes away no matter how hard I try. Just watching him drink water is making the space between my legs get tingly. When the bottle's empty, he pulls it from his mouth, the back of his hand goes to his lips, and he swipes them. As soon as his head turns, his eyes land on me and a look I'm starting to become familiar with fills his eyes.

"How'd you sleep?" he rumbles.

I stand there staring at him, trying to comprehend what he just said over the lustful haze that's filling my head.

"You put up blinds," I say when I finally find my words and then want to smack myself for being an idiot.

"I know how tired you've been," he says, his eyes going soft.

"That was very sweet, and I actually slept really great. When I woke up, I thought I'd overslept and missed work."

His smile makes the breath catch in my throat.

"I thought you would be at work," I tell him, trying to think of something else to say besides, *"Please kiss me."*

"Yeah. I have to leave for a couple of nights. Justin has a lead for me, but my flight isn't until after midnight, and I wanted to make sure you would be okay being here alone."

My heart plummets. I don't want him to leave, but I know his work is important. Plus, I would look really stupid if I were to beg him to stay. "I'll be fine. Don't worry about me." I wave him off, trying to do the same with the feeling of loneliness starting to fill my chest. I've forgotten what that feels like; I haven't felt it since I moved here.

He shakes his head and takes two long steps until his body is crowding mine. "I like worrying about you."

"Why?" I ask softly, my eyes drawn to his mouth.

"Honesty, I don't know."

I look at him and my hands go to his chest when I feel like I might fall over from the heat in his eyes.

"What I do know is I want this"—his finger presses lightly into my chest above my heart—"more than I've wanted anything, and that right there tells me everything I need to know."

"Oh," I breathe. The words aren't deep or particularly meaningful, but something about the way he said it, with such sincerity, has me leaning deeper into him.

His hand goes to the back of my neck and the other around my waist. I expect him to kiss me, but instead, he just pulls my head into his naked chest and the rest of me tighter against him.

We stand there for a long time with our arms wrapped around each other. I want to ask what he's thinking, but I'm too afraid to break the moment. Instead, I listen to the sound of his heart beating rhythmically against my ear as I memorize the thud and double beat along with the way his chest feels when it expands against my cheek. This is a moment I know I can recall the next time I need comfort.

"When I get home, we have a date."

"Maybe."

I smile as I hear his low growl. "I'm not even pissed that you wanna fuck with me right now." He pulls my head away from his chest, his hands go around my neck, and his thumbs slide under my jaw, tilting my head back. His mouth lowers and my eyes start to flutter closed. "Every time you fuck with me, it makes me wanna fuck you. One day, we're going to get to a point in our relationship where you'll say something to set me off and I'll bend you over right where you stand and punish you for misbehaving or talking back."

My clit starts to pulse. I can feel my breathing increase, my chest meeting his on each deep inhale. He closes the gap between us, his lips touching mine. When his tongue touches my bottom lip, my eyes close and I get lost in his kiss. By the time he pulls his mouth from mine, I've never hated clothes more than I do right now. I have the urge to take off my sweatshirt and plaster my chest against his.

"I gotta shower," he says, resting his forehead on mine.

"Sure." I nod, my eyes still closed.

He chuckles and shakes his head against mine. "If you don't wanna come shower with me, baby, you need to hop off."

I open my eyes, seeing that my fingers have somehow gotten tangled into his hair and my legs have wrapped around his waist. I bite my bottom lip, place my hands on his shoulders, unwrap my legs, and hop down. "Sorry." I shake my head, trying to clear my needful haze.

"Don't apologize." He kisses my nose then forehead. "I'll be back down to say goodbye before I leave."

"Okay." I nod again.

His hand goes to his chest then runs down his abs. My eyes follow its movement until they drop lower, seeing his very apparent erection outlined through his sweats. My eyes get big and lift to his when he starts to laugh.

"Jesus, you're cute." He shakes his head, running a hand down his face. "I gotta go before you end up on the counter." His voice sounds deeper than normal, and I nod again. "Baby, you gotta move," he says, his hands fisting at his sides.

My gaze drops to his hands before shooting back up to his eyes when he growls. I don't know what's going on, but I immediately step aside so he can get out of the kitchen. I watch him walk away, his head bent as he mumbles something under his breath.

"Coffee," I whisper to myself.

I PULL UP to the house, seeing a strange car parked out front. My pulse starts to speed up as I wonder who it could be. Kenton messaged me when I was at work, letting me know that he had arrived at his destination safely. I didn't ask where he was; I figured that, if he wanted me to know, he would tell me. I worry that he's in danger, and maybe his leaving has something to do with my situation. I don't want him hurt because of me, but I trust that he knows what he's doing. After all, he's been doing it for years without incident.

I slowly pull into the driveway, trying to angle the car in case I need to make a quick escape. As soon as I'm able to see the front porch, I spot Justin sitting on the top step with a black duffel bag at his side and his head bent towards his phone. His head comes up when I get out of the car and slam the door.

"Hey ya, roomie," he says, giving me a goofy smile.

"Roomie?" I ask, looking at the bag next to him and then noticing the sleeping bag he has along with it.

"Yep. Boss man told me to stay here with you," he says, pointing a finger at me while standing. "I'm here until he gets home."

"That's not necessary." I start shaking my head frantically. Justin seems like a nice kid, but I'm not sure I can deal with him for more than a few minutes without wanting to strangle him.

"Aw, come on! It's going to be a great time. If you're nice, I'll let you paint my nails. I even brought my own color," he says, pulling a bottle of black nail polish out of his pocket.

"I'm not painting your nails," I huff out, wondering why the hell he would be carrying it around with him in the first place.

"Okay, you don't have to. I can do it myself." He shrugs, putting the bottle back in his pocket before bending down to pick up his bags.

"You don't need to stay here," I repeat.

"Have you met my boss?" He raises an eyebrow. "He is scary. If he calls and says, 'Justin, I need you to stay with Autumn until I get home,' I say, 'Okay, no problem, boss man.'"

"No offense, but I think I'm just as safe alone as I would be with you. Actually, I think I'm better off on my own. If you're here, I have to worry about both of us."

"You should never judge, sweet cheeks. I was a sniper. I know how to kill someone with one finger, and I guarantee nothing will happen to you while I'm here."

Wow, okay. Didn't see that coming. So I'm probably safer with him, but I still don't want him here. "I think I should call Kenton," I tell him, pulling out my cell.

"He's gone to ground," he singsongs.

"What does that mean?"

"It means he is unavailable until he's available."

"But what if you need to talk to him? What if *I* need to talk to him?"

"If there's an emergency and he needs to get back here, there's a code," he says conspiratorially.

"What's the code?" I ask, watching as he pulls out a set of keys from his pocket, opening the front door.

"No way, sweet cheeks. You don't need to know the code."

"What is it?" I put my hands on my hips, glaring at him.

"I can't tell ya." He shrugs, stepping into the house, and as soon as he's inside, he turns, grabs my arm, and drags me with him. "Now, boss man said I have to be on my best behavior and to not say anything stupid or try anything on you…unless I want to see what it feels like to be neutered. I thought that was taking things a little too far, but he didn't feel the same." He smiles, walking into the living room to set his bags down. "Also, I'm sorry to say you're going to have to keep your hands to yourself and control the urge to molest me." He flexes his arms, and I close my eyes and groan.

"I'll try to control myself," I say, opening my eyes, wondering if there is a way out of this. *I'm going to kill Kenton.*

"That would be appreciated. I wish things were different, but I like my balls just the way they are. Plus, I don't think you want to explain to my mom why I can't give her grandchildren."

Oh, God. Maybe I should make a move on him to save the world from him reproducing. "I need to go to bed," I tell him, shaking my head.

"I'll be here." He pulls out some kind of gaming console from his bag and sets it on the coffee table. Then he pulls out a controller and some wires, but what I don't see are clothes.

I watch him for a few minutes as he connects the system to the TV, and after he has everything hooked up, he sits down on the couch, pulls out a pair of headphones that have a mic, puts them on, and then turns on the game.

The second it loads, the loud sound of guns firing fills the room and men wearing camo appear on the screen. I look at the TV then at Justin and shake my head before leaving the room. I don't care if Kenton has gone to ground; I need to text him to let him know that I'm going to kill him when he gets home. Then I need to go to bed. I go upstairs, pull out my phone, and send Kenton a text.

Me: *I hope you make it home safely so I can kill you when you get here.*

I press send then bite my lip, wondering if I should apologize. I know he has my best interest at heart, but I do not want a babysitter. I toss my phone on the bed, grab some clothes from the dresser, and make my way across the hall to shower. When I get back to my room, I go directly to my phone and press the button, seeing that I got a text back.

Kenton: *Sweet dreams, baby.*

That's it? He didn't even address my threat. I huff out a breath, shake my head, toss the phone onto the bed, and pick it right back up to send another text.

Me: *Ditto.*

I hit send then feel stupid, wondering if I should've just left it alone.

I WAKE UP in complete darkness for the second morning in a row. My first thought is Kenton. I miss not having him hold me. I don't know how it's possible to miss sleeping with someone after only having it for a few nights, but I do. I stretch out and look at the clock. It's three thirty. I need to get up, send some e-mails, and pay a few bills before I have to get ready for work.

I got an e-mail back from Sid the other day, and I could tell even through e-mail that he was upset I hadn't called him. Link also told me that I should try not to have too much contact with anyone in Vegas. He's worried I could somehow be tracked. I think this is a little over the top, but what do I know?

I don't miss home as much as I thought I would. I really don't miss my old life at all. I know that Link can tell that I'm thinking about moving to Tennessee. The last time I spoke with him, he told me that he would be willing to have my stuff packed up and sent out to me if that's what I want. The idea of making this my permanent home is exciting and scary. I just want to make the right choice.

I get out of bed and pull on a pair of sweats before opening my door. The first things I hear are explosions and yelling coming from the living room below. I slept for over eight hours, and I wonder if Justin sat downstairs playing that game the whole time. Then I wonder how the hell he's supposed to 'look out for me' when he probably wouldn't hear if someone were to break down the front door.

"I made coffee!" Justin yells over the TV as soon as I make it to the bottom landing. I wonder how the hell he heard me when the stairs didn't even squeak. "Told you—you are safe with me," he teases loudly as soon as I finish my thought.

I shake my head and walk into the living room, seeing that the whole space is covered with food wrappers and open bottles of soda. I have no idea how he consumed so much food in such a short amount of time. I take a seat next to him on the couch, pull a bag of Doritos from the coffee table to my lap, shove my hand in the bag, pull out a handful, and stuff my face.

"What game is this?" I ask through a mouthful while watching a guy get his head blown off.

"Call of Duty," he mumbles. "These fuckers are campin'!" he shouts into the mic while the guy on the screen looks around him, trying to find whoever is shooting at him.

Before I know it, I'm yelling at the TV every time Justin gets shot at. I get so lost in the game that I don't even realize how late it is until I look at the clock and see that it's already after eight at night and I haven't done anything with my day besides eat junk food and lie on the couch.

"I gotta get ready for work," I tell Justin.

He grunts and nods. I get up and go to the office to get online. After I pay my bills, I check my e-mail, and the first one is from Sid.

Angel,

There is so much I should have told you, so many things I should have said. I want to hear your voice. Please call me. My number hasn't changed.

XX Sid

I close my eyes and lay my forehead against the desk. I do not want to deal with this, but I know I need to let Sid know that there's nothing between us and never will be. I feel bad, but I know I'll feel worse if I let him believe even for a second that I felt anything for him.

"What's going on?"

I lift my head and look at Justin, who is standing in the open doorway of the office.

"Nothing."

"It's something," he says, coming in and setting a cup of coffee down on the desk in front of me as he takes a seat and raises an eyebrow.

"Thanks." I take a drink of the coffee and sigh with happiness.

"So, what's going on?" he repeats, and I know there is no way he is going to let it go.

"My old boss sent me an e-mail and wants me to call him."

"That's nice," he says, leaning back in the chair.

"I think he believes there's something between us," I say quietly, shaking my head.

"Boss man won't like that." He smiles, rubbing his eyes.

"Kenton won't care."

"I beg to differ, sweet cheeks." He shrugs. "I've known Kenton for a long time and have seen plenty of women come and go—"

"I don't want to know this," I cut him off, feeling a ball of jealousy beginning to form in the pit of my stomach.

"Do you want to know how many times I came to stay when Cassie was living here and Kenton went out of town?"

"No."

"Do you want to know how many times he asked the guys to swing by her job to check on her or any of the other women he's been with?"

"No," I repeat again, that warm feeling settling in.

"Do you know how many women he's become possessive over?"

"No," I whisper.

"The answer to all of the above is *zero*. You are the first woman to have him tied in fucking knots, and I know you're going to say it's because he's looking out for you, but I guaran-fucking-tee it that's not the reason."

"Please don't say anything else," I mumble.

"Why are all women the same?" He shakes his head, running a hand through his long hair. "Women are always talking about how men are so afraid to commit when the truth is you guys send the most fucking confusing signals. One minute, you want us, and the next, you're running away."

I raise an eyebrow and he shakes his head again.

"E-mail your boss and let him down easy. If you don't and Kenton finds out about him, *he* will let him know and won't be nice about it."

"I think you're blowing this out of proportion."

"You think so?" He smiles and gives a small, humorless laugh. "Kenton had one of his best friends by the throat for calling you a sweet piece a few days after they saw you at the hospital. It took three dudes to pull Kenton off him. I've never seen him react like that over a female."

I have no idea what to do with that information. I'm not even sure I want to know what all of that means exactly.

Justin continues. "All I'm sayin' is whether you want to be or not, you're his, and he won't like your ex-boss sniffing around."

"Did you beat the game?" I ask, trying to change the subject.

"You never beat Call of Duty." He smiles then looks out the window.

"Have you heard from him today?" I ask softly, thinking about everything he just told me and really wanting to talk to Kenton. I want to know that he's okay. I really want him to know that I'm thinking about him and miss sleeping with him.

"Not after your text last night, though I'm surprised he messaged you back. But that only proves my point—you're the exception."

"You know I sent him a text?" I ask, surprised and slightly annoyed while ignoring everything else he just said.

"His phone goes thorough my computer. I get all his messages. It's easier than waiting for him to send me the info I need. In this business, a second can mean the difference between landing a case and getting hurt." He stands up and leans on the side of the desk.

I don't want him hurt, so I'm glad they're taking every precaution necessary. Then I wonder what kind of texts Kenton gets daily where he needs that kind of precaution.

"Oh God," I whisper in horror when I realize that Justin probably saw my drunken texts to Kenton. "Do you read all his personal messages?"

He smiles and nods. "Yeah. The ones from his mom are the best." He starts to laugh, and I can only imagine the kinds of texts Nancy sends Kenton. I'm sure they're something like, *Did you eat your vegetables? Are you taking your vitamins? Do you have clean socks and underwear?*

"I like Nancy."

"She likes you too," he says softly, making me wonder what he knows.

I look away and try to swallow the lump in my throat.

"I'm gonna go back out and finish my game while you send your e-mail."

"Sure." I try to smile, but I know that it's one that doesn't meet my eyes. I wiggle the mouse around until the screen lights back up and press reply on Sid's e-mail.

Sid,

I don't want you to think that I haven't appreciated you or your friendship over the last few years. I also don't want you to think that I don't care about you, but I don't think we have anything else to talk about.

I wish you all the best,
Autumn

I press send and hope that he understands. I know he may think that he cares about me or wants a relationship with me, but I've had a front-row seat to Sid's dating life over the last few years, and if he really wanted something serious with me, I doubt he would've paraded all of those women in front of me.

I close down the computer and yell to Justin as I'm passing the living room that I'm going to get ready for work. He says something back that I don't really understand due to the loud sounds coming from the TV.

Kenton

"FUCK, MAN. GOOD to see you," Link says as soon as he spots me when I exit the airport.

I pull him in for a one-armed hug and pat him on the back, and he does the same before we separate. He pops the trunk for his SUV. I toss my duffel bag in and then walk around and climb into the passenger's seat.

"I wish you were here under different circumstances," he says, running a hand over his head and using the other to start up the car.

"Me too, brother." I pull out my phone and see a message from Justin letting me know that he's at the house and Autumn is home safe from work. I don't think it'll be long before she messages me, telling me off about Justin being there.

"The police really wanted to call Autumn, but I told them she's in Europe and I would get a message to her as soon as possible," Link says.

"Fuck," I clip. "I don't want her to know her place was broken into."

Yesterday, while I was still wrapped around her in bed, Justin called and woke me up to tell me that Link had been trying to get ahold of me to let me know that Autumn's condo had been broken into. I didn't want her to know what was going on, but I needed to see for myself if I could find out what had gone down and if the break-in had anything to do with the shooting at the club.

"Chances are the two things are completely separate. Someone probably noticed that her place has been empty for a while and wanted to see if they could find anything worth pawning," Link deduces.

Those are my thoughts too, but I'm not going to chance it. I know the local PD is trying to find out what's going on, but they're taking way too fucking long. "I'm not leaving this shit to chance. While I'm here, I need to see the tapes from the night of the shooting."

"They're at the club," he says, pulling onto the highway. "Sid's there tonight. He'll let you look them over. I figure you can sleep for a while, and then we can head to the club later."

"Sounds good."

We drive in silence for a few minutes, and I know that he's dying to ask about Autumn. I'm just waiting for him to say something, hoping it doesn't piss me off when he does.

"How's Autumn?"

I smirk, looking over at him. "A pain in my ass."

"She got to you, didn't she?" he asks softly, tapping his thumbs on the top of the steering wheel.

"Yeah, man." I shake my head. "She's not what I expected."

"She's thinkin' about movin' to Tennessee."

"I know," I reply, feeling a hint of jealousy that she talked to Link about it.

"Don't hurt her, man. She's a good woman," he says.

I feel a growl start to vibrate my chest. I know there's never been anything between them, but that doesn't mean it doesn't piss me right the fuck off that he feels like he can look out for her.

"Don't," I say, hoping he gets it.

"There's a lot you don't know."

"I know she has a sadness inside her that she tries to fight, but it's so deep that she gets lost in it and has a hard time finding her way out. I know she freaks when she's tickled and has a hard time letting people in. I know she has a boy she lost, and the loss still haunts her. But I also know that she smells like flowers, loves to be held even if she denies it, is cute as fuck when she's angry, and is funny as hell when she lets down her walls. I may not know everything, but I know enough that I want to know more," I tell him, hoping he gets that this isn't some passing fuck to me.

I also hope that he understands that, yes, he may know more than I do, but she is mine to worry about now. I don't like explaining myself to people, but I want him to comprehend that she is not a conquest; she is mine, and I take looking out for her very seriously.

"When she's ready for me to know everything, she will open up to me."

"Right," he replies, no sarcasm to be found in his tone.

"Tell me about Sid." I know that Autumn worked for him, but I don't know what kind of man he is or if he keeps his business on the up-and-up.

"He's a good dude. I've known him for the last five years. He's good to the girls at the club, always willing to help them out." He pauses and takes a breath. "He has a soft spot for Autumn."

"Have they had a relationship?" I grit out.

"Autumn doesn't date. Sid's been tryin' to get in there for years, but she hasn't ever clued in or returned any of his feelings."

That makes me feel somewhat better about meeting him, but it doesn't mean I want to sit back and have a beer with the guy. "Do you think he was in on what went down?"

"Nah. He wouldn't put anyone in that kind of danger. He knew three of the men who came into the club for the meeting, but the fourth was not someone he planned for. From what I understand, the fourth man was a guy by the name of Terry Waters. He was the owner of two of the largest strip clubs in Vegas. The police had been working on building a case against him for sex trafficking and prostitution."

"Jesus." I shake my head, wondering what the fuck to do with this information.

"They think he was the target," Link explains, and I see that his knuckles turning white on the steering wheel.

"So the rest were just casualties?"

"Basically." He shrugs.

My phone beeps and I click my messages, seeing that it's from Autumn. I smile before I even read her message. I know she's pissed about Justin being there, but I want to make sure she's safe while I'm out of town and don't want her at home alone. I don't think the shooter has any clue where she is, but I know that Cassie is still on a rampage. The good news is that, as soon as Cassie gets my message from Finn, she will no longer be an issue, but until things get sorted, I don't want her fucking with Autumn while I'm gone, especially after I found out that she's the one who posted the video of Autumn on YouTube after they'd been at the same club.

Am I pissed that Autumn was letting some guy do body shots off her? Hell yes, but I know she was completely smashed when it happened. I also acknowledge that she never had a chance to experience that kind of thing before. Do I wish it had been me licking salt off her tight, little body? Fuck yes, I do, but I know only me and my mouth will be allowed to touch her from now on.

I look at the message from her and laugh before quickly replying. We pull up to Link's apartment and I realize that I'm fucking beat from the last few days. Autumn's schedule has mine all fucked up.

A few minutes later, I'm already toeing off my boots, ready to collapse on his guest bed, when he tells me from the doorway, "I have some shit to take care of, but I'll be back later, and we can head to the club then."

"Sure, man. Thanks," I tell him. Then I listen as he walks down the hallway and shuts the front door. I pull out my phone, see that she replied with one word—*Ditto*—and smile and close my eyes.

"Sid, this is Kenton. Kenton, this is Sid," Link introduces us later that night.

I look Sid over, and the first thing I notice is how put together he is. I imagine that he spends more time getting ready than most women do. His suit is tailored, his hair is combed over to the side, each piece styled just right, and his fingernails even look manicured.

"Nice to meet you." He sticks out his hand and I grasp it with one of mine, giving him a firm shake.

"You too." I nod, looking around inside the club, understanding from the decor where it got the name The Lion's Den.

"Kenton needs to see the tapes from the night of the shooting," Link says, bringing me back to the conversation.

"You working with the police?" Sid asks, looking me over.

"Kenton's the friend I was tellin' you about," Link informs him, and Sid's eyes come back to me.

"You think you can find the shooter?"

"I'll do what I can." My main concern is Autumn and keeping her safe. I don't care about any of the other shit.

"Follow me."

We walk down a long hall and into a dark office, where there is a large desk in the center of the room and large computer monitors lining one wall.

"We didn't get the guy on tape. He avoided all the cameras in the building and the two outside." He starts up the tapes from the night of the shooting.

There are no shots of the man in question, but there are images of Autumn running through the club, and even through the grainy images, I can see the terror on her face. "Where were the bouncers?"

"Two were out front and one was at the door," Sid answers.

"Did they see the shooter?" I ask, looking at the different screens to pinpoint the security on duty.

"No." He shakes his head then looks at the screen paused on a picture of Autumn.

"How did he get the drinks that were being delivered to the private party?"

"That's something we haven't been able to figure out. The bar registered and filled the drink orders but never had them delivered."

"So someone who works for you was in on it?" I ask, trying to get him to see that he can't trust anyone right now.

"I'm not sure," he says, running a hand down his face. "I want to say I trust everyone who works for me, but unfortunately, I can't."

"I'm gonna need to talk to the other bouncers," I state.

"Both the guys who worked that night are on now. You can use my office," he offers.

"Thanks," I tell him before he heads out of the room to bring the guys back.

"What are you thinking?" Link asks.

"How well do you know the guys who were on that night?" I ask instead.

"We're friendly, but not friends," Link says as I lean against the side of the desk, looking at the still image of Autumn.

I hate that she's involved in this shit. I don't like the idea of someone on the inside being involved in what went down. That means that they know who she is—and possibly *where* she is.

"My guess is that one of them has something to do with the shooter being a ghost. Have you told anyone where Autumn is?"

"Hell no." Link shakes his head, his eyes coming back to me. "I haven't even told Sid that information. He told me he e-mailed her and she wrote back, but she didn't let him know where she was."

That makes me feel marginally better, but I still don't like the idea of her being in contact with the guy. "When the guys come in, we're going to play it cool. I'm going to ask some questions about what went down and see if they have any leads for me. Most of the time, when someone is involved in something like this, they try to make up for their sins by overly playing the good guy."

"I'll follow your lead," Link says, and he does just that. He's the guys' source of familiarity and comfort.

It doesn't take long for me to figure out that Mick is hiding something. After about twenty minutes, I thank them for their time and let them know that I will be around if they remember anything else. As soon as the office door closes, I look at Link, who shakes his head and closes his eyes.

"I'm gonna let Sid know we're out."

"I'll meet you outside." I head out the front of the club and pull out my phone to send a quick text to Justin to let him know what's going on. With this new development, I'm going to need his skills to pull up some info on Mick.

About an hour later, Link and I are in his home office, sorting through the information we obtained at the club, when I receive Justin's email.

"What does it say?" Link asks, looking over my shoulder at the report Justin sent me on Mick.

"From what Justin was able to find, old Mickey-boy has been having money problems. He was three months behind on his rent, had about ten thousand dollars worth of credit card debt, and took a title loan out on his car in the amount of two thousand bucks. Two weeks before things went down at the club, he deposited thirty thousand dollars cash into his account. Did he say anything about hitting the lotto or winning at the casino?" I spin the chair around and lean back.

"Nah, he never said anything like that," he mumbles.

"If he had, would he brag about it?"

"Mick?" He nods. "Hell yes, he would brag about it."

"Looks like we need to have another talk with him." I shake my head and look up at the ceiling. After letting out a long sigh, I stand and we head out to Link's SUV.

We park across the street from Mick's place and wait for him to show up. About two hours after we arrive, he pulls into the driveway, and Mick and a stumbling blonde get out of his car and start heading inside. I get out of the truck and slam the door closed, and when Mick turns in my direction, even in the dark I can see his eyes widen when he spots me and Link walking across the street.

"What are you doing here?" he asks, taking a step back towards his closed door.

"Darlin', you're gonna need to call a cab," I tell the blonde.

She nods, pulls her phone out of her purse, and starts walking away without saying a word.

"What are you doing here?" Mick repeats, watching his date walk to the end of his driveway.

"Open the door. We need to talk."

"I'm not letting you in." He looks at Link then back at me and swallows.

"You can either open the door and we'll talk about this shit inside, or you don't open the door and I call the cops, tell them what I know, and we can see what they think. What do you think they'll say when I tell them you deposited thirty grand cash into your account? Do you think they will wonder how a bouncer at a club was able to get that kind of dough?" I ask, creeping closer to him, watching him swallow thickly again. "Link, you're cool with the local PD, right?" I ask, looking over my shoulder at him.

"I have a few friends on the force," he replies, pulling out his phone.

"We can talk inside," Mick mumbles, pulling out his key and opening the door.

As soon as we get inside, I notice that everything is new, from his couch to his kitchen appliances.

"Nice place," Link voices loud enough for me to hear.

"Can we get this over with?" Mick says, walking into the kitchen. He grabs a beer from the fridge, holds one out to me, and then offers one towards Link.

I shake my head, and Link does the same.

"Let's talk about how you got thirty thousand dollars," I say to start.

"I won at the casino." He shrugs, looking away.

"You don't want to lie to me." I take a step towards him while blocking the kitchen exit. "Now tell me how you got the thirty grand."

"I can't tell you that." He retreats as I take another step towards him. "You don't understand, man." His head drops forward, his hand going through his hair. "These dudes are fucking scary… A lot fucking scarier than you. They'll kill me."

"You're right. They will, but they'll probably do that anyways." I lean back slightly and pull out my phone from my back pocket so I can bring up the message from Justin. "The men you're protecting are part of Lacamo, one of the biggest crime families in the United States. You mean nothing to them." I show him the email with a sketch of the suspect along with a picture of one of the most notorious Mob hit men, who matches the sketch perfectly. "I'm guessing you have no real understanding of what you've done."

"I didn't know what was going to happen." His face pales as he looks over the pictures.

"Have you told them about Autumn?"

He shakes his head, but his eyes don't come back to me. Fury fills my veins as I realize the kind of danger my woman's in now.

"You piece of shit," I growl, shoving him into the counter. My hand goes around his neck and I can feel his pulse beating against my fingertips. I know that, if I squeeze his throat a little tighter, one less asshole will be breathing. "You're gonna tell me exactly what you told them and how you get in contact with them."

"I only told them her name," he chokes out, my hand going tighter. "I never told them anything else about her, I swear." His nails claw against my hand and his feet skid against the floor, trying to get leverage.

Link's hand on my arm is the only thing that stops me from killing the fucker where we stand. I take a step back while shoving him away. I run a hand through my hair, trying to compose myself enough to think of my next move.

"Call in your friend from the local PD and tell them to pick up this piece of shit," I say, looking over at Link.

"I told you what you wanted to know. Please don't call the cops," Mick whines.

I turn my head in his direction and he lowers his eyes. "As much as I want to leave you here and let you get what you deserve, you may be the only one who can stop these sick fucks, so that means I need to keep your punk ass safe until this shit's taken care of." I scrub a hand over my mouth as Link makes a call to his friend.

It takes two hours to get everything settled with the cops and Mick to be taken into custody. When we leave the local precinct, we make a plan to go to Autumn's condo to have a look around. Once inside, I can tell that the person who broke in wasn't looking for shit to pawn. Everything that has any value is still here. The only things gone through are papers, which tells me that whoever broke in was looking for information.

"Nothing here will point them to Tennessee," Link says, shoving a stack of papers into the desk.

"True, but she needs to change her number and stop using her e-mail. I don't want whoever this is to have any way to track her down."

"You gonna tell her what's going on?" he asks quietly.

"I don't have a choice." I look around again before walking over and opening her balcony door.

The sun is just starting to set over the mountains, causing an orange-and-red glow to fill the horizon. After taking a seat in one of her deck chairs, I pull out my phone and send a text to Justin, telling him the latest development. Then I send a message to Autumn, letting her know what time my flight would arrive so she would be dressed and ready to go out. I also tell her to make sure to wear the red lipstick she wore to the club.

Just thinking about how she looked that night causes my cock to jump. I need to see how fucking long it would take to kiss that red off her mouth. Looking out at the sunset again, I can't help but smile. I'm not buying a new bed for my room until she's willing to help me pick it out and share it with me. Until I can convince her to move into my room, we will be staying in hers. I look down at my phone when it beeps.

> **Justin:** *Autumn is safe in bed. I'm running a cross-check on the names you sent. As soon as I know anything, I'll send you the info.*

I know Justin is a good kid, but I still hate that he's there with her right now instead of me, even if I'm the one who ordered him to. I beat back the jealousy I feel and focus on what I need to do next.

> **Me:** *I get back tomorrow. Cancel all her e-mails/accounts and change her number. Now.*

> **Justin:** *Already on it.*

I look over my shoulder when I hear Link come out. I know he's gonna want to know my next move, but until I get more info, my hands are tied.

"You good?" he asks, taking a seat across from me.

"Yeah." I lean back, closing my eyes. "I need to make a few calls and see if I can get some info from a friend of mine before I head home."

"I don't envy you right now, man," Link says.

I open one eye, look at him, and smirk. A pissed-off Autumn is a thing of beauty, and she's going to be riled as hell when I get home.

Chapter 7
A Whole Lotta Like...

"**W**HY'S MY PHONE off and my e-mail not working?" I yell as I stomp into the living room, where Justin is still playing Call of Duty. I don't know how I know, but I know he has something to do with it.

"You're gonna have to wait to talk to boss man," he mumbles, never taking his eyes off the TV.

"I'm asking you, so tell me why my phone is off, I no longer have an e-mail, and even my Facebook is gone…and I haven't gotten on that thing in over eight months!"

"About that—you are not very photogenic. I think you should take some classes or something."

"Are you frigging serious right now?" I pick up one of the throw pillows off the couch and start hitting him over the head with it.

"Stop! You're making me lose the game!" He grabs the pillow out of my hand, tossing it across the room.

I start to run for it but then turn to see that he's not even moving from his spot on the couch. My eyes travel from him to the TV then his Xbox.

"You better not," he says, standing.

I lunge for the game system, ready to rip it out of the wall, when I'm tackled, but somehow, Justin flips us, taking the brunt of the landing, making me land on top of him, my thighs on either side of his waist. I reach for the pillow on the floor next to me and start to lift it above my head.

"What the *fuck* is going on?"

I close my eyes and press my lips together when I hear Kenton's voice, and when I open my eyes, I glare at Justin before standing up and facing the door of the living room. I fight the urge to run to him when our eyes lock. I've missed him these last few days, and he looks even hotter than normal with the extra scruff darkening his jaw, making it appear squarer.

"I asked a fucking question. What the fuck is going on?" he asks, taking his eyes off me, pinning Justin with a ferocious scowl.

"That's what I want to know." I cross my arms over my chest and glare first at Kenton and then at Justin, who glares back at me as he goes to stand next to his boss.

"Your girlfriend's crazy," Justin mumbles to him loud enough for me to hear.

"Shut up," I hiss.

"No, you shut up," he retorts immaturely.

"No, you shut up," I repeat, taking a step towards Kenton.

"Jesus, what the fuck?!" Kenton shouts, making me jump back.

"Why's my phone disconnected along with my e-mail and Facebook?" I ask, directing my haughtiness at Kenton this time.

He looks at me for a long moment before his head drops forward, his hand going to the back of his neck. "We need to talk," he says, lifting his head, looking me over. Then his eyes go to Justin. "Thanks for helpin' out," he says begrudgingly.

"No prob, boss," Justin says and starts to gather all of his stuff up, shoving it all back into the same bag he showed up here with.

When he's finished packing everything, Kenton walks him to the door, where they have a quiet conversation before Kenton pats him on the back and opens the door.

"See ya around, Copper," Justin says over his shoulder.

I give him a wave, and he smiles before heading out of the house, the front door closing behind him.

As soon as Kenton faces me again, his eyes turn dark and his jaw starts to tick. "Come here."

"Wh-what?" I stutter, looking at his clenched fists and the pulse of his neck, which is beating rapidly.

"Come here," he repeats, the tone of his voice making me freeze in place.

"Why?" I ask softly.

"First, I haven't seen or touched you in days and need to reassure myself that you're good. Second, I need your help getting the image of what I just saw out of my head."

His words have my feet moving before my brain even has a chance to catch up. I do a face-plant into his chest, wrapping my arms around his waist and breathing him in. Every breath I take eases some of the anxiety I didn't even know I was feeling.

"What's going on?" I whisper into his chest. His muscles tense and I'm not sure I want to know anymore.

"Let's sit down." He takes my hand in his and leads me to the couch, where he tugs me down into his lap. "Your place in Vegas was broken into."

"Shit," I whisper. "What was taken?" I don't really have anything of value, so I'm not too worried, but it still doesn't feel good knowing that someone broke in.

"Nothin'," he says, surprising me.

"What do you mean?" I ask, searching his face.

"Found out that Mick was the inside source at the club the night of the shooting." He runs a hand down my back. "He told them who you are, and we're guessing it was them who broke into your place."

I don't want to believe that Mick was involved in what happened, especially because he and Tessa were sleeping together, but I'm not really surprised. Mick is a self-centered asshole who doesn't care about anyone but himself.

"Okay, so what do we do now?" I wonder out loud. I can't think of anything I left behind that would lead anyone here, but I can't be sure.

His eyebrows come together in confusion and his hand travels to the back of my neck then up into my hair, fisting it. "You're not gonna cry?"

"No," I reply, feeling my own eyebrows pull together, wondering why I should cry.

"Warrior," he says quietly, his eyes going soft, making my heart pound a little harder. "I have a guy who's connected to the organization that planned the hit. I sent him a message and am just waiting for him to get back to me."

"What do you think they're going to do?"

"Not sure, but I doubt they want the kind of publicity they'll create if they try to send their guy after you."

"What do they care about publicity if they are who you say they are?"

"They're in control of half of Vegas. They may be Mob, but even they have an image to uphold," he explains.

"They killed innocent people," I remind him on a whisper. The thought of people like that caring what others think about them is laughable.

"They planned the hit, but their hands are clean." He shrugs.

I look into his eyes and see an understanding that confuses me, and I wonder if he's ever used that excuse. I lift my hand and run it along the roughness of his jaw. "Are you okay?" I ask him, seeing the weariness around his eyes.

"Yeah, but I'll be even better when this shit's over."

I hear the tiredness in his voice and wonder how much sleep he's gotten since he left. I push my fingers through his hair and his eyes start to close at the contact.

"You should take a nap," I tell him softly. "We can figure out everything else later."

"You gonna take one with me?" he asks.

Without thinking, I nod and he maneuvers me so that I'm straddling him. My breath leaves on a whoosh, my hands go to his shoulders, and his go to my ass. Our mouths are so close that I feel each of his breaths against my lips. I expect him to kiss me, but instead, he stands up off the couch. My legs wrap around his waist and I bite my lip when

I feel the hard length of his arousal against my core through the thin material of my shorts.

When we reach my room, he pushes open the door and gently lays me on the bed before stepping back and taking off his boots and shirt. I watch, mesmerized, as his arm and abs flex when his fingers go to the button of his jeans and he pulls them down. I can see his hard-on outlined through his boxers, and my eyes travel up his body to his eyes, which look sleepy. I scoot back in the bed as he shuts off the light, and I feel the bed compress and his weight hit my side.

I try to ignore the ache between my legs as I lie on my back with his arm around my waist, his breath hitting my neck and his thigh over my legs. I try to calm down, but his hand lifts my shirt and my muscles clench. I expect him to grab my breast or touch me sexually, but he surprises me yet again when his hand just lies against my skin. All of my nerve endings are tingling in anticipation, and then I hear his light snore. My body relaxes and I take a deep breath, letting it out slowly before drifting off to sleep.

"Wake up, baby."

I feel a featherlight touch travel down the side of my face. My eyes flutter open and connect with Kenton's. "Hi," I say, blinking against the light coming in from the now open blinds in the room.

His fingers run down the underside of my jaw then up along my ear. "You sleep okay when I was gone?" he asks, his eyes focused on his fingers traveling over my skin.

I think about lying and telling him that I slept great and didn't miss him at all, but something about the moment has me blurting out the truth. "I missed sleeping with you."

"Yeah?" His eyes search my face as I nod and close my eyes, feeling too exposed. "I slept like shit." His words make my eyes open and search his face. "Hated that I couldn't be here to look out for you and Justin was doing my job. I didn't like that another man was in the house with you."

"I wouldn't—" I start to tell him that I would never even think about Justin like that, but his finger covers my lips and his head lowers towards mine.

"I know you wouldn't. I still didn't like it." He takes away his finger and lowers his face towards mine.

The first touch of his lips is soft, and my eyes flutter closed as his hand runs along my jaw to the back of my neck. I whimper when his tongue runs along my bottom lip before nipping it with his teeth. My hands find their way into his hair so I can hold him to me. His hips shift and his hand at my hair travels down along my side then up and under the shirt I'm wearing, settling just below my breast.

As his mouth devours mine, I pull my mouth from his, pressing my head back into the pillow, lifting my chest, trying to get his hand to move. His thumb sweeps over my nipple; the slight contact has me moaning loudly.

"I need to see you," he rumbles, pulling away. His hands go to the hem of the shirt, pulling it off over my head and tossing it to the floor behind him.

I start to cover myself, but his hands capture mine and tug them above my head. His eyes travel down my body, and when they come back to mine, the dark hunger I see makes me hold my breath. His mouth lowers towards mine again, his tongue plunging between my lips, not giving me a choice but to kiss him back. When his mouth leaves mine, traveling down my neck, he sucks my collarbone, causing my hips to lift and my chest to rise higher. His mouth starts a slow trek around my breast before I feel warm, wet heat cover my nipple. My body arches off the bed, and one of his hands leaves mine above my head and travels down to cup my other breast, his fingers rolling over my nipple, causing a moan to climb up my throat.

My hand goes to his shoulder, holding on as his hand navigates down over my stomach, causing my muscles to contract and wetness to gather between my thighs. The first feeling of his fingers along my pubic bone has me panicking, but want quickly takes over as one slides under the edge of my shorts and panties and then down to roll over my clit.

"Soaked," he growls, his head lifting and his eyes locking on mine.

His finger lowers, entering me slowly as his eyes watch me closely. I don't know whether to pull away or to lift my hips for more. When his hand leaves me, I cry out, only to be startled when I feel my panties and shorts being tugged off. Before I have a chance to think, his fingers are back and he adds his thumb, rolling it over the bundle of nerves that has me clawing at his shoulders.

"I really want to fucking taste you, but no way can I do that yet." His jaw locks and a look of desperation fills his eyes. "My control is slipping, so I need you to come for me."

I don't understand what's wrong, but as if he spoke directly to my body, I come on a cry, my head falling back and my eyes closing. The pull from below my belly button expands and explodes through my body. When the feeling subsides, I lift my head, still trying to catch my breath.

"Fucking exquisite," he whispers, his eyes meeting mine, his fingers still lazily stroking between my legs.

I bite my lip, wondering what to do. I have never experienced anything like that before, and it's been years since I've had sex. I feel completely out of my league and overwhelmed.

"Don't," he states firmly, making my eyes travel back to him. "Do not leave me here. Not right now." His hands leave me as he crawls up my body, cocooning around me.

I clear my throat and shake my head. "I wasn't. I mean…I just don't know what I'm doing, so I feel—"

"Overwhelmed," he states, running his nose along mine. "That's why I didn't do all the things I really want to do to you. I could see it in your eyes that you were unsure." He kisses my forehead and rolls to his side, pulling me with him. "How long has it been?" he asks softly, gliding his fingers down my spine then back up again.

"A little over ten years." I close my eyes in embarrassment and only open them when I realize that not only is his body tense, but he doesn't seem to be breathing. "Are you okay?" I get up on my elbow so I can look at his face.

"Fuck," he mutters as his eyes open. "How the hell have you kept yourself away from men for the last ten years?"

"It's not hard when you're not interested," I answer truthfully, looking away from him.

"Until me."

I hear the smugness in his voice and my eyes go back to him, narrowing when I see the smirk on his face. "My tastes could always change."

"They won't," he says confidently.

"They might," I huff, and his smirk turns into a full smile as he rolls on top of me.

"They won't," he repeats, this time kissing me silent.

"We're not going out," Kenton says as soon as I walk around the corner into the kitchen.

He's wearing a dark-burgundy button-down shirt that looks like it's custom-made for him. With the top button released, the shirt is tucked into a pair of black slacks that hug his thighs and show off his lean waist. I don't know how it's possible for him to look just as hot dressed up as he does in jeans. Seeing him like this has me craving to see him in a suit.

His eyes do a head-to-toe sweep, and I stumble slightly when our eyes lock. The look in his eyes is so dark and hungry that I can't even take a breath. After he kissed me quiet earlier, he got out of bed and got dressed, telling me that he had some stuff to do, but we had a date and to make sure I was ready. I nodded, unable to talk, and watched as he left the room.

I got up, made some coffee, and ate a piece of toast before heading back upstairs to get ready for my first date. I took an extra-long shower, making sure I shaved everything from the neck down and scrubbed every inch of my body. I chose a dark-blue wrap dress that hugs my curves and shows some cleavage without being slutty. The shoes are what completes the outfit—gold stilettos with a strap across the tops of my toes and a thick band around my ankle. I did my makeup the same way I'd done the night I went to the club—simple with dark-red lipstick.

"You're really testing my self-control." Kenton's rough voice brings me back to the present—along with his hands, which have found their way to my waist. "But then, if I don't take you out, I can't show you off." One hand slowly slides up my waist to the bow that is holding my dress together. "You're like a dessert I get to unwrap and eat at the end of the night." His fingers wrap around the loose length of the ribbon, giving it a gentle tug. "Let's go before I say fuck it and unwrap you here in the kitchen and take you on the counter."

I'm not opposed to skipping dinner and being dessert now. After what happened earlier, I know I won't put off being with him.

He smiles like he read my mind and shakes his head. "Dinner, then dessert."

My pussy contracts and I bite my lip to stop from moaning. He leans forward, his finger going to my chin, pulling my lip out from between my teeth, kissing me softly.

"I wouldn't mind skipping dinner," I tell him when his mouth leaves mine.

He laughs, shaking his head and taking my hand. "We're both gonna need our strength." He walks us out to his car, opening the passenger's side door for me before shutting it and jogging around the car to slide behind the wheel. As soon as we make it down the driveway, his hand interlocks with mine on my lap.

"So, where are we going?" I ask once I find my voice again.

"An Italian place a couple of towns over. They have the best eggplant parmesan I've ever eaten in my life."

"I love Italian," I tell him.

"I know." He smiles, squeezing my fingers.

"How do you know?"

"All those frozen dinners you bought are Italian." He laughs, making me smile and my cheeks heat up in embarrassment.

"I'm not good at cooking." I shake my head and look out the window.

"I can teach you how to cook," he says softly, squeezing my hand.

"I would like that." I've always wanted to learn how to cook, but every time I've tried, it's been a disaster, so I've given up.

We talk the rest of the way to the restaurant about his favorite things to cook and how he learned. I knew that his aunt Viv and uncle own the diner I had gone to the first time I met Viv, but I didn't know that he used to work there during the summers when he was younger.

When we arrive at the restaurant, he finds parking along the busy street and leads me inside. The interior is dim, with mood lighting that makes the space feel much more intimate. The tables are covered in white linen cloths with a single tea light candle in the center of each. The host leads us to a small table in the back of the restaurant, but when he begins to pull out my chair, Kenton stops him, taking the chair and holding it for me until I take a seat. He then takes his own seat across from me.

"Would you like to see the wine list?" the waitress asks when she arrives at our table.

I look up at her and see that her eyes are glued to Kenton. I know that, if we're going to try and build something lasting between us, I need to get a hold on the jealousy I feel when other women admire him, but that doesn't mean I have to like it.

"Would you like a glass of wine, baby?"

My eyes travel from the waitress to Kenton, and I shake my head. I don't want anything tainting tonight.

His eyes darken with approval and never leave mine as he answers the waitress. "Just water for now."

She nods and leaves us to look over the menus.

"Do you know what you're going to have?" he asks after a few minutes.

"I don't know. Everything looks so good," I tell him, my mouth watering in anticipation.

"Everything here is delicious. My parents used to bring me and Toni here when we were growing up."

My throat clogs at the happy memory of him and his family. A wave of sadness hits me over the fact that I have none to share with him.

"Stay with me, baby. We're here together." He takes my hand in his, some of his strength seeping into me through our connection.

I look into his eyes and nod as he brings my fingers to his mouth, pressing a kiss to them. "I'm okay," I say after a few seconds.

He nods but doesn't release my hand. Even when the waitress comes back to the table to take our order, he still holds on to me but changes the subject. We talk about my job and the request I put in to change shifts; we also talk about Justin and how he started working for him.

He keeps the conversation away from family and anything else he thinks might have me retreating. I know what he's doing, and I appreciate it more than he knows. During dinner, I realize that he has a way of reading me that no one else ever had. That in itself tells me everything I need to know about being with him.

"Are you ready for dessert?" the waitress asks when she arrives back at our table after clearing our empty dishes.

I squirm, remembering what he said to me in the kitchen about being dessert when we got home. His eyes flare and his tongue comes out, running along his bottom lip.

"Yes," Kenton replies, his eyes on mine. "You ready for dessert, baby?"

I know his question isn't about food, and I squeeze my legs together and nod.

"We'll take a piece of tiramisu to go, please." He pulls out his wallet, handing her his card.

After he gets his card back along with a dessert box, we get back into his car, and the lust is so thick that I swear I can taste it as he pulls out into traffic. His hand goes to my knee then travels up my thigh and under the hem of my dress. When I feel his finger slide over my core, I gasp.

"Fuck, you sat across from me the whole time like that?" he growls, his finger running down my bare center again.

"Kenton," I cry when his finger circles my clit.

"Jesus, baby." His fingers circle my entrance then travel up to run around my clit, keeping me on the edge of the orgasm I feel building, torturing me. I grab his wrist, trying to pull it away. His arm flexes and his hand cups me over my pussy. "This is mine. I get to play with it any time I want, any way I want to."

His words have me panting. I turn my head to look at his profile and his eyes come to me. The want and determination I see has me removing my hands from his wrist, sitting back, and spreading my legs slightly.

"Good girl." He keeps up the same pace and movements, and this time when I feel the orgasm building again, I expect him to pull away like he's been doing. Instead, two fingers swiftly enter me and I lift my hips higher, meeting his hand. His fingers curve and I come; my head rolls against the headrest and my legs squeeze his hand, which is lodged between my legs.

I wonder how he's able to drive while controlling my body. I look back over at him once I come back down from the high of my orgasm. I have no idea what happened to my inhibitions, but he makes me want to give myself to him, makes me want to please him. I watch as his fingers leave me and he slowly puts them in his mouth. His eyes close like I'm the best thing he's ever tasted before coming to me for a second then going back to the road again.

"Yes. That pussy is mine."

I press my legs together and pray that we make it to the house without me climbing into his lap and causing an accident. When we pull onto the dirt road that leads to the house, I sigh in relief and hear him hiss out a breath when I lean over and wrap my hand around his cock, feeling it throb against my palm.

"So is this mine then?" I ask teasingly.

The car comes to a stop, and he looks at me. "I'm yours. All of me is yours."

His words hit my chest and the look in his eyes makes the last of the barricades around my heart crumble into dust. I swallow and lick my bottom lip, never breaking eye contact.

"And I'm yours," I tell him.

His eyes close and his forehead touches mine. "That makes me a very happy man." His hand moves to the underside of my jaw, tilting my head to the side, and his mouth slants over mine, taking it in a deep kiss before tearing away. "Inside. Now."

His door opens and I fumble with my seatbelt, getting it unhooked right as my door is opened. I'm out of the car in a heartbeat, and we rush up the stairs. My mouth goes to his neck as he fumbles with the keys, trying to get the door open. Once inside, he shoves me against the wall, his hands going to the tie on my dress. I expect him to rip it apart. Instead, he drops to his knees, his eyes locking on mine as he slowly pulls the ribbon, causing the dress to fall open, exposing one side of my body.

His fingers move to the small button on the inside of the dress, undoing it quickly, making the dress open completely. He looks me over then pulls the dress off my arms, letting it drop to the floor, leaving me in nothing but my sheer bra and heels.

"Best gift I've ever unwrapped," he mumbles, running his hands along my sides then to my ass, pulling my hips forward to kiss me above my pubic bone.

I start to pant as I watch his tongue come out and lick up my center. My head falls back as his hand lifts my leg over his shoulder. My hands go to his head for leverage as he shoves his face between my legs, his mouth sucking my clit before releasing and licking it in fast strokes.

"Oh God," I breathe as two fingers enter me and my body starts to shake. My one heel on solid ground makes me teeter. "Wait," I cry, feeling myself start to fall.

His mouth never leaves me as he quickly maneuvers my other thigh onto his other shoulder, my back and him the only things keeping me from hitting the floor. His mouth takes me hard, sucking and licking until I explode. My hands fist into his hair, holding on for dear life as I fly into the abyss of a mind-shattering orgasm.

When I come to, we're heading up the stairs. My head is on his shoulder and his hands are under my ass, holding me to him. He opens the door to my room and lays me on the bed. I quickly take off my shoes before lying back on the bed so, just like earlier today, I can watch him undress. The only difference is that, this time when he gets to his pants and unbuttons them, he pulls them and his boxers down at the same time. I hold my breath when I see his size. He's long and wide, and there's no way it's going to fit inside me.

"It'll be tight, but we'll make it work." The familiar words and the smile on his face cause me to smile and my body to relax.

My eyes roam from his eyes down his body, watching as he strokes himself. He walks slowly to me, his muscles flexing with each step. I scoot back up the bed as he crawls to me, his legs spreading my hips wide.

"You're so gorgeous, baby."

His body covers mine, his hands going behind my back, where I feel him unhook my bra then drag it down my shoulders. Once my breasts are free, he lowers his head and pulls first one nipple into his mouth and then the other. I writhe under him, running my hands down his back to his ass, trying to pull him closer. I can feel more wetness surge between my legs as he torments my breasts. I grab his hair in my hands and pull his mouth away.

"I need you," I breathe.

His eyes grow even darker and his fingers slip between my legs again. His hand leaves me, but then I feel the head of him at my entrance as he slowly starts to enter me, Then he stops, his body suddenly going still.

"What's wrong?" I gasp, adjusting to his width.

"Condom... We need a condom."

His words sound pained, and I search his face before deciding what to say. "I'm on the pill. I've been on the pill since I was seventeen."

"Fuck," he clips, making me jump and wonder if I said something wrong. "I'm clean, baby, but I want to make sure you're really okay with this." Both of his hands go to my hair, pushing it away from my face, his eyes looking me over.

"I want this."

"Jesus," he groans.

One of his hands goes to the underside of my thigh, lifting it up higher around his waist while slowly sinking into me. I breathe out against the slight pain, trying instead to concentrate on how good it feels. He starts to move in slow, steady strokes, his lips never leaving mine. I lift my hips higher, wrapping myself completely around him, needing to be as close as possible.

"So perfect. Your pussy is so fucking perfect," he says as he slides out only to slide back in, making me moan. Our skin starts to slicken with sweat, causing his body to slide smoothly against mine. "I'm not gonna be able to hold off," he says, pulling his mouth from mine and pressing his forehead into my collarbone.

I feel right on the edge as his fingers roll over my clit. I want to come, but I'm so consumed by every other emotion I'm feeling that I can't let go. Instead, I concentrate on the way my body's feeling. I hold him closer, just enjoying the closeness of the moment and how connected I feel to him. His hips jerk, and I feel him grow even bigger before he groans, his mouth latching on to my neck.

"You didn't come," he breathes against my skin after a few moments.

"It's okay," I say softly, running a hand down his back. "It was great."

"'Great'?" He chuckles, pulling his face out of my neck. When he looks down at me, he shakes his head. "That's not gonna work for me."

I don't even get a chance to ask him what he's talking about before he picks me up out of bed and walks us to his room, straight into his bathroom, where he starts up the shower, pushing me inside before following me in. He pulls me under the water, tilting my face back. His fingers work through my hair. When his hands leave me, I open my eyes, watching as he grabs a large sponge off the shelf. Then he pours some body wash onto it, lathering it up, causing the room to smell like him.

He gently washes me, paying close attention between my legs, where I can still feel him. When he's done, he washes himself before tossing the sponge to the shower floor. I think he's going to get out, but instead, he moves us under the rain coming from the showerhead on the ceiling so that hot, steamy water falls down on us. Then he pulls me to him, my back to his front.

His hands start at my shoulders, rubbing in slow circles, then travel down my arms to my hands, where he pulls them up and behind his head. His fingers run down the inside of my arms, over the tips of my breasts, down my stomach, and over my hips. One hand moves to my center, rolling over my clit, and the other slides back up to my breasts, alternately toying with my nipples. My whole body relaxes into him, just enjoying his touch.

"I love touching you," he whispers.

The word 'love' makes my stomach flutter. I know I'm on the edge of love with him, and it won't take much to push me over.

"Feel what you do to me?" He licks my neck, his hips shift, and his cock slides between my legs from behind.

I lower my hand to where his is playing with me, and I feel the head of his cock near my clit. He pulls his hips back and forth again, and I feel him in my hand every time he moves forward.

"I need to be inside you, baby." His words sound pained as his hand moves mine out of the way, and on the next thrust forward, he enters me.

"Yes," I breathe.

"This time, you're gonna come with me inside you." He runs his chin up my neck, the scruff on his jaw causing goose bumps to break out on my skin.

One hand cups my breast, first softly. Then it pinches and pulls my nipple as his other hand slowly moves between my legs. My pussy tightens when his fingers tug my nipple hard.

"Fuck. You like that?" He does it again, getting the same reaction.

It doesn't take long to feel the knot in my lower stomach start to unravel. I lean forward, putting my hands on the tile wall in front of me. One of his hands slides around my waist, hitting my clit, and the other goes to my nipple, pinching it. My orgasm is sudden and all consuming. His name leaves my mouth on a cry, and in the distance, I hear mine roared as I float away into euphoria. When I come back to myself, I'm sitting in his lap in the middle of the shower, my face in the crook of his neck.

I lift my head and look up into his eyes, giving him a tired smile. "That was amazing." I run my fingers along his jaw then up and around his lips.

"That's what I like to hear." His tone is soft, along with his eyes, and I shake my head at his smugness.

"I'm in like with you," I tell him, getting lost in his eyes.

"Yeah?" His eyebrow rises and he kisses my forehead. "I'm in a whole lotta like with you too, baby," he says softly, pulling my head back down to his chest.

We sit there for a few more minutes before he stands us up, quickly rinses us off before turning off the shower, and then pulls a large towel out of the cabinet to wrap around me, getting one for himself off the hook on the back of the door. I watch as he dries his body, my mouth going dry as a tingle begins stirring in my core again.

"Stop looking at me like that."

I jump and quickly look away at his words, feeling my cheeks pinken as I start to dry myself off. Hearing him laugh, I turn my head, looking over my shoulder.

His eyes drop to my ass and he shakes his head. "It's gonna be a long night," he mumbles.

I look down at his hard-on before lifting my eyes to his again.

He wasn't wrong; it was a very long night.

Chapter 8

It's Not Past Tense

I WAKE UP when I feel lips touch my shoulder, a hand slide around my waist, and warmth hit my back. I smile into my pillow then roll over to face Kenton.

"I didn't mean to wake you." He pulls me up his body so I'm lying on his chest.

"Yes, you did." I laugh, cuddling into him while breathing in his scent.

It's been three weeks of us being an 'us.' At first, it was difficult living together plus being in a new relationship, but things have seem to have fallen into place. He's still an ass every now and then, but he's *my* ass.

The day after our first date, Kenton woke me up early, dragging me out of the bed and into the shower, where he proceeded to make love to me before telling me to get dressed because we had to go shopping. I got dressed in a pair of shorts and a light T-shirt before meeting him downstairs. I was exhausted, a little sore from being kept up the night before, and in no mood to go shopping, but he seemed so excited about it that I couldn't exactly tell him that I hated shopping and to go alone.

When we got in his car, we headed to Nashville. I'd expected him to take us to the mall, but instead, he took us to a large furniture store.

"Why are we here?" I asked, looking at the store in front of us then over at him.

"I need a new bed," he said, hopping out of the car.

My heart fell into my stomach. We had just had sex for the first time yesterday, and he was buying a new bed to leave mine already? I waited until he opened the door for me to get out. I wanted to claw his eyes out of his head for being such an ass, but instead, I swallowed down the hurt I was feeling, determined to find some other way to get back at him.

He took my hand in his, leading me inside the furniture store. A man in his mid-thirties with a bad comb-over and an even worse suit greeted us as soon as we entered the store. I looked around, trying to clear my head as Kenton and the guy spoke quietly.

When Kenton grabbed my hand, twining his fingers with mine, I was admiring a king-size bed with a canopy top. The set also came with beautiful side tables that were round in the middle with thin legs that curved out and a dresser and armoire that were similar. All the wood was dark with notches in it, making it look like it had just been chopped down in the forest. I could imagine a princess sleeping in that bed amongst the furniture.

"Do you like this one?" he asked.

I looked over at him then back at the bed. I could see him in it as well. The ruggedness of the wood was manly enough that the whimsical element to the design was toned down.

"It's really nice," I said softly, not knowing how I felt about picking out a bed that would basically guarantee that he wouldn't be sleeping with me anymore.

"Is it something you would buy for your own room?"

"Yes," I told him truthfully.

"Ralph, we'll take this one."

Ralph nodded and we followed him to the register, where he rang up the order. The whole set was over six thousand dollars, and Kenton pulled out his wallet, pulling out a shiny black card and handing it over to Ralph without even an ounce of regret on his face. When we were done, Ralph told us that he would have it delivered this afternoon.

When we left the furniture store, I thought for sure we would head home, but he drove us to a bedding and home goods store, leading me inside and right to the bedding department, telling me to pick something.

"What do you mean 'pick something'? It's your bed. You pick something," I told him, crossing my arms over my chest in order to not punch him in the gut. My feelings were hurt. All I wanted to do was go home. I knew it was dumb, but that didn't mean that I didn't feel like crying about it.

"I need help," he said, a smile tugging at the corner of his mouth.

I bit my lip, looked around at every bedding set, and one caught my eye. It was white with a large design of a tree on it, and it had a green border that was made out of silk ribbon. I knew it would look amazing with his new bedroom furniture, but I also thought it was too feminine for a guy's room. I walked over to the wall of blankets, grabbed a Bed in a Bag set that was mostly browns and blacks, and handed it to him. His eyes went from the bag to my face and then narrowed.

"What?" I asked, wondering what was wrong with the set I'd picked. I'd done what he'd asked me to, so what was his problem?

"You would have this in your room?"

"No, but this isn't for my room," I said, pointing at myself. "This is for your room." I shrugged and started to walk away, but I was grabbed by the back of my jeans, and his hands slid along my stomach.

"Who do you think will be sleeping in my bed with me?" he asked against the shell of my ear. He'd found out the night before that that was a very weak spot for me.

"I don't know," I said, feeling stupid tears sting my nose. I didn't want to think about anyone in his bed.

He turned me in his arms and I ducked my head, not wanting him to see the emotions I was sure were written all over my face.

"What's going on?" His concerned voice caused my eyes to lift. I shook my head and started to look away, but his hand cupped my cheek, forcing me to look at him. "You're the most difficult woman I have ever met." He shook his head and started to laugh. My eyes narrowed, and he looked over my face before laughing harder.

"What the hell is funny?" I hissed.

He stopped laughing and his voice became serious. "You're in my bed. I want that to be the place you sleep from now on. I also want it to be somewhere you're comfortable. That's why I wanted you with me today."

"Oh," I mumbled, my belly fluttering.

"Now, what are we getting?"

I bit my lip and walked over to the set that had caught my eye. I picked it up then put it down when I saw the price. "Maybe you should just get that other one," I told him, seeing the much cheaper price boldly displayed across the front of the picture on the bag in his hand.

"Jesus." He shook his head then walked over and picked up the one I really liked. "I hate shopping, so this will go a lot faster if you just pick the shit you like so we can get the fuck out of here."

"Don't be an ass," I growled, making him smile.

"Do we need sheets?"

"Yes," I hissed then stomped over to the sheets, picking up two sets—a black one that would match the tree printed on the comforter and one green set the same color as the ribbon on the border. The whole time I stomped around, I listened to Kenton laughing. I rolled my eyes but couldn't help the smile that formed on my lips when his arm swung over my shoulders and his lips touched my temple.

The feeling of him taking a deep breath brings me back to the present, and I tilt my head back slightly to look at him.

"Is everything okay?" I ask sleepily.

"All's good. Justin just left. He said you went to bed late 'cause you were up eating junk food while watching him play Call of Duty all night."

"He's such a tattletale." I shake my head.

Justin has become like a brother to me. We bicker and argue constantly, but he also makes me laugh so hard that I can't breathe. I adore him for the way he looks out for Kenton and love that he is such a great friend. He stays with me every time Kenton is out of town. Between him and the rest of Kenton's men, there isn't a time when my whereabouts are unknown or I'm not supervised. I hate having people constantly in my space, but I know that, in order for me to be safe right now, I need them.

"I missed you," I say softly, pressing my nose into his chest.

"Missed you too, babe." His hand travels down my back, over my ass, and between my legs. One finger dips inside my pussy before rolling over my clit.

"Kenton," I moan as he takes my mouth in a deep kiss, rolling me to my back and entering me.

By the time we both come, we're exhausted and fall back asleep.

I snuggle into Kenton and wrap my arms around his waist when I hear the doorbell ring in the distance. "They'll go away," I tell him, not ready to get up. I feel like I just fell asleep.

"I gotta get it. It could be Mom."

Crap, he's right. It could be his mom, because while he's out of town, she or Viv stop by for coffee most mornings.

"Did you tell her you are home?" I ask, knowing that, if she knows he's home, she would normally give him at least until the afternoon before calling or showing up.

"Nah, so she's probably here to see you."

"I'm up. You should sleep." I throw my legs over the side of the bed then find the T-shirt he had on yesterday. I pull it on over my head before bending and grabbing my sweats off the floor.

The loud slap on my ass has me jumping in place and glaring at Kenton, who is now up and wearing a pair of jeans with the top button undone.

"What was that for?"

"You stick it in my face, babe, and I'm going to slap it," he says with a smirk, opening the bedroom door.

I jump on his back, wrapping my legs around his hips and my arms around his neck while biting his ear and neck, making him laugh as he tries his best to tickle me off him, making me giggle while heading down the stairs.

"What the fuck?" I hear whispered.

I lift my head at the familiar voice, shocked to see Sid standing on the front porch. My arms and legs start to loosen from around Kenton's waist and neck, and I drop to the floor.

"Sid?" I ask, concerned, taking in his disheveled appearance.

"I knew she was with you." His eyes narrow on Kenton. "I fucking knew after your last visit, but this sealed the deal."

"You were in Vegas?" I ask Kenton and glare.

He crosses his arms over his chest, looking down at me for a second before his eyes go back to Sid. "Why are you here? More importantly, how the fuck did you find me?" Kenton asks him.

"It wasn't that hard," Sid says, glaring.

I look between the two of them then settle my eyes on Kenton. A million questions fly through my head, but the biggest one is why the hell he was in Vegas and didn't say anything to me. "Why were you in Vegas?" I try, hoping to get an answer.

"He had a meeting at my club yesterday," Sid says, and my head swings in his direction.

"Meeting?" I mumble, looking between the two of them.

"Motherfucker," Kenton growls, taking a step towards him.

"She should know what's going on," I hear Sid say, and I look back up at Kenton.

"What happened?" I ask.

The last time he went to Vegas, my place had been broken into. I have no idea who he would be meeting with besides Link, but I don't think that's what this is about.

"We'll talk soon," Kenton says, the vein in his neck ticking.

"Why don't you tell her now?" Sid looks from Kenton to me, his eyes going soft. He starts to take a step towards me, but Kenton blocks his way, putting his hand on the door. "She's my friend," Sid complains.

"She's my woman."

"Okay, please put your giant penis away for a minute," I tell Kenton, elbowing him in the side before looking over at Sid. "Why are you here?" I ask him softly, wondering if he's in trouble or something.

"After your last e-mail, I wrote you back. When I didn't hear from you, I wrote you again, only for it to come back to me saying you'd deleted your account." He runs a hand over his head, and this time, his eyes go to Kenton. "I knew you were with him after yesterday, so I got his address and came to talk to you."

"Why?"

"You know I've always been in love with you, Autumn. Don't be stupid."

"'Don't be stupid'?" I whisper. "So, all the women you paraded around in front of me?" I ask.

"Meant nothing." He shrugs. "I just wanted you to realize you wanted me. I wanted you to fight for me."

"Wow," I say softly, shaking my head. "You're telling me you were in love with me and brought women around so I would be jealous and fight for you…instead of telling me how you felt and *you* fighting for *me*?"

"You're so closed off. You were always in your head. I was trying to break through to you."

I look at Sid then Kenton.

"Don't look at me, babe. I don't know what the fuck to say about this shit."

"Sid, you're a great guy, but you don't love me."

The differences between Kenton and Sid are striking, the biggest being that Kenton has fought for me since the beginning. He's never let me get too far when I've tried running away. He's also never brought women around to try to get me to accept my feelings for him.

"Like I said in my last e-mail, I care about you, but not like that. I hope you can understand," I tell him softly, hoping that he gets that there is nothing—nor will there ever be anything—between us.

"You're serious?" he asks.

I bite my lip and nod. I watch regret pass through his eyes before he shakes his head then turns to look off into the distance.

"I guess this is goodbye then?"

"Yeah," I reply, not understanding the feelings I have inside, why this is so hard. Deep down, I wonder what would have happened if he would've actually tried to get to know me. I step up to him and wrap my hands around his waist, giving him a hug. "Thank you for everything," I whisper. "One day, you're going to find someone worth fighting for."

His arms squeeze me a little tighter, his chest expanding on a breath. "Have you?"

I know exactly what he's asking, and tears sting my nose. I nod into his chest and step back into Kenton's embrace.

"You hurt her and I'll kill you," Sid says before turning and heading down the steps.

Once he's in his car and pulling away from the house, I turn to look at Kenton. "So what happened in Vegas?" I cross my arms over my chest.

His eyes drop then meet mine again. "Let's go sit down."

I follow him into the living room, sitting on the opposite side of the couch from him. That way, he can't distract me with his touch.

"I met up with the boss of Lacamo. They agreed you're off-limits," he says softly, and my whole body stills at the news I have been waiting to hear.

"So it's over?" I ask on a whisper. I can't believe that, after all this time, all it took was one meeting for this whole thing to be resolved.

"It is," he says, looking at me from across the couch.

I can't understand why he looks so worried when I know that this news will make things easier for him as well. He has been running himself ragged working his normal cases while trying to keep me safe. Then, my head starts to fill with thoughts about my life, why I'm really here, and what this news means for my future.

"So, I can go home then?" I ask, looking down at my hands.

"No."

The word is rough and causes me to lift my head. "What do you mean 'no'?" I search his face, wondering what he's not telling me. If I'm no longer in danger, I can return to Vegas, even if the thought alone makes me feel sick.

"Exactly what it sounds like—no, you can't go back to Vegas." His hands ball into fist on his thighs. "This is your home."

"This is *your* home," I murmur and swallow, feeling my heart pound against the inside of my ribs.

"Since you've been here, this has become my home, but before you, it was a place I slept at night. You have given me a reason to come home."

"You want me to move in with you?" I whisper, hope blooming in my chest.

"Yes, I want you to move in with me."

"You're serious?"

"Yes, baby." He laughs, shaking his head.

"What about my place in Vegas?"

"Sell it...keep it... I don't give a fuck what you do with it."

I stand up, glance around the room, and then look back over at Kenton, who looks worried. My heart does a flip from knowing that he really wants this; he really wants me.

"Are you sure about this?"

"Without a doubt. One hundred percent sure."

"What will your family say?"

"'When are you getting married?'" he replies. I feel my eyes get big and my mouth fill with saliva. "One thing at a time," he says gently, and I nod.

I'm not sure if he's in love with me, but I think this feeling I have for him is love—or some form of it. Never really having been loved before, I don't know what it really feels like. I know that what I feel for him makes what I felt for my son's father pale in comparison. I know that I want to spend all my time with him, and he's always my first thought when I wake and my last thought when I go to bed at night.

"Okay."

"Okay?" he asks, searching my face.

"Yes, okay. I'll move in with you," I tell him, a smile creeping onto my face.

"Yeah?" His lips twitch, and I nod before running at him and climbing onto his lap. His arms wrap around me as I press my mouth against his. "Shit," he groans, pulling his mouth from mine.

"Why are you stopping?" I try to pull his mouth back to mine when I hear someone knocking on the door. "Oh."

I smile as he sets me aside and adjusts himself in his jeans before standing. I sit there for a second and then get up to follow him to the door. After he looks outside, his eyes come to me before pulling the door open.

"You're home?" Nancy says, smiling. "If I would have known that, I wouldn't have come so early."

"It's fine. We were up." He kisses her cheek, letting her into the house.

"Why were you up?" She looks between the two of us, her eyes twinkling, and I know she's going to say something that will have me turning red. "You know, I want my grandchildren to have our family name. I think it's about time you two stop playing house and just get married."

All the air leaves my lungs at the word 'children.' I grab the table closest to me for balance. When a wave of dizziness hits me hard, I'm surprised that I don't hit the ground.

"Jesus, Mom! Autumn just agreed to move in, and now you're trying to scare her off." He shakes his head then looks at me. "One thing at a time," he says gently, reading my face.

I nod and swallow against the lump in my throat. I could see myself having his child. I can picture a little girl with his dark hair and golden eyes. She'd be a daddy's girl and he would adore her. Her life would be so different than mine was when I grew up up.

"You okay, baby?"

I feel a hand on my cheek, and I shake the thoughts out of my head. I look into his concerned eyes and take a breath before nodding.

"You're moving in?" Nancy asks. The surprise in her voice has me getting up on my tiptoes to look over Kenton's shoulder. I smile when I see the look of approval and the wide smile on her face as she looks between us. "So I'm guessing everything has been sorted out?" She looks at Kenton, who nods. "I knew my boy would fix it." She shakes her head then ducks by Kenton and grabs my hand, pulling me with her to the kitchen.

"What are you doing, Mom?"

"Well, now that it's official, we need to talk about redecorating. This place was okay when it was just you, but now that Autumn's going to be living here for good, we need to make some changes."

"We don't need to talk about that, Mom. Autumn can make any changes she wants to, but we don't need to have a sit-down about it."

"Honey, until you give me a wedding to plan and grandbabies to play with, you're going to have to give me something."

"Jesus. I'm going to the office." He looks at me then his mom and shakes his head. "You gonna be okay here with her?"

"Of course she will be okay with me," Nancy scoffs. "I'm going to get coffee started and call Susan to see if her boys have anything on their schedule." She looks at me then my clothes. "You should get dressed so we can go downtown and head to some stores. I need to get an idea of what you like. I hope we can do the kitchen right away."

"Mom, seriously, slow down," Kenton warns.

"Do you know how long I've waited for you to find a decent woman…someone I could stand being around, someone I would be proud to call my daughter?" She puts her hands on her hips and narrows her eyes. "I want the wedding and the grandkids, but I can't have that right now. So instead, we're going to be redecorating this house so that, when the time comes, you're ready."

"You know that, when me and Autumn get married, it will be up to her to plan the kind of wedding she wants, right?"

"Of course it will be her planning it." His mom shakes her head and starts down the hall.

I stand there in shock, my body coiled tightly. He said *when*, not *if*, we get married, like he knows for sure that it's going to happen.

"Breathe, baby," I hear on a laugh. I look up and my eyes automatically narrow when I see that he's chuckling. "Told you she would be planning a wedding when she found out you were moving in."

"You said *when*." I shake my head.

"What?" His eyebrows come together in confusion and his hand goes to my waist, dragging me to him.

"Nothing."

"When what?"

"Nothing?" I say, and it comes out sounding more like a question.

"Autumn." His tone has my head coming up and my heart beating double-time.

"You said *when* we get married, not *if* we get married," I repeat. The words are circling inside my head.

"Yeah?" His eyes narrow further, making me squirm.

"When, Kenton…you said *when* we get married, not if," I say again, trying to drive home what I'm getting at.

"Of course we're getting married," he says in a tone that makes me squirm.

"What?"

"Babe, what the fuck do you think is going on between the two of us?" He shakes his head, putting his fingers under my chin, titling my head farther back. His mouth touches mine, his teeth tugging on my bottom lip. "You make me crazy." He kisses me. Then his eyes search my face. "We'll talk tonight."

"We don't need to talk," I say immediately.

"You don't need to talk. You just need to listen."

"Joy." I sigh, trying to think of a way to get out of this.

"When I get home, we'll talk."

"I can't wait," I say sarcastically and yell, "Ow!" when he smacks my ass hard. "Your mom's here," I remind him when he gets the look in his eyes that tells me I'm about to get bent over.

"Keep up the smart mouth and I'll fill it with something that will keep you quiet," he whispers in my ear, causing goose bumps to break out over my skin.

"I thought you needed to go into the office," I breathe, closing my eyes.

The image of me on my knees in front of him flashes behind my closed lids. Every time I have tried to take him in my mouth, he's stopped me, saying that he needed to be inside me badly.

My hands slide around his waist and my head goes to his chest, where I listen to the rhythm of his heart. "I'll see you when you get home." I squeeze his waist and feel his lips at the top of my head.

"See you when I get home," he says quietly.

"Okay," I reply, and he kisses me once more before jogging up the stairs.

"You got it bad," Nancy says, making me jump.

I turn around and look at her. Standing in the doorway, she looks me over before looking up the stairs at where Kenton just disappeared.

"I would send you up to get dressed, but he's up there now, and if you go up there with him, I have a feeling neither of you will be back down for a while."

I feel my face heat up and I look at the ground.

"Come have some coffee." She laughs, turning and heading back into the kitchen.

I follow behind, wondering if she gets off on making me squirm.

Once we've had coffee and Kenton comes back downstairs to kiss me goodbye, he tells me that I can message him any time and he'll send someone to rescue me. I would normally laugh about that, but I have a feeling that he's being completely serious.

The minute the door closes behind him, Nancy pushes me up the stairs to get dressed. She lets me know what we're going to be doing, not that she gives me a choice in any of it. I have a feeling that the only way I could disagree is if I pop out a kid or start planning a wedding, and neither of those things is going to happen for a while, so I'm stuck picking out appliances—or at least agreeing with what she picks out.

I SIGH AS I sit down in the booth across from Nancy. I think we've gone to every home improvement store in the state. If I never look at another oven or fridge again, it will be too soon. I feel my phone vibrate in my bag, so I pull it out and slide my finger across the screen when I see that Kenton is calling.

"Hey," I answer.

"Hey, babe. I just wanted to call you really quick and let you know I'm gonna be late."

I feel a frown touch my lips at his words and the anxiety in his voice. "Is everything okay?" I ask softly.

"Sophie's place was broken into when she was home. I'm with Nico and the cops now."

"Oh my God, is she okay?"

"She's fine. A little shook up, but she's all right."

"Who broke in?" I ask in shock.

Nancy grabs my free hand, giving it a squeeze.

"We're not sure, baby. As soon as Nico gets Sophie home, I should be on my way."

"Okay, I'll talk to you then."

"Later, baby."

"Later," I say softly.

My mind goes to Sophie and Nico. I haven't met Sophie yet, but I have met Nico. He looks scary but is very sweet. The two times we've talked, he told me all about Sophie, and I can tell just by the tone of his voice when he speaks about her that he is in love. I can only imagine how worried he is right now.

"Kenton said Sophie's was broken into," I tell Nancy, setting the phone down on the table.

"Oh my," she mumbles. "I'm going to call Susan." She picks up her phone.

I watch as she makes the call, and I know that, by the time the phone is hung up, the Maysons will be on a mission. I'm just not sure if it's going to be what Nico wants. He doesn't seem like the kind of guy who'd want everyone over after something like that.

"Susan's going to call Nico's dad and tell him what's going on. He's a cop and may be able to get some stuff sorted before my son or nephew end up in jail."

I feel my eyes get big. "Why would he go to jail?"

"Honey, Kenton works with cops but isn't a cop." She shakes her head, grabbing my hand again. "He can still be arrested if he does something the police find to be criminal."

"Holy shit." I stand, grabbing my bag, ready to go save Kenton before he gets into trouble.

"Where do you think you're going?" She grabs my hand and tugs me back down into the booth next to her. "Let me tell you something. Kenton will always do whatever he wants. There is nothing his father or I—or now you—can say to change his mind."

"I don't want him to get into trouble," I breathe in distress.

"I don't really believe he will get into trouble, but a mom's job is never done. I will always protect my family."

Her words bring tears to my eyes. She's a great mom who loves her kids. Even with as old as Kenton and Toni are, they are still able to lean on her when they need something.

"You're family now too, honey," she says quietly, "and I will protect you as I would protect my own children. That includes looking out for my son so he can continue to look out for you."

I feel a tear falls down my cheek.

Her hand comes up, holding my face, her thumb wiping the tear away. "Now, what do you say we have some cake?"

"Sure." I nod, swallowing against the lump in my throat.

We sit there in silence while we each eat a large piece of chocolate cake that is so dense that it's more like fudge. I have a large glass of milk with mine, and Nancy has a glass of wine. When we're done, we pay the tab before climbing into Nancy's Jeep.

I don't know why she doesn't say anything, but I know why I can't. My emotions are too exposed; too much has happened today and I need some time to regroup. It isn't until Kenton sends a text telling me that he's on his way home that I feel some of the tension in my belly dissipate. Right then, I know that I'm no longer in like with him; I'm head-over-heels in love with him.

I WAKE UP on a scream when I feel myself being shaken. My throat feels like it's on fire and my skin feels damp with sweat. I look around in the darkness, holding my chest, trying to remember where I am, when the light is switched on and I see that Kenton is looking at me worriedly. I lower my head, covering my face with my hands, taking a few deep breaths as I try to get my heart rate back to normal.

"You were screaming like someone was killing you," he whispers, sliding in behind me.

I feel my stomach drop and my insides twist with anxiety. I haven't had a nightmare in years. When I first left home, I would get them often, but somehow, they stopped. I forgot what it feels like to wake up scared, so scared that I want to turn on every light then hide under the covers.

"Sorry I woke you," I whisper, trying to pull away from his touch, humiliated that I woke him, that he witnessed that.

"Jesus, don't do that. Do not fucking pull away. Not right now. Not when whatever it was you were dreaming about is still clinging to your skin and has seeped into mine."

The bed moves behind me again and my hands are taken from my face. He pulls me down so I'm on my side, facing him, our faces so close that I can feel each of his breaths.

His arms wrap around me and his thigh slides over my legs so I'm surrounded by him. "Talk to me."

I try to sort out what to say to him in my head. How can I possibly explain what just happened when I don't understand it myself? "I don't know if it's a dream or a memory," I say softly after a few minutes. I press my face into his neck and press my body closer to his.

"What happens?"

I take another shuddering breath and shake my head. "I'm in water. It's not very deep 'cause I'm sitting in it and it only comes up to my waist. I have this doll in my hand that has blond hair, and I'm dunking her underwater, singing a song to her." I swallow again, and this time, I feel bile at the back of my throat. "I don't know what happens, but I feel hands on my head pushing me down. I can't breathe and I try to scream but end up sucking in lungfuls of water."

I take a breath just to remind myself that I can. My mom was never a good mom; she was abusive but never left a mark. She always made sure there was never any evidence pointing to her being less than perfect. To everyone who knew us, we lived the perfect life. We had the perfect home, the perfect yard, and she was the perfect mother, who had perfect hair, clothes, and makeup. Everything about her was perfect, and she made sure I was perfect—at least what everyone saw of me.

"Do you think that really happened? That she tried to drown me?" I wonder out loud, feeling his body wrap tighter around mine and his muscles tense. We've talked some about how it was for me growing up. I try to avoid talking about it as much as possible, even though he asks often. I just don't like the look that comes across his face when we do discuss it.

"Do you?" he asks gently.

I take another deep breath, tucking my face into his neck, letting his warmth and smell take away the last of the nightmare. "Yes." I nod, feeling his arms go tighter before he lets me go and gets out of bed, muttering a quiet, "Fuck," under his breath.

"Oh God," I whimper, feeling sick. I sit up, holding the sheet to my bare chest, looking around for quick escape. Tears start to sting my nose and I fight them back, knowing that there is no way in hell I will cry in front of him. Not now.

"Fuck!" is roared, and I turn my head just in time to see one of the new bedside lamps fly across the room, hitting the sliding glass door.

The lamp bursts into thousands of pieces while the door somehow doesn't shatter. "Fuck, fuck, fuck," he chants, pacing back and forth, running a hand through his hair as I try to think of something to do or say to calm him down.

"I'll leave," I tell him quietly, fear settling in my gut.

His pacing doesn't change, and his fists clenching and unclenching tell me everything I need to know about his state of mind. I start to wonder if I do this to people, if I make them want to hurt me.

"I'm so sorry," I whimper.

His head swings my way, and his eyes look me over, going from hard to soft. "Jesus, baby." He comes towards me and I hold up my hand, trying to ward him off. His eyes drop to my hand then move back up to my face. "I would never hurt you."

I know this; I know deep down that he wouldn't, but I just watched him freak out, and that has put some fear in me.

"Never," he repeats, and that's when I notice that my body is shaking so hard that the bed is vibrating. "It was either the lamp or track down your mom and put a bullet in her."

I feel my eyes widen as he shakes his head.

"I would kill her, baby. Without a second thought, I would end her. I know you don't understand, but this is me. I protect the people I love. I hate feeling helpless when I know I can fix this. Knowing that someone who has harmed you is out in the world, walking around, does not sit well with me. It goes against everything I am to let her get away with what she did to you."

"You love me?" I ask, ignoring everything else he just said, my mind zeroing in on that one fact.

His eyebrows rise and he shakes his head. "What do you think we're doing here?"

I swallow and shrug my shoulders at his familiar words.

"Baby, you need to start looking at what's going on around you."

"You never told me."

"I show you every day," he says, looking dumbfounded.

"You should have told me you loved me." I resort to getting angry. Why the hell are guys so damn stupid?

"Love."

"What?"

"I *love* you. It's not past tense. I love you now and will love you until my heart stops beating."

My belly flips and I shake my head. "I'm in a whole lot of love with you too."

"Why didn't you tell me?" he asks, his eyes narrowing.

"I didn't know until today." I shrug, pulling the sheet up higher on my chest.

"What?"

"I didn't know."

"*I* know you love me," he says, and I'm sure he did know, because he knows what love feels like.

"I have loved—*really* loved—only one person, and that was my son." I look around, trying to think of a way to explain it to him. "My love for him was different. It was one-sided and pure of any other emotions. Then, today, you sent me a text message, and when I read that you would meet me at home, something in me clicked into place. I have never had that—a home or someone to go home to. That's when I understood what I'm feeling. You're my home. You're the person I belong to."

"Stop," he growls, and I know that he understands now.

"You're the glue that holds all of my broken pieces together," I say quietly.

"Autumn—"

"You love me for me," I whisper, and I know he's done when he plows into me, his body knocking mine backwards onto the bed, caging me in.

"I said shut it." His mouth comes down on mine, his tongue seeking entrance.

I open my mouth under his. My hands go to his back, feeling his warm, smooth skin under my fingers. His fingers go to my center, where he pulls my panties to the side. Then his fingers run down my slit, causing my hips to jerk at the contact.

"Lift your hips."

I do what he says, raising my hips off the bed. His hands pull my panties down my thighs, his weight leaving me only to drag them off me. As soon as they're gone, his fingers go right back to where they were, making my hips shift and jerk once again.

"I think it's time I get your mouth. What do you think?"

My pussy convulses, sucking his fingers deeper.

"My girl likes that idea," he says, licking up my neck before rolling to his back.

I watch as his hips lift and he pulls his boxers down, kicking them off the bed. His hand wraps around his cock, stroking twice and causing a bead of pre-cum to seep out of the tip. My mouth waters and I lick my lips. His groan has my eyes going to his as I bend forward on my knees to lick the tip. His taste bursts on my tongue, and I want more, so I wrap my hand over his and close my lips over the tip, swirling my tongue around it.

His fingers run over my cheek, around my ear, and down my neck, shoulder, back, and ass before hitting me just right. I moan, taking more of him into my mouth.

"Com'ere," he groans, shifting my hips over his head. The second his tongue touches me, I cry out, forgetting what I'm supposed to be doing. "You stop, I stop," he growls, slapping my ass. I moan, taking him as deep as I can, causing him to hit the back of my throat, which makes me gag.

I can feel his fingers holding me open while he licks and sucks, not missing any part. I feel my orgasm approaching and know that it's going to be huge. My hips start bucking against his face, my hand working fast with my mouth. Do I know what I'm doing? No, but I know him, and I know the noises he makes when something feels good. I know we're both close, but then he lifts me off his face with an order of, "Ride me."

I start to turn to face him, but his hands hold my hips in place.

"Reverse, baby."

I can feel more wetness build between my thighs. One of his hands holds his cock upright, the other wrapping around my hip. I position myself over him and sink down hard. My head flies back and a loud moan leaves my mouth. *I just found my new favorite position.*

The head of his cock hits my G-spot on each downward thrust. His hands slide around my waist, one going up to cup my breast, the other down to roll over my clit.

"Shit. I need a mirror."

I look over my shoulder and down at him. His eyes are at half-mast and his cheeks have a slight pinkness, and I know I did that to him. I made his hot even hotter just by fucking him.

His hand wraps around my hair, pulling my head back, and I hold the position for a minute before leaning forward. My hands go to his shins as I start to ride him hard and fast. I can feel myself getting closer the harder I ride. When his hips start lifting to meet mine, I cry out my orgasm as he grunts his.

"Wow," I breathe into the crook of my arm, where my face had ended up.

"Fuck yeah. Perfection in everything you do, baby."

I smile into my arm before lifting myself off him and turning around to lie against his chest with my chin on my hands. "I love you," I tell him, looking into his eyes, my finger tracing first one eyebrow, then the other, and then around his lips, which I love so much.

"Love you, baby." He leans up, kissing my mouth. "I gotta clean up. You wanna come, or do you want me to bring you something?"

"I wanna come," I smile.

"Smartass." He smiles back, smacking my ass lightly and shaking his head.

I follow him into the bathroom, where he cleans me up before smacking me on the ass as I walk back into the bedroom. I don't even bother saying anything when he does it; I know it's pointless to tell him to stop. Instead, I pick my panties up off the floor, toss them towards the closet, and grab a new pair from the drawer before stepping into them.

"I fucking love those."

I look down at my underwear and feel my eyebrows draw together.

"When the fuck did cotton panties with flowers become sexier than lace shit? Do not fucking ask me, but those are hot, and you in nothing but them is even hotter."

I roll my eyes and pull them up my legs before climbing into bed. "You're such a guy."

"But you love me," he says, and I smile.

"I do. I don't know what that says about me, but I do love you."

"It says you're smart." He turns off the light and pulls me to him so my head is on his chest and his hand can wrap around my hair like it always does when we sleep. "You gonna be able to sleep?"

Hearing the concern in his voice has me pressing closer to him. "I'll be okay. I haven't had one in a long time," I tell him quietly, tracing random patterns on his chest.

"I wonder what triggered it."

"I think talking to your mom last night," I say softly.

"What did she say?" he growls.

"She told me about your work."

"You already knew about my work," he says, confused.

I press closer. "I know, but I guess I never thought you could get into trouble."

"Baby, if we were having this conversation a few years ago, I wouldn't be able to tell you that you have nothing to worry about, but I'm no longer reckless. I take risks, but they are all calculated, and the worst-case scenario is thought of and worked around before every situation." His hand moves to my cheek. "I don't want you to worry about any of that. Things can always go wrong, and if they do, we figure it out when it happens. Yeah?"

"Yeah." I nod against his chest.

"Night, baby."

"Night," I whisper, listening to his heartbeat, letting it lull me to sleep.

Chapter 9

Shit Hits The Fan

"SHHHHH," I WHISPER to the little ball of fur I just set down on the floor of my old room. He whines at me, and I can't help but pick him up again to give him a cuddle. "Sorry, baby, but you need to be in here until I can figure out how to tell Kenton about you," I tell my new puppy before setting him down on the ground.

I was at the mall when I walked past a pet store. I looked into the window of the shop and a little white fur ball caught my eye. He was tugging a large, red chew toy around the pen that was full of wood chips while all the other puppies fought amongst each other. I went into the store to have a closer look at him, and the minute I stood next to the pen, his head came up, his eyes met mine, and I fell in love. He ran to me, his little puppy body so round that he had a hard time running straight. I picked him up and started laughing. He was so wiggly and loveable, and I knew right then that I was taking him home with me.

I look around the bedroom, making sure there's nothing for him to get into while I'm downstairs trying to think of a way to tell Kenton that we got a dog. The last few months have flown by. Not long after I agreed to move in, Kenton and I took a trip out to Vegas, packed up my condo, and put it on the market. When we got home from our trip, Nancy got her nephews to come over to gut the kitchen. It took about a month for them to completely renovate it.

The counters are now dark granite, the appliances are stainless steel, the cupboards are dark wood, and the floors are slate. Nancy wanted to redo the dining room, but after the kitchen ordeal, I was over renovating for a while. We did get a new set for the deck—a large, metal table and six chairs—and we also got a large, round outdoor bed that has a top that flips over to block out the sun. It's the perfect place to read a book or make love under the setting sun, which has happened more than once when Kenton's caught me out there reading.

I come out of my thoughts when I hear a quiet snore. I look down and see that Tubs is sleeping. I shake my head, laying him on his bed before closing the door carefully behind me, hoping that he doesn't wake up until I can tell Kenton about him.

I hear the alarm system sound, letting me know that the front door is open, and I run down the stairs. My feet hit the bottom landing with a loud thud when I jump off the last step.

"You're home," I say breathlessly as soon as his head turns my way.

"I am," he says suspiciously.

I feel myself start to squirm under his gaze, and I dig my nails into my palms to keep from blurting out about Tubs. I need to figure out how to tell him, and I'm thinking a blowjob may ease the blow. A smile twitches my lips at that thought and his eyes start to narrow.

"What's going on?" This time, the words are impatient.

"Nothing," I reply immediately, and his eyes narrow further.

"Then why are you over there and not here?" He points to the floor in front of him.

I go to him like I normally would, lift up on my tiptoes, and tilt my head back, waiting for him to bend to kiss me.

"Okay, what the fuck is goin' on?"

"Um…I… Well, we…um," I start, trying to tell him about Tubs, when all of a sudden, there's a loud bang upstairs and both of our heads tilt towards the ceiling for a second before he looks back down at me. When our eyes meet again, I see hurt hit his eyes. Then rage.

"Stay here," he growls, setting me away from him before I can explain what's going on.

"Wait!" I yell when I see him pull his gun out from behind his back. I run after him up the stairs and yell, "No!" as he pushes open my old bedroom door when he sees all the others are open.

"What the fuck?" he asks, stopping dead, causing me to run into his back.

I slide around him into the room, seeing that Tubs has pulled the lamp off the bedside table and onto the ground. Luckily, it didn't break. I pick him up and pull him into my chest.

"Bad puppy," I mutter, kissing his furry little head.

"What is that?" Kenton asks.

My eyes go to him and I smile. "This is Tubs." I hold him out to Kenton and he wiggles in my hands, his tongue coming out, trying to reach Kenton's face. I look from Tubs to my confused man, who is looking at the dog like he's some kind of alien.

"How did it get here?"

"He got here in my car," I say, bringing him back to my chest, petting him behind his ears when he whines.

"Put him back in your car and take him back to where he came from."

I lift my eyes and narrow them. "I'm keeping him."

"Baby, do you know how much work a puppy is?"

No, I don't know, but I talked to a very sweet girl at the pet store and she made sure I had everything we needed—from food to a rhinestone-studded collar.

"It's a lot of work," he says, watching me.

"But I love him," I pout, tucking his tiny head back under my chin.

His eyes drop to my mouth then to Tubs. "Fuck." He shakes his head then reaches out his hand, petting the top of Tubs's head. "What kind of dog is he?"

"American Eskimo," I whisper as he takes Tubs from my hands and pulls him to his chest. My heart melts at the sight of him cuddling the puppy.

"Okay, baby."

"What?" I ask, thinking, *This is way too easy.*

"We can keep him."

"Really?" My eyes go wide.

"I'll probably regret this after the first time he pisses in the house, but yeah, we can keep him," he says, bending towards me, kissing the smile off my face. "None of that," he tells Tubs when he tries to get in on our kiss.

I laugh and wrap my arms around his waist, looking up into his eyes. "Thank you, honey." I give him a squeeze.

"You owe me."

"Anything you want." I smile and his eyes heat.

"Remember you said that," he says with a wicked grin, but then I remember the look on his face before he ran up the stairs.

"Did you think I had someone here?" I ask him, my eyebrows coming together, thinking the look of hurt I caught.

"No, but you were acting strange, and then the crash happened, so I didn't know what to think."

"I wouldn't do that to you," I tell him softly. The thought alone feels like a lead weight in my gut.

"I know that"—his hand comes up, cupping my jaw—"but sometimes when you have something that seems too good to be true, you start waiting for it to crumble to pieces around you." My breath catches in my throat and tears fill my eyes. "You, Autumn Freeman, are the most important thing in my life."

"Stop," I choke out.

"I love you, baby."

"Love you too," I sob, burying my face in his chest, and Tubs takes the opportunity to start licking me, making my sobs turn into laughter.

Kenton tilts my head back again, kissing me. "Where's his kennel?" he asks when his mouth leaves mine.

"Kennel?" I ask dizzily.

"Where he sleeps," he prompts.

"Oh, I got him a bed." I point to the large, fluffy dog bed that is now in the middle of the floor, where I'm sure Tubs dragged it.

Kenton looks at me then the bed and shakes his head. "Get his leash and collar."

"Why?" I ask, going over to the bags I put on the bed with all his stuff in them. I dig through until I find his baby-blue collar with rhinestone studs and his leash that matches. I turn around, my head bent as I take the tags off both items.

"Hell no!"

I jump at his voice and lift my head. "What?" I ask, looking down at my hands, where his eyes are pointed.

"He's a boy."

"I know," I say, feeling my eyebrows draw together. "That's why I bought blue." I hold up the collar and leash so he can see them better.

"It has sparkly shit on it."

"The girl at the pet store told me they're the 'in' thing. I even got him a couple of shirts that are blue," I tell him.

"Scratch that. We have two stops to make—one to Petco and the next to wherever the hell it is you bought all that crap so we can return it."

"We don't need to return his stuff."

"It was one hundred degrees outside today with eighty percent humidity. He's covered in fur. When the hell would he wear a shirt?"

That's a good point, but I don't want to give in; the things I bought are cute. "He can wear them around the house." I shrug, walking towards him with the collar undone so I can put it around Tubs's neck.

"He's not wearing shirts around the house." He shakes his head, pulling the stuff out of my hand and giving me Tubs.

I turn and watch him go back over to the bags of stuff I bought, look through it, and mutter the whole time. By the time he's done, all he keeps out is the dog food.

"Let's go." He puts his hand on the small of my back, leading me out of the room then down the stairs to his car.

When we get home that night, Tubs has a new kennel, a few toys, and a plain, black leash and collar, but I did make it out of the store with a new harness that has blue hearts on it, much to Kenton's disapproval.

5

"STOP HIM!" I shout, running after Tubs, who is racing away from me with one of my bras hanging from his mouth.

Kenton blocks his path and bends down, picking up the fur ball, who is still gnawing on my bra, and when Kenton tries to take it from him, he starts acting like it's a game of tug-of-war.

"Bad puppy," I tell him, unlocking his jaw with my fingers and grabbing my bra, which is now covered with dog slobber. "It's not funny," I snap at Kenton when his laugher follows me as I go back into the bathroom, tossing my bra into the hamper before going to get a new one out of my underwear drawer.

"I told you having a puppy is a lot of work," he says, walking into the bathroom behind me.

"I know, but he's so cute," I say, putting my bra straps over my shoulders and hooking the clasp behind my back.

He starts to laugh again, but this time, the vibration of his laughter is against me as he slides his hands around my waist. "You sure you gotta go to work?" he asks, kissing the skin of my neck.

"I wish I didn't." I move my head to the side so my neck is more exposed to his mouth.

"Stay home with me."

I hear the plea in his voice and turn in his arms, looking up at his face. I know that, after what happened with Sophie and Nico a few weeks ago, he has been on edge and hasn't wanted me too far away from him, and it's not surprising. Having someone you know and care about kidnapped and then having to help rescue them would do that to anyone.

I've tried to reassure him that nothing like that will happen to me the only way I know how. The cops are still looking for the hit man, but the men who hired him gave their word that I'm not on his list, and as stupid as it may be, I believe them. After all, they are the ones who paid him. Kenton and I talked though, and he knows that, if they catch the guy, I will testify against him for what he did. I never made any deals, and there's no way I could refuse to be the only person to help the families of the five people I watched get murdered in cold blood get justice.

"I love you," I say, coming out of my thoughts. I wrap my hands around the back of his neck and press my mouth to his before he has a chance to reply. If I only knew what was going to happen in a few hours, I would have kissed him a little bit harder and held him a little bit tighter, but that's the thing about life—you never know what's going to happen, so every moment you have, you need to act like it's your last.

"WHY ARE YOU here?" I stop outside the emergency room doors as soon as I see Sid standing there. My heart starts beating wildly as I scan the parking lot, trying to see if there is anyone else around.

"I want to apologize."

"That's not necessary." I shake my head, pulling out my keys as I make my way to my car. I have never been afraid of Sid, but something is off. My insides are twisted into knots. I ended up having to work a double tonight, so the darkness isn't helping with the fear turning in my gut.

"I would never hurt you." the pain in his voice is evident, and I slow down, turning to face him.

As soon at my eyes meet his, a car squeals around the corner of the building, coming to a halt behind Sid, who looks stunned for a second before his eyes get big as he watches a man jump out of the driver's side door and pull a gun from behind his back. I'm frozen in place as I watch the scene unfold in front of me.

"Run!" Sid roars, causing me to come out of my freeze.

I look around, gauging if I should try and make it into my car. I realize I won't be able to get there in time and start to take off on foot towards the emergency room entrance. I hear one shot then a grunt, and

I know it was Sid getting shot. I don't even pause. I keep running, but I don't get far before I'm grabbed around my waist. I start kicking my legs and clawing at the arm wrapped around me, but due to the fabric covering his skin, I can't do any damage.

"No!" I yell as my face is shoved into the hard ground. I feel a gun shoved into my cheek so hard that I know I will bruise. I've heard stories about people coming back from flatlining, but I've never experienced it myself, so I don't know what it feels like, but I swear I die in this moment. I feel two shots as pain explodes in my body, but after that, all I feel is myself floating away.

Kenton

"MAN, KENTON. FUCK." Justin's distressed voice sounds over the line as soon as I put my phone to my ear.

"What?" I ask. I've been on edge all day; something has felt off since I woke up.

It took everything in me to let Autumn go to work. I knew that, if I tried to stop her, she would've flipped the fuck out, but something isn't right. I've been in contact with her all day. She even joked during the last call that I must really miss her, 'cause I wouldn't stop phoning.

"I need you to get to Vanderbilt," Justin says with forced calmness.

My gut tightens, and I know before he even says it that it's Autumn. "Tell me she's okay."

"I don't know, man. I'm gonna meet you there," Justin tells me, and I can feel the pain in his voice as the words leave his mouth.

"I'm on my way," I clip, hanging up, and I race out of the office, jump in my car, and head downtown.

When I pull into the parking lot of the hospital, I see that the news cameras and police cars have settled around the entrance of the emergency room. I spot Finn near the front doors in the crowd. I pull my car into the ambulance parking lot and get out, ignoring the yells from everyone around me. I toss Finn my keys before running into the building.

The minute I make it around the corner, the nurse's station comes into view, and unlike most of the times I've been here, it's completely empty. I run down the hall to where they took Finn the night he had been shot and stop dead when I reach the door. My eyes lock on Autumn through the small, glass window.

Her shirt is off.

Her skin is covered in blood.

Doctors and nurses are surrounding her.

My legs start to get weak and my stomach starts to turn. I swear I feel my life ending as I watch them work on her. I hear, "Code red," from the other side of the door as someone pulls a set of paddles off the wall.

"You can't be here," someone says as I feel a hand on my shoulder and turn my head. "This is a personnel-only area."

"That's his girlfriend."

I look over the nurse's shoulder and see Justin coming down the hall towards us. *Girlfriend?* Yes, she's my girlfriend, but she's also my future…and she is lying on the other side of that door, covered in blood, and they are calling a code red. *FUCK!*

"He's still not allowed back here. You need to wait in the waiting area."

I try to look back in the room, but this time, the nurse blocks the door. "I need to be with her." My voice is gruff to my own ears. As a man who hasn't cried since he was young, I'm shocked to feel wetness on my cheeks.

"I'm sorry, hun, but you still can't be here," she repeats compassionately this time. "Come with me and I'll show you where to wait, and as soon as we know anything, a doctor will be out to speak with you and her family."

Family?

I'm her family.

She's my family.

I'm her goddamn family!

I look at the ground, shaking my head, my hand going to the back of my neck. I can still hear loud voices from the other side of the door, but I can't make out what they are saying.

"I need to be with her," I repeat, but this time, I don't know if I'm saying it for me or for the nurse.

"Those doctors in there will do everything within their power to help her, honey. Right now, you just need to be strong for her."

I don't know if I will ever be strong again if she doesn't make it. I shake my head at my own thoughts. If she doesn't make it, I'm not sure what I'll do. My whole life with her flashes before my eyes—the way she smiles, the look she gets when she looks at me, her kindness and generosity to everyone she meets. All the things we would miss out on, like her wearing my ring, our wedding, her having my child, and the little moments you take for granted every fucking day because you always think there will be a tomorrow.

I knew my own piece of heaven was too much to ask for. I fucking knew it was too good to be true.

"Come with me, hun."

I don't even know that I'm following her until I hear Justin tell her that Autumn's his sister when she asks if there's anyone she should contact. He tells her that he'll call everyone. I don't even know if I'm breathing when my parents show up. It isn't until my mom wraps her arms around me that I feel something.

"She's strong, baby," Mom whispers to me.

"I won't make it without her."

"You won't have to," she replies softly, and I feel her tears seeping into my skin.

I pull away and put my head between my legs, praying for the first time in years. I pray to every god out there or anyone who will listen.

"Are you all the family of Autumn Freeman?"

I stand up immediately, taking in the room for the first time since I got here. My family, some of Autumn's friends, and my men are all sprawled throughout the room.

"I'm her fiancé," I tell the doctor, walking towards him.

His eyes take me in, and then Justin is at my side. "I'm her brother."

"Do you want to talk in private, or can I speak openly in front of everyone present?"

I looked around again at all the people in the room. "We can talk here," I tell him.

"Let me start out by saying she is stable but still in critical condition."

I feel my legs get weak and I let out a long breath.

"She suffered two gunshot wounds: one to the shoulder that hit a major artery and one to the face. The one to the shoulder caused her to lose massive amounts of blood, and the one to the face went in her cheek through her lower jaw, shattering it." He takes a breath. "She's a very lucky woman. Though the injuries are significant, we do expect her to make a full recovery."

I lean my head back, saying a silent thank-you to whoever answered my prayers before looking at the doctor again. "When can I see her?"

"Right now, she's being moved to the ICU. After we get her settled into her room, we will let you know when you can see her."

"Thank you," I mumble.

"She will only be allowed visitors for fifteen minutes at a time, and no more than two people in the room with her." I nod and he keeps going. "Her recovery is going to be a long one. The amount of damage to her jaw alone will take months to heal. I have to tell you…if it weren't for the man who attacked her assailant, this conversation would probably be a lot different."

"What?" I ask, wondering what the fuck I missed over the last few hours while I sat here feeling like my world was ending.

"A man named Sidney Sharp was there when the attack occurred. He was shot in the chest but was able to make it to your fiancée and somehow stop her assault."

What the fuck was Sid doing here? "The gunman?" I ask aloud.

"He got away. The police are looking for him."

I take a breath, letting it out slowly. I need to keep it together long enough to see that Autumn gets better, but then I'm going to track down the stupid fuck and kill him.

"Did Sid make it?" I ask.

"He's in the ICU now but is expected to recover as well."

"Thanks, Doc." I shake his hand then go back to my seat. I lean my head back and close my eyes. Whoever did this is going to fucking die, and I don't give a fuck who or how many people I have to kill to make that happen.

Chapter 10

The Slaughterhouse

Kenton

"They agreed she was off-limits," I remind Justin, sitting back in my chair.

We were going over what happened at the hospital after watching the tapes from the night of the shooting. I hated seeing the video of Autumn getting shot, but it was the only way to know exactly what happened. The video footage was grainy and the images distorted, but I could still make out what happened. Autumn is adamant that the shooter from the club is the guy who shot her, and I will always trust her over anyone else.

It's been two weeks since everything went down. I've been working leads as they come in, but most of my time has been spent with her since she woke up from the medically induced coma they'd been keeping her in. She can't talk because they have her jaw wired closed, but she does recognize everyone and has been able to write things down, and that's the most important thing in all of this.

The first time I saw her after I was let into the ICU, it took everything in me to stay upright. Her head was wrapped in gauze, only her lips and eyes visible. She looked like a science experiment gone wrong. There were tubes and wires attached all over her body, leading to the machines that were surrounding her bed.

I used every muscle in my body to get my legs to move me to her. When I reached the bed, I fell to my knees at her side and dropped my forehead to the top of her hand. I stayed like that for a long time, just thankful to feel the warmth in her hand and hear the sound of her breath.

When I lifted my head and my eyes looked down at her empty finger, I knew I would put my ring where it belonged, where I should've put it months ago, but I had been concerned that I was moving too fast for her. Now, I don't care. I know she loves me, and I know that the love I have for her is something I've never felt for another person and what that meant for us.

So that night, I talked to my mom and she gave me my grandmas' ring, the same one that's been in our family for generations'. The oval-cut sapphire ring has diamonds around the center stone and down the band. It's the ring I knew would sit on the finger of the woman I love since I was old enough to understand its meaning.

I went to the hospital the next day, and like it was meant to be, I slid the ring on her and it fit perfectly. I knew that, when she woke up, she would have a long road to recovery, but I also knew that we were going to go on with our lives together and there would be no more putting stuff off until tomorrow.

"Man, he's the only person I can think of who would have the balls to hurt her," Justin says, bringing me out of my head.

"Get Kai on the phone." I run a hand through my hair, frustrated that this shit is happening. I feel torn between needing to be with Autumn and needing this finished so we can move on with our lives knowing that there is no longer a threat once she's out of the hospital.

"On it." He stands up and leaves the office.

I turn my head and look at Finn.

"Where do you want me?" he asks.

"Go to the hospital, talk to Sid, and see if he told anyone about his visit here."

"Done." He stands but stops at the door. "How's Autumn?"

"She's doing better than they thought she would be at this point."

"What did she think of the ring?" he smirks.

I smile for the first time in hours and shake my head. "She hasn't taken it off and thrown it at me, so I'm taking that as a good thing."

"She loves you, man. You're both real fuckin' lucky." He shakes his head and I see something flash in his eyes before he leaves the office.

I don't know what that was about and don't have time to find out right now, but it looks like, when the water calms, I need to have a sit-down with my boy.

I run a hand over my head before picking up the phone when I see that Justin is calling. "Yeah?"

"Kai will be calling any minute."

"Thanks."

"You heading to the hospital soon?" he asks.

I look at the clock and check the time. "Yeah. They should be moving her out of the ICU today and I want to be there."

"I'll see you there at some point," he mumbles.

Justin has been at the hospital as much as I have. I can tell that the thought of losing Autumn from his life has affected him as much as it has me. He isn't in love with her, but he loves her like a sister and is one more family member she didn't have before but has now.

"See you." I hang up. A few minutes later, I answer the phone, looking at the clock again. "Yeah?"

"I was told you need to speak with me," Kai says, and I lean forward and feel my muscles tense.

"I need you to set up another meeting."

"I'm sorry about your situation, but—"

"Do not fucking tell me you can't get me a meeting," I cut him off, feeling the phone cracking in my hand. "This is my woman. I need this shit done so when she comes home, she knows she's safe. Get me the meeting."

"You're putting me in a very bad position."

"What would you do if this shit happened to your woman?" I growl.

"Kill every single motherfucker who even thought about hurting her," he replies back, his tone dark.

"Give me what I want."

"I'll make the call, but you owe me," he replies.

Kai isn't the kind of guy I like owing favors to, but at this point, I would make a deal with the devil to get what I need. "Thanks, man."

"I'm very sorry about what happened."

I hear the sincerity in his voice, but that does nothing to ease the fury that's been pumping through my veins since this shit went down.

"Me too. Call me when it's set up." I hang up and shove my phone in my pocket before heading to the hospital.

"YOU TOLD ME she was off-limits," I tell the two men sitting across from me. "You said you were putting a leash on your fucking dog." I got into Vegas two hours ago on Sven's private plane after I learned that Paulie Amidio had agreed to have a sit-down with me.

"Do you know who you're talking to?" Paulie Amidio Jr. asks, sitting forward.

His father, Paulie Sr., puts his hand on his shoulder, pulling him back. Anyone can tell they are family. They are both dressed identically in black suits, both have dark hair slicked back from their faces, and both have dark skin and crystal-blue eyes.

"We were under the impression that it was over. Unfortunately for all parties involved, Vincent didn't feel the same." Paulie Sr. starts rubbing the bridge of his nose.

"Where is he now?" I ask. I don't care what the fuck is going on in their organization; the only thing I care about is getting this shit settled.

"My men are looking for him now," he says, and his son nods.

"I need a list of the people he associates with." I will find him myself if I have to.

"Do you think this is Match.com?" Paulie Jr. asks, and it takes everything in me not to shoot him in the fucking head. This little fuck is greedy for power. I saw it during our first meeting, and I see it now.

"Son," his dad says in a harsh tone.

"Fuck that, Pop. This is bullshit," Junior says, starting to stand.

His dad wraps his hand around his arm and pulls him back down into his chair. "This is my fucking family. You do what I say when I fucking say it," Senior tells him, slamming his fist onto the table in front of him. When the younger man's eyes come to me, I see embarrassment and anger, but he covers it quickly, ducking his head. "I'll get you the information you asked for, but if you find him, you bring him to me," Paulie Sr. compromises.

"What are you going to do with him?" I ask, because in my mind, death is the only option at this point.

"That's family business," he says vaguely.

"That's not going to work for me. He put two bullets in my woman. I want him six feet under," I state, trying to keep my cool.

"He won't be a threat to you after I get him." His tone is cold, and I immediately nod.

"I'll be waiting for your call," I tell him, standing and leaving the room.

Kai doesn't follow me out into the parking lot right away, so I take the time to call my mom and check in. She gives me an update about Autumn and Tubs, telling me that both are okay and Autumn seems to be doing a lot better today; she got out of bed and took a shower. That's all great news, but it would be better if I were there to see it for myself. Autumn was upset that I was leaving, and I could see it in her eyes that she was afraid, but I needed to see to this situation myself. I'm not leaving anything to chance.

"TELL ME WHERE the fuck Vincent is," I growl, digging my thumb into the open wound on Alfeo's thigh. I have been at this for over two hours and still have nothing.

I picked up Alfeo outside his place of business in Vegas at a house known for selling pussy. Normally, I would turn my eyes at this, but

Justin got back to me with information, and this house has been on the cop's radar for the last year. They've beentrying to build a case against Alfeo. Seems he has a preference, and that preference is for young girls who are mostly runaways and high school dropouts with nowhere and no one to turn to. He gets them addicted to blow and then puts them to work.

"I'm not telling you shit," Alfeo says as spit and blood fly out of his mouth.

"That's not the right answer." I pull the knife I shoved into his left thigh out and slam it into his right one.

His scream fills the small space, and I shake my head. For a man who acts so fucking hard, he sure as fuck screams like a chick.

"I'm getting really fucking sick of this game. Tell me what I want to know or I'll put a bullet in your fucking head."

"Fuck you." He tries to sit forward, but the ropes around his arms and legs hold him in place.

I pull out one of the guns Sven gave me from behind my back and hold it to the side of his head. "Last chance."

"Like I said before…fuck you," he spits.

I pull the trigger, letting one off into his shoulder. I don't want to give him another chance, but he's been one of Vincent's sidekicks since they were young. I only have three men who've been in contact with Vincent over the last three years, so I don't have a lot of options.

"You shot me!" I make out through his screams of agony.

"And I'll do it again if you don't tell me what the fuck I need to know." I put the gun back to his head.

"I don't have anything for you, you piece of shit!" His eyes go wide with panic.

"Well then, Alfeo, our time here's up." I pull the trigger.

This time, the bullet goes through his temple and his brain splatters all over the wall. *I will never get used to the stench that comes along with killing someone,* I think as I go to the sink, wash off my arms and hands, and then begin thinking about my next move.

"What's next?" Kai asks.

I look at him then Sven over my shoulder. Both of them have been at my side since I left the meeting. They helped me get Alfeo to the basement I brought him to but have stayed back and let me handle this my way. I'd expected Kai to go back to Hawaii, but he came out of the club when I was hanging up with my mom, his face contorted with rage. I didn't ask him what it was about, but I had a feeling the small woman I'd gotten a glimpse of him kissing a couple of minutes before his men had taken her away as we'd gone inside had something to do with that look. Sven, I knew, would have my back. The minute I called him from Tennessee telling him that I needed his plane, he was on it, coming to pick me up.

"We're going to find Carlo to see if he has anything to say," I tell them.

"You gonna kill him too?" Kai asks.

"Yep." I look Kai dead in the eyes without saying anything else. These men are all fucking scum and do not deserve to breathe.

"Just making sure," he says, and I see his lips twitch.

I shake my head and listen as he makes a call to have someone come clean up my mess.

"Do you feel like we've been here before?" Sven asks Kai from behind me.

I ignore them and pull the blade out of Carlo's leg. I tilt my head back and forth, working out the kinks in my neck.

"I told you I don't know where he is!" he shouts and then starts to cry.

"When the hell did men start all this crying bullshit?" Kai asks, stepping forward. "Your man has no loyalty to you. Tell us where he is and this will be over," he says, getting down to Carlo's level.

"So you can kill me? Fuck you!"

"You're going to die one way or another, but think of it this way: you do the right thing and, when you get to the other side, God may have mercy on you," Kai says, but I disagree with him. This guy here is as bad as his friends. He has a history of beating women that goes back ages. His last girlfriend was in the hospital for a month after what he had done to her.

"I haven't spoken to him," he swears.

"Bullshit." I lift the blade I pulled from his thigh and slam it through his chest. He gasps for air, and I can almost visualize his lungs filling up with blood. "Tell me!" I roar, losing patience.

He starts coughing and his body begins to convulse out of control in the chair.

"Now you killed him and he didn't even tell us anything," I hear Sven say, but my eyes are locked on Carlo's mouth as I lip-read the word 'slaughterhouse.'

"Where's the slaughterhouse?" I ask Sven.

His eyebrows come together and his hand goes to his suit's pants pocket. He pulls out his phone and types something in it before looking at me again. "There's a club named The Slaughterhouse downtown."

I pull the blade from Carlo's chest and watch as his body fights for air, hearing Sven ask, "You gonna end him?"

"He'll die." I wrap my knife up in a thick piece of cloth and tuck it into my bag.

"Remind me not to piss you off, Mayson," Kai mutters as Sven laughs.

※

"WHAT KIND OF fucked-up place is this?" I shout over the music as we walk into the club.

The room is dark, with an eerie, red glow. Hanging from the rafters, acrobats of both sexes are naked and dripping blood onto the crowd below them. Around the room, there are spotlights that shine down on different BDSM scenes being played out.

"Well, we now know where they got the name from," Kai says as we make our way through the groupings of people in various states of undress.

After the cleanup crew came and got rid of Carlo's lifeless body, I sent Justin a message and had him look into The Slaughterhouse. His search turned up the name of a woman named Abigail Soscia. She's a twenty-six-year-old woman who has a police record as a prostitute but has been clean for the last ten years. How she got the money to open this place is the information I'm interested in.

We make our way to the bar and Sven leans across, talking to the bartender. Then his eyes come to me and he lifts his chin towards the door at the side of the room. As soon as we make it through the door and head down the hall leading to the bottom of a set of stairs, a guy who I'm assuming is a bouncer comes down the stairs and blocks my path, crossing his arms over his chest.

"Move," I tell him, not in the mood for bullshit. I need to get home to my woman, and the only way I can do that is to get this shit handled.

"No one goes upstairs." He glares. "Go back to where you came from. This part of the building is off-limits."

"Look, I know you got a job to do, but you do not want to piss me off right now."

He raises an eyebrow, obviously finding me lacking.

"A word of advice—move," Sven says, and the bouncer's eyes go to Sven and then Kai before coming back to me.

"Fuck this," Kai says, and his arm swings around my head and cold-cocks the guy right in the jaw. I watch in slow motion as his eyes roll back in his head and his body folds to the floor.

"That's one way to do it," Sven mumbles.

I step over the guy. When we reach the top of the stairs, we see that there are three doors, one on each side of the hall, and a set of blood-red double doors at the end face us. I head straight for them while Sven and Kai stay behind, blocking the first two doors.

I knock once, putting my hand on the gun in the waist of my pants, and I hear something mumbled from the other side, footsteps, and then a lock being turned. The door swings open and a tall woman with dark-red hair, which I can tell is natural 'cause it looks almost identical to Autumn's, wearing a pair of jeans and a black, skintight T-shirt looks at me with wide eyes.

"This area is off-limits," she says.

I scan the room behind her and see that it's an office with a desk, a chair and a couch. I can't see any doors, so I know she's alone.

"We need to talk." I start herding her into the room.

"No, we don't. *Justice!*" she yells, backing up.

I'm sure Justice is her bodyguard who is currently taking a Kai-induced nap.

"Do you know a guy named Vincent?"

Her eyes flash with understanding and she shakes her head, looking around the room.

"Where is he?" I ask as she goes behind her desk, trying to put space between us.

"I don't know," she whispers.

"Where is he?" I roar, my hand going to the top of her desk, sweeping everything off.

Her chest is moving rapidly as her eyes go from me to the floor. I look to where her eyes are pointed and they land on a photo that is now on the floor lying faceup. The painted, black, wooden frame shows off the photo of a little boy, a man who I know to be Vincent, and Abigail. They look like an everyday American family, all of them wearing the same dark jeans and white button-down shirts. They are sitting out in an open field of grass, and Abigail is looking down at her son with a smile on her face that says he is the love of her life. Vincent has a smile on his face as well, but his seems forced, and even through a picture, I can see the kind of man he is, almost like he has no soul.

"How long have you been together?" I nod towards the picture. Her eyes come to me and tears begin to fill them. "He shot my fiancée at close range two times, once in the face and once in the shoulder," I tell her, reminding myself why I'm here. "I won't stop until I get him. I'm sure you know I'm not the only person looking for him. I'm sure members of Lacamo have been here looking for him. I would hate for something to happen to you or your boy 'cause you're protecting him."

Her face softens and her hands wring together. "I found out he was having another affair two weeks ago and kicked him out. Last I heard, he was staying with his latest piece in the penthouse at The Guardian."

I pull my phone out and send a text to Justin. It takes two minutes to get a message back letting me know that the penthouse has been rented out for a little over a week to a woman named Layla Harden. I look up from my phone after reading the message. I have a feeling that anyone who has any kind of relationship with Vincent at this time is in danger. He has screwed over the wrong people, and those people's moral compasses are fucked up.

"You need to get your boy and get out of town for a little while."

"I have a business to take care of." She shakes her head.

"Find someone you—" I'm cut off mid-sentence when there is a loud bang in the hall followed by a lot of grunts.

We both turn towards the door when it's thrown open. I pull my gun as the bodyguard from downstairs crashes into the room with both Sven and Kai trying to hold him back. If this situation weren't so serious, I would laugh.

"Justice, stop! I'm okay!" Abigail shouts, covering her mouth as she watches Kai and Sven attempt to take this guy down.

His eyes go to her, and I can see worry etched in his face. "Get the fuck off me!" he barks, batting Sven and Kai off him. He storms over to her, holding her face and looking her over. "You okay?"

"Yeah," she answers as tears slide down her cheeks. "I have to get out of town."

I watch understanding light across his face, and he nods, looks over at me, and says, "You're lucky I didn't have my gun on me or you would have a bullet in your head."

"Justice." She slaps his arm, bringing his attention back to her.

"Babe," he replies softly, and her eyes lower from his as a light blush creeps across her cheeks. "I know a place we can go. Dex will love it."

"I don't think that's a good idea." She looks away.

"No more bullshit, Abi."

"I told you I can't see you like that," she tells him.

"And I told you I don't give a fuck what you say anymore. I know you feel the same way I do."

"But Dex…" she whispers, closing her eyes.

"I love that kid. I've been a part of his life since he was born. Do not use him as an excuse," Justice growls.

"As sweet as this moment is, we've got shit to do," Sven says, breaking in.

I look at him and nod.

"I'm sorry about your fiancée," Abigail says sincerely. "I know it doesn't make it any better, but I'm sorry, and the Vincent I fell in love with years ago would have been sorry too."

I doubt that, but love is blind.

I turn to look at Justice and pull my card out of my pocket. "If you find you can't keep her and her boy safe, you call me."

His eyes narrow, but he takes the card with a nod of his head.

"Are you going to kill him?" Abigail asks, looking at me.

"No," I say, telling her the truth.

"Amidio is looking for him, and I doubt he wants to have afternoon tea. If I were you, I would find a way to prepare your boy for what's to come," Kai tells her.

She nods and understanding flits across her face before she grabs Justice's hand.

"Let's roll," I tell Kai and Sven.

I WATCH FROM down the hall as the small housekeeper I just paid a thousand bucks walks up to the large double doors at the end of the hall and knocks.

"Housekeeping!" she shouts through the door.

When I see the door open and a woman wearing nothing answer, I make my move, pulling my gun and heading down the hall. The housekeeper runs away and the woman, who I'm assuming is Layla, screams at the top of her lungs when I shove her inside. Vincent comes around the corner with a towel around his waist and a gun in his hand.

"Drop it," I grumble.

"Fuck you." He raises the gun towards me and an almost silent shot goes off from behind my back. He falls to the ground, clutching the hand he was holding the gun with to his side.

I turn my head, expecting to see Sven or Kai, but it's one of Amidio's men who has his gun raised. Kai and Sven are both behind the other three members of Lacamo, looking ready to kill.

"You following me?" I ask.

He shrugs, and I walk over to Vincent, putting my boot to his hand, which is trying to pick up the gun, and I crush a few bones. He grunts pulling his hand to his chest.

"We'll take it from here," one of Amidio's other men says, bringing Vincent to his feet.

His face is now pale from the amount of blood he's lost; I'm sure an artery was hit. One of the men brings over a towel, wrapping it around Vincent's wrist while the others start to clean up the mess.

"We had a deal," I remind them.

"Deal still stands. Right now, boss has some questions for him. We'll be in touch," he says as he and another man drag Vincent from the room while another man talks to Layla, who is crying hysterically.

"Now what?" Sven says, looking between Kai and me.

"Now, we wait."

It isn't until two in the morning that Kai gets a message to head downtown. When we arrive at the location, I'm surprised by the amount of cars gathered outside.

"What the fuck is going on?" Kai asks, looking over at his man, Frank, in the driver's seat. How the hell he got the name Frank when he's Hawaiian and looks like he could be a sumo wrestler is anyone's guess.

"Don't know. You want me to come in with you?"

"Nah." Kai shakes his head, looking around at all the cars. "These men know not to fuck with me." He gets out of the SUV and bends over, pulling something out from under the seat and putting it in the waist of his pants. "Keep it running and use your gun if you have to. If something seems off, leave, get Myla, and head to my parents'."

"You just said they know not to fuck with you," Frank tells him, pulling his gun from his inside coat pocket.

"Doesn't mean they aren't stupid, brother," Kai mutters, slamming the door.

"Myla won't be happy," I hear Frank say as I slam my door.

When we get to the building's entrance, one of the guys from the hotel earlier meets us out front and escorts us inside and down a hall.

"What the fuck is going on?" I ask when we're taken into a large room.

It is full of men of all different ages yelling at the top of their lungs as a man in the center of the room pulls a pair of metal cutters from his pocket and walks to Vincent, who is strapped to a chair. He picks up Vincent's hand and touches each of his fingers with the tip of the clippers before settling on one.

Vincent doesn't even flinch when his finger is clipped off and it rolls across the floor. His body is now black and blue, and he's bleeding from his nose, mouth, and other wounds. I can tell just by looking at him that he's in shock. The good in me fights to the surface, not wanting any human being to suffer like he is, but then I remind myself of the shit he's done and how much pain he's caused and the urge to end his pain is beat back as anger is put in its place.

"You're up next," Paulie Jr. says, walking up to me and handing me a knife. "What's going on?"

"Payback. He betrayed a lot of people, and all those people get their pound of flesh before he's ended," he explains.

"Take this back." I hand him back the knife and pull my gun.

"You can't kill him, and you only get one hit," Junior tells me.

"I won't." I walk past him to the center of the room.

Vincent raises his eyes, but at this point, with the kind of damage that's been done to his body already, I would be surprised if he even understands what's going on. When I reach his side, I put the gun to his shoulder at the same place he shot Autumn. Then I think about her face, the damage that's been done, and how, regardless of how much she heals, every time she looks in the mirror, she will be reminded of what happened. I pull the gun away from his shoulder and walk around to the front of him. My hand moves to his jaw and I pull it open.

"I told you, you can't kill him."

I ignore him, put the gun in Vincent's mouth, and lean it to the side so the muzzle is sitting against the inside of his cheek. I feel a gun come to rest at the side of my head, and I start to say something when Kai comes over and whispers inaudibly to Paulie Jr., making him back up.

"You shot my girl," I say quietly, tilting his head back and forcing his eyes to mine. "You know I could kill your son and wife and you can't do shit about it," I taunt only loud enough for him to hear.

His eyes widen and I know he understands. Before he can respond, I pull the trigger, and blood and flesh spray out across the room and onto some of the people who are standing too close.

A loud cheer goes up as I make my way back to Sven and Kai. When I reach them, I notice a man talking to Kai. He's young—I would guess mid-twenties. He's wearing a suit and his blond hair is pulled back into a ponytail. His posture is casual, but the expression on his face is anything but.

"We good?" I ask, stepping into the mix when the man presses his chest into Kai's.

His eyes come to me and he looks me up and down before looking back at Kai. "Tell Myla I send my love," the guy says, starting to walk off.

I put a hand to Kai's chest when I see a look I've become familiar with over the last few weeks come across his face.

"You don't even get to say my wife's name!" Kai growls, grabbing the guy around the throat.

Wife? I look at Kai's hand and notice for the first time that a very thick band is wrapped around his left ring finger.

"What's going on here?" Paulie Sr. asks, walking up and putting a hand on Kai's shoulder.

"Just making a few things clear," Kai says, shoving the guy away from him. The guy looks like he wants to say something before thinking better of it and walking away. "Let's get the fuck out of here," Kai says, shrugging off Senior's hand.

I look at the older man and give him a chin lift before leaving the warehouse.

"You okay, man?" Sven asks Kai, and he nods, but I notice that his body is still tight and his fingers have started rolling his wedding band around his knuckle. I don't say anything, but I do watch closely as he and Frank have some kind of silent conversation. Sven looks at me and shakes his head, saying, "I'm gonna call and have the plane ready."

"Thanks, man," I tell him, sitting back. I pull out my phone, sending a message to Autumn, telling her that I love her and I will be home soon. It didn't take long for her reply to come through. The simple "*I miss you*" message has me smiling to myself. A few more hours and I would be home with my woman, leaving all this shit behind us.

Chapter 11

Future, Meet Past

Autumn

I LOOK IN the mirror and turn my head to the side, taking in my face. My jaw is still slightly swollen, but for the most part, I have healed completely. I know I'm the one who said that I hated being beautiful, but when I was able to see myself in the mirror at the hospital for the first time, all I could think about was how disgusting I looked. My face was swollen and deformed, my lips cracked from being so dry. It wasn't so much that I cared what I looked like, but I was worried Kenton would see me and the look of love I was so used to receiving from him would turn into something else. I didn't want that.

I should have known better though. The first time he saw me without the bandages covering my face, his hand gently cupped my cheek while his eyes told me everything I needed to know. I knew he loved me before everything happened, but now, I will never doubt it again.

I look down at my hand and remember when I saw my engagement ring for the first time. I was sitting up in bed, my head swimming due to the pain medication I was on, but Kenton was there to see me and I never wanted to go without spending a single second with him. We were talking. Well, he was talking; I was writing everything down on a white board they had given me. My face was bent towards my hand when my eyes caught on something on my finger. At first, I thought it was a bug, but then my eyes focused on the sapphire and diamonds and my breath caught in my throat, making me feel like I was going to pass out from lack of oxygen.

"Breathe, baby," I heard him urge, and I gulped down a lungful of oxygen as my eyes filled with tears. "Will you marry me?" His hand covers mine on the whiteboard before I could write YES. "I already told everyone you're my fiancée, so you have to say yes. Maybe I should take your pen from you so you don't have a say," he mumbled, and I growled. "So what will it be? You gonna make an honest man out of me?"

His hand left mine and I wrote MAYBE in large, bold letters on the board.

"You must feel better if you're fucking with me." He smiled and my heart contracted. "Now, will you please just fucking say yes?"

If I could have smiled, I would have. My head bent and I wiped the board off before writing YES across the whole surface. The smile that lit up his face was one I would never forget until the day I die. His fingers went to the ring, rolling it back and forth on my finger.

"We're getting married," he whispered. I nodded, feeling tears fill my eyes. "Thank you." His forehead touched mine. I lifted my hand and held it against his cheek.

I shake my head out of my thoughts when I hear something coming from down the hall. I peek my head around the corner just in time to see Tubs running with a pair of Kenton's boxers, taking them with him down the stairs. I shake my head and go back to getting ready, figuring that Kenton can deal with him. I hear Tubs bark and Kenton growl, and I start to laugh.

When my eyes go back to the mirror, I see the dimple in my cheek I didn't have before the shooting. My hand lifts and my finger runs over the mark. It's funny how something that seems so innocent can come out of something so painful.

I clear my head and finish getting ready. Tonight is the night I marry Kenton. Well, kind of. When I got out of the hospital, Kenton wanted to go right to the courthouse and get married, but I wanted to at least have his family there to witness us starting our lives together.

He didn't agree with me. He didn't want to put it off another day, so we compromised. We got married two days after I was released, and he promised me that, when I was completely healed, he would throw me a huge reception, where I could wear a dress and he would wear a suit, and that way, I could have the wedding pictures I really wanted.

I finish my hair and makeup, and when I hear someone coming up the stairs, I smile as Tara calls out my name.

"In the bathroom!" I yell, touching up my lipstick.

"Your dog molested me when I walked into the house. I think it's time you got him fixed."

"We can't. Not yet anyways. Only one of his balls has dropped," I tell her, walking into our bedroom.

"Seriously?" she asks, and I can't help the laugh that escapes me.

"Seriously, but don't bring it up in front of Kenton. It's a sore subject."

"What's a sore subject?" Kenton asks, walking into the room, wearing his usual jeans and T-shirt. I cannot wait until later—when I get to see him in his tux.

"Your dog having one ball," Tara teases him.

His eyes narrow and I shake my head.

"What time are you heading to your mom's?" I ask in a rush, knowing what's coming if I don't change the subject.

"I'm leaving now. I just came up to kiss you," he says sweetly.

I smile as he walks towards me. His eyes move from my mouth to my cheek and then to my eyes. I see pain cross his features, but he quickly covers it. He told me the other day that he loves my dimple, just hates what it reminds him of. I can't imagine being in his position, thinking he was going to die. He hasn't talked much about what happened while I was in the hospital, but before he left, I could sense that he was ready to snap at any moment.

Since he got back from Vegas, he's seemed much more at ease. He hasn't told me what exactly went down when he was away, just that I was safe now. I asked about the police and what they were doing, but all he told me was that sometimes justice isn't provided by law enforcement. What that means is anyone's guess.

His mouth touches mine in a soft kiss, bringing me back to the moment. When my eyes meet his, I take a deep breath, willing myself not to cry.

"I guess I'll see you at the altar." I smile, and he shakes his head, kissing me again.

"You're already my wife," he says against my mouth.

"I know," I whisper then start to giggle when I hear Tara making gagging noises. I look around Kenton at her. "You know I have seen you with Finn, right?" I ask her, watching a blush creep across her cheeks.

She and Finn got together while I was in the hospital. She had been in the ER while I was being worked on and was a wreck when they took me to the ICU. Finn found her sitting in the hospital chapel and didn't leave her side. Since then, they have been inseparable. It's funny to watch him with her. He never lets her leave his side when they are in the same room. Life is crazy sometimes. The guy who seemed to take life as a joke has done a complete turnaround.

"Oh, shut it," she growls, picking up a pillow from the bed and tossing it at me.

I laugh and Kenton kisses the smile off my face. This time when he pulls away, it takes a few minutes to pull myself together enough to finish getting ready.

"YOU KNOW YOU don't have to do this, right? We can run away and live on a beach somewhere, drinking from coconuts and using banana leaves as clothes," Justin says.

I look at him and raise an eyebrow. "First of all, that's sick. I don't want to even see you without a shirt, much less wearing nothing but a banana leaf. Second, you're like a brother to me, so that's just weird. And third, I'm already married to Kenton, so it really doesn't matter if I walk down the aisle or not at this point."

I watch his eyes go soft and he puts his arm around my shoulders, pulling me into his side before kissing my hair. "I love you too, sis, and

I'm honored to walk you down the aisle."

"If you mess up my makeup by making me cry, I'm going to kick your ass," I tell him, putting my arms around his waist and laying my head against his chest.

When I was little, I used to wonder who my dad was. My mom never talked about him, and if I did bring him up, she would get pissed, so I learned quickly not to ask questions. Kenton asked me if I wanted him to look for him, but I don't know if I want to do that. When Nancy and I talked about the wedding—or renewal of vows—she asked who I wanted to walk me down the aisle. At first, I said no one, but then I thought about all the people I have gained as family here. Then I thought about Link and wished he would be here to do it, but he was taking care of the club for Sid. Then I thought about Justin, how much he means to me, and how important he is in my life, and I knew it had to be him. We may not be blood, but I know deep down we are family—maybe not in the traditional sense, but in every way that counts.

"All right. Let's go before you get my suit all wet," Justin says as we hear the music begin.

I look at myself in the mirror that's propped up against the side of the door one last time, making sure my dress is still in place. The white lace dress with cap sleeves that drapes under my shoulders hugs my body, showing off every curve until it reaches mid-thigh and bellows out similar to a mermaid's tail. I fell in love with this dress immediately when I tried it on at the bridal shop.

I pull the veil over my face and down around my shoulders, taking a deep breath. Tara looks at me and smiles, and I smile back as she opens the door. I take in the backyard of Kenton's parents' house. There are chairs on the grass, where all of our family and friends are seated so they can watch us say our vows. At the end of the aisle, Kenton is standing under a large arch that's been covered in tulle, lace, and flowers. My breath catches in my throat when I look at him in his tux. He is always gorgeous, but right now, as his eyes take me in, I have to do the same. His broad shoulders are covered in black material that shows off the expanse of his chest and the strength in his arms. His hair looks like he has been putting his hand through it all day, and the dark hue around his jaw that is always visible only adds to his hotness.

He asked me if he should shave, and I told him that, if he did, he wouldn't be getting lucky until his scruff grew back. He laughed and smiled, picked me up, put me on the bathroom counter, and ran his jaw along my inner thigh before looking up and whispering, "Told you you would love it." Then he proceeded to shove his face between my legs, making me scream out his name. He was not wrong; I loved the way I could grab fistfuls of his hair to hold him in place and the way the roughness of his facial hair felt between my legs.

I come out of the memory as I make it to the end of the aisle, and Kenton takes my hand from Justin. When I look into his eyes, his travel down my body and he mouths the words, "Holy shit." I smile bigger and look into his eyes.

"Dearly beloved, we are gathered here today to witness the union of Kenton and Autumn," the pastor says, and my eyes go to him. "Is there any—"

"We're already married, so you can skip the part about anyone not wanting us joined together," Kenton says, cutting the pastor off, and I feel my cheeks get pink as everyone in the crowd starts to laugh.

"Okay, we'll skip that part," the pastor says, looking at Kenton and laughing. He continues the ceremony, and when he asks Kenton if he will have me as his wife, Kenton's eyes come to me and I see the same look in his eyes that I saw the first time he said, "I do." Every ounce of love he has for me is there right on the surface for me to see.

I don't even remember saying, "I do," when my veil is lifted and Kenton takes my mouth in a kiss that is way too hot for all of the people who are there to witness it. His tongue delves into my mouth, his body pressing against the length of mine. One hand is on my ass, his other hand on the back of my head, forcing it to the side so he can get deeper. I moan into his mouth as I feel his erection press into my belly.

The moment is broken when the catcalling and clapping starts.

He rips his mouth from mine and his lips go to my ear. "You're so fucking lucky my whole family's here."

I close my eyes tighter and press my legs together the best I can to temper down the throb that's started in my core. When I open my eyes, I'm almost bent backwards and Kenton still hasn't stood up.

"What are you doing?" I whisper, looking at everyone watching us.

He presses his hips into my waist, letting me know why we're stuck. After a second, he stands us up and wraps his arms around me.

"How long until you can walk without me guarding you?" I ask him while trying not to laugh out loud.

"Glad you think this is funny, babe, but I have no idea how I'm going to make it through the rest of this party. You in that dress is a recipe for blue balls," he mumbles, giving me a squeeze. "If the cameraman wasn't at the end of the aisle waiting to capture this moment, I would say fuck it, but I don't think I want our kids looking at our wedding album one day and asking what's wrong with my pants."

I start to laugh and bury my face in his chest. It takes a minute or two for me to get my laughter under control, and by the time I've calmed down, his hard-on is no longer pressing into me. I tilt my head back and he leans down, kissing me one more time. This time when his mouth leaves mine, his hand goes behind my back and his other under my legs. I squeal as he lifts me into the air, shouting, "My wife!" More applause breaks out and I shake my head, looking out over the crowd at everyone I have come to know and love.

I LOOK AROUND the backyard and smile. It's now dark, and there are twinkling white lights running overhead across the entire area. The center of the yard has been turned into a dance floor with tables set up along the edge, each with a large centerpiece in the middle made out of large glass bowls with candles floating in them and stones at the bottom that match the forget-me-nots and white roses I carried in my bouquet. The whole backyard looks like something out of a romance novel.

"I'm so happy for you and Kenton," November says, bouncing

April, one of her little girls, on her thigh while another runs around us.

Her and Asher's other kids are off running around with the rest of the kids at the party. Kenton told me that the Maysons are trying to take over the world with their offspring, but I didn't believe him until there were kids running around the backyard.

"Thank you," I tell her, smiling at the little girl on her lap. She holds her hands out for me to take her, and I look at November, who nods. "Hi." I smile, looking into her cute little face.

She pats my cheek with her hand then pulls herself closer to me, laying her head against my chest. I feel tears start to sting my nose then look around when I feel someone watching me. My eyes meet Kenton's and his go from mine to the little girl, who is now fighting to keep her eyes open as she plays with the stones of the necklace I'm wearing.

"Looks like you're going to be joining the club soon," November says.

"Oh, no, I don't think so," I murmur before looking down at the sleeping baby girl in my arms then over at Kenton, who hasn't taken his eyes off me. The look in his eyes makes my belly flutter, and the word, "Maybe," comes out of my mouth before I can think better of it.

November starts to laugh, and I look at her and smile.

"Autumn, you're needed out on the dance floor," I hear through the speakers set up around the backyard.

My eyes go to the dance floor, and Kenton is standing there in the center with his hand reaching out to me. I get up from my chair, handing a sleeping April to her mom. I walk to the dance floor, my stomach in knots. When my fingers touch Kenton's, his hand wraps around mine and he pulls me into him just as *All of Me* by John Legend starts to play. Tears fill my eyes as I listen to the lyrics of the song. When Kenton's lips whisper words of how he loves all my curves, edges, and imperfections, my face goes into his chest and the lyrics of the song sing to my soul like they were written just for us.

When the song ends, Kenton looks over my shoulder and nods, and I turn my head to see who he's looking at. Sid is standing off to the side, his hands in his suit pockets. I put out my hand to him and he shakes his head, walking towards me. He saved my life the night I was shot. If he hadn't been there, I have no doubt I would have been shot again. I put my hand in Sid's as I feel Kenton kiss my hair. He still doesn't like Sid, but he now tolerates him.

I finish my dance with Sid and go right to Kenton. His arms wrap around me and I look up into his eyes, saying a silent, "Thank you."

The rest of the night is a complete blur. I don't know if I will ever be able to get my shoes off; they feel like they are imbedded into my feet. I have laughed and danced more tonight than I ever thought possible. When all the men went to the dance floor, I almost fell out of my seat laughing, watching them dance to *Larger Than Life* by the Backstreet Boys. I couldn't imagine a more perfect night.

"You're not going to fall asleep on me, are you?" Kenton asks as he kisses the top of my hair.

"No way. I want to see where we're going for our honeymoon," I tell him, leaning my head back to see his face.

"You won't know until we land."

"What do you mean?" I know they tell you where you're going when you check in at the airport.

"Sven's letting us borrow his plane as a wedding present."

"Wait. So you're telling me we're going on a private plane?" I ask, my mouth hanging open.

"What can I say? I've always been curious about the mile high club," he says with a shrug. A smile forms on my lips and his eyes drop to my mouth. "You like that idea?"

"I kinda can't wait to show you your surprise," I reply.

"If it has anything to do with you naked, then I can't wait either." He bends down, pressing his mouth to mine.

"You'll just have to wait and see," I say breathlessly when his mouth leaves mine.

By the time we get into Kenton's car and head to the airport for our honeymoon, my eyes are so heavy that I'm not sure how I will keep them open. I make it onto the plane and find a seat as Kenton talks to the stewardess and pilot. I can't imagine living the life Sven does, but he always seems so down to earth. I adjust my wedding dress and lean my head back, just wanting to close my eyes for a few minutes before I go take the dress off.

I wake up, feeling a kiss to my lips then forehead. My eyes slowly open and Kenton's face is the first thing I see before I look around, seeing the sun streaming through a set of open doors. Bits and pieces of last night come back to me, but most of it is hazy.

"I missed all the good stuff, didn't I?" I ask.

"You slept like the dead, babe." He chuckles, kissing my nose.

"I even slept through you taking off my dress." I close my eyes in disappointment. I had on a beautiful, strapless, lace bra and panties that matched it. I know he says that he loves my plain undergarments, but even I thought I looked hot in what I had on under my dress.

"I loved the lace, but I prefer you as you are now," he says softly, his hand moving under the sheet along my belly then up, cupping one breast before traveling down to run along the top of my pubic bone. His tongue runs over my nipple and he pulls away, blowing on it and watching as it puckers. "Yes, I love you like this."

He smiles, pulling my nipple into his mouth. This time, the heat has me arching back and grabbing a handful of his hair. His mouth travels from my breast, up my neck, and to my mouth, where he kisses me deeply as his tongue delves into my mouth. His long, thick fingers slide between my folds and down over my clit before entering me, curling up, and then hitting that spot that makes my toes start to curl.

"Yesssss," I hiss.

"Already so hot and wet for me." He bites my earlobe before licking and sucking down my neck. He moves so that his body is over mine and his thighs are pushing mine apart. His hands hold each of mine, pulling them up near my head. I lift up, biting into his chin. His mouth takes mine, and I moan when I feel the head of his cock touch my clit before it lowers, bumping against my entrance. Then the tip slips inside before pulling out, going too far. My mouth pulls from his and I try to lift my hands, wanting to grab his ass to pull him into me.

"Please," I beg.

"So sweet," he whispers, bending his head, biting and sucking one nipple before moving to the other one and torturing it the same way.

My hands are fighting to get free, wanting so badly to grab him. His hands shift to hold on to my wrist, forcing my hands flat down on the bed. His hips shift forward and he enters me again, this time thrusting fast and hard. My hips rise up to meet his, my legs wrapping around his waist.

I start to feel that deep tingle in my core, but just when I know I'm going to come, he pulls out, his hands release mine, and his body shifts. Then his hands push my thighs farther apart and his mouth lands on my center, pulling my clit between his lips. I come on a scream, my hands holding on to his hair as I ride out my orgasm.

His mouth lifts, and before I even come down from my high, he flips me to my elbows and knees and his hand slides up my spine to the back of my neck, pressing my head deeper into the mattress. Then his hands go to my hips and lift them higher, and he surges deep inside on a swift thrust.

"God, yes," I moan and start to get up on my hands when they are grabbed from the mattress, pulled behind my back, and used to pull me back into him so hard that the slapping of his skin against mine causes a slight sting against my ass.

"Give it to me, baby. Give me what I want." He thrusts harder, and this time when I start to feel the pull to come, he releases my hands and pulls me up against his chest. His mouth moves to my ear. His hands separate, one zeroing in on my clit, the other pulling one nipple. I come hard and fast, bucking against him. "Fuck, yes," he mumbles in my ear, his thrusts slowing until he plants himself deep inside me, where I can feel him pulsing.

His hand releases my breast, traveling up my neck and turning my face towards his before he takes my mouth in a deep kiss. He pulls out of me, making me whimper, then flops down on the bed, pulling me down on top of him. I lie there in silence for a few minutes, listening to the sound of water while feeling the slight breeze coming from outside glide across my damp skin.

"Where are we anyways?" I ask, getting up on an elbow so I can look down at him.

"Go look out the door." He smiles, and I debate on whether or not I want to get up before pulling myself away from him.

I find his shirt at the end of the bed and quickly slip it on over my head before walking to the doors. The closer I get to the doors, the brighter it gets outside. My breath catches as I take in the view before me. There is a pink beach that leads to water so blue that it looks like a painting.

"Oh my God," I whisper and feel hands slide around my waist. My hands slide over Kenton's and I tilt my head back so I can look into his eyes. "Where are we?"

"The Bahamas." He smiles, bending down to kiss my mouth.

"Is the beach pink or are my eyes playing tricks on me?"

"It's pink."

"Wow." Who would have thought there was a place in the world with pink-sand beaches?

"What do you say you put on that bikini I saw in your bag and we go snorkeling?" he asks.

I smile and nod before completely turning around in his arms. "Thank you for this." I get up on my tiptoes, press my mouth to his, and then duck under his arm, running back into the room so I can put my suit on. I hear him laugh and the sound only makes me smile bigger.

The rest of our honeymoon is spent either in bed or on the beach. I can't imagine it being any more perfect.

"Babe, get the door!" Kenton yells from his office.

I roll my eyes and drop the shirt I was folding to the bed. "You could say please!" I yell back, bouncing down the stairs with Tubs right behind me. I hear him laugh but don't hear him say please.

We have definitely fallen into the role of a married couple—except I don't cook or clean. We have a housekeeper who comes once a week, and Kenton cooks dinner most nights, because anytime I get near a stove, it's a recipe for disaster.

I swing the front door open and my world tilts. "Mom," I whisper in shock. Before I realize what's happening, her hand is coming across my face in a slap so hard that my head flies to the side.

"How dare you?" she hisses, lifting her hand again. I can hear Tubs going crazy.

"I have never hit a woman in my life, but I will tell you right now. You touch her again and I will put you down," Kenton growls while stepping between my mom and me.

My hand hasn't moved from my cheek. I can still feel the sting of her slap, and my body heats up. My vision blurs—not with tears, but with rage. I have been through hell and she shows up here not out of concern, but out of self-preservation. I know exactly why she's here.

Kenton found my father not long after we got home from our honeymoon. At first, I wasn't going to contact him, but after a long talk with Kenton and Nancy, I decided I had nothing to lose. If he didn't want to talk to me or have a relationship with me, it wouldn't hurt any more or any less than if I didn't reach out to him. So I called him, and to say he was adamant that I was a scammer is an understatement.

It wasn't until Justin sent him a copy of my medical records that he called me back. He told me that my mom told him that I'd died when I was three and that I had been cremated. He said that he still had the urn that he believed my ashes were held in. He explained that my mom moved out of the area they lived in a few days after she dropped off what was supposed to be my remains to him, and he never heard from her again.

"Do not come between me and my child," my mom hisses, trying to get around Kenton.

I don't even know what comes over me, but the rage I have felt since I was young gives me the strength to get around Kenton's body, which I swear is expanding before my eyes.

"How dare I? *How dare I?*" I shriek at the top of my lungs. "I'm sure you're here because my father contacted you. How dare you keep him from me?! How dare you tell him I was dead and let him believe his only child was killed?"

"Do not talk to me like that. I did what was best for you. He was nothing."

"Why? Because he didn't fit into your perfect little world?"

"He was a garbageman," she says snottily.

"And you slept with him for over two years!" I yell, my hand balling into a fist at my side. I feel heat from Kenton at my back, his presence offering me strength. I know that, with him, I will be able to face any demons I have.

"He wasn't good enough for me or you."

"He loved me!" I scream, and without thinking, I smack her. My hand stings from the impact, but seeing the red tinge to her cheek somehow makes me feel better.

Her hand goes to her face and her eyes get big. "You little bitch."

"I'm not that scared little girl anymore, Mom," I tell her when I see her hand start to rise again. "You hit me and I *will* hit you back."

Her hand reluctantly drops to her side and her eyes start to narrow. "He's suing me. After all these years, he showed back up in my life and threatened me. My fiancé left me and it's all your fault."

"I hope he wins, and your ex is obviously a smart man," I hiss, and then I take a step back and slam the door in her face. My heart is beating out of control and I can feel the adrenaline pumping through my system, begging me to open the door and kick her ass.

She starts to yell, and Kenton picks me up, growling, "Stay," before setting me away from the door and opening it. "You're trespassing. I have a gun and will shoot your sorry ass if you don't get the fuck off my property, and don't even think about coming back. There will be a restraining order in place before the night's up." He slams the door closed then puts both his hands to the frame, his head lowering between his open arms.

I can tell by his breathing alone that he's trying to control the urge to go back out there and make good on his threat, whether she's leaving or not.

"I want to kill her," he whispers.

I duck under his arm, put my face near his, and wrap my arms around his waist. "I know," I whisper back. I can feel the anger rolling off him in waves so strongly that it's almost hard to stand. "Do you think she'll come back?" I ask.

"She will never get near you again." He stands, his hands come up to hold my face, and his thumb moves over my cheek, which still feels hot from the slap. "I may not be able to kill her, but I swear she will not have the life she has now by the time I'm done with her."

I can tell that there's nothing I can do or say that will change his mind. I don't even want to try to get him to let it go and let her move on with her life like nothing happened. She knowingly ruined my life—and my father's—and it's going to take a long time to build a relationship with him.

"I need to call Justin. Are you gonna be okay?" he asks after a few minutes.

"I'll be fine," I tell him softly.

He bends down, pressing his lips to mine in a quick kiss. I watch him walk away before heading upstairs to finish what I was doing. I somehow feel like a weight has been lifted and I was given my power back after what happened with my mom.

"It's done," Kenton tells me, coming into the kitchen, where I'm making a peanut butter and jelly sandwich.

I look at the clock, seeing that he has been in his office for about five hours now. When my eyes go to him, I can tell that the stress and anger that were on his face before are now gone. I know that, with him as my man, I never have to worry about anything. He will always work to make the world a safe place for me.

"I love you," I tell him, watching his face go soft.

"I know, babe."

I smile bigger and go to him, wrapping my arms around his waist. "Now what do we do?"

"What do you mean?"

"There are no bad guys after me, and I'm sure you got rid of my mom for good, so now what do we do for entertainment?" I ask, and he starts walking me backwards until my back hits the counter.

"Now, we see how long it takes for me to plant my kid in you."

"Really?" I whisper.

"Hell yeah," he growls back, his mouth crashing down onto mine.

I have to say that I like the way he looks at keeping us entertained.

Epilogue

One Year, Three Months, Six Days, Twelve Hours, Fifteen Minutes, And Thirty-Six Seconds Later. Approximately.

I LOOK IN the mirror, my hands going to my waist, where my stomach has started to expand. I love this. I love knowing that our baby is growing inside me. We were worried for a while after we started trying to have a baby because I didn't get pregnant right away, but the doctors all assured me that sometimes it just takes time. It was worth the wait. When I took that pregnancy test and saw the positive sign for the first time, I thought I was going to pass out from excitement. Kenton just looked stunned, like he couldn't believe it had finally happened.

"Baby, seriously, we're going to be late if you don't move your ass," Kenton says, walking into the bathroom.

Our eyes meet in the mirror and mine narrow. "I would be ready if I didn't puke every ten minutes and pee every five from your child. So if you want to blame anyone for my lateness, you need to look in the mirror."

"Babe, I got you up four hours ago knowin' you get sick in the mornings and you need time to wake up and use the bathroom a million times before we can leave the house."

I feel my eyes narrow further and my fists start to clench at my sides.

"I wanna meet my kid, baby," he says gently, a small smile forming on his lips as his hands come around my waist, his thumbs moving over my bump. All the annoyance I was feeling seconds ago leaves, and then tears start to fill my eyes. "What am I gonna do with you?" he asks, taking in the tears filling my eyes.

"Love me," I say as he pulls me into his chest. These pregnancy hormones are killers. One minute, I feel like I'm on top of the world; the next, I want to kill someone. Luckily, Kenton loves me all the time.

"So today's the big day, huh?" the nurse says, handing me a dressing gown. I look at her and smile, nodding my head. "Well, I'll just let you get changed, and the doctor should be in in a few minutes." She closes the door behind her, and I start to get undressed.

"Are you nervous?" Kenton asks.

I turn to look at him, my eyebrows coming together. "Why would I be nervous?"

"You know, what if it's a girl?" He shrugs.

I smile and start to laugh. All of his cousins have girls; it seems their firsts are always girls. I don't know what's bringing this on now, but we've talked about the sex of the baby before and he's always said that he would be happy with whatever we have as long as he or she is healthy.

"What's bringing this on?" I ask him as I finish getting undressed and putting the gown on before hopping up on the table.

"I talked to Nico last night. He was telling me how different it feels having girls than boys and how, with the girls, he's worried nonstop, but with his boy, his emotions have seemed to even out some."

Nico and Sophie had a little boy a few weeks ago. I'm sure it is different having boys, but I can't imagine it being that different. "So now you're worried?" I guess.

"I think about you nonstop all day long," he says softly, causing my breath to pause. "I just worry that I won't have enough of me left over."

I let out a breath, and my heart lightens. "You have the biggest heart of anyone I know." I hop off the table and go to him, pushing my fingers through his hair. "No matter if we have a boy or girl, I know you will find room for all of us."

His head tilts back and his eyes meet mine. "Love you, babe."

"Love you too." I bend my head down and kiss him just as the door opens and the doctor walks in.

"How are you guys today?" Denise, our doctor, asks.

Kenton stands to greet her with a hug, and Denise smiles and hugs him back with a pat to his cheek. Denise is about seventy years old and should probably retire, but she told me the first time I met her that she will probably be working until the day she dies. She's the same doctor who delivered Kenton and would be delivering our baby if everything goes as planned.

I go back to the table and hop on top, lying back before answering, "We're really good." I smile at her, running my hand over my stomach.

"Well, you look really good, and all the work-ups we did look perfect. I just need to check you over to make sure everything looks okay, and then we can see what you're having."

"Sounds good," I say.

She smiles at me and then Kenton before proceeding with the internal exam. Then she lets me put my pants back on before having me lie back on the bed again. She tucks a paper towel under the edges of my leggings and lifts my shirt farther up, exposing the rest of my stomach before squirting lubricant there.

Kenton comes to stand next to me, wrapping his hand around mine. The loud sound of a heartbeat pulses through the room, and I watch the dark screen next to my head, trying to make out our baby. When I see the figure emerge through the black, tears start to fill my eyes as they always do when I see our child.

"Look at how big he is already," Denise says, and my eyes go to her before my head tilts back so I can see Kenton's face.

"We're having a boy?" I ask when I don't see Kenton react at all. I wonder if he even caught on to what she just said.

"You are." I hear the smile in her voice as Kenton's head tilts down and he looks at me.

"Well, Daddy, what do you have to say about that?" I ask him.

"Thank you." He bends, kissing my mouth. Before he pulls his lips away, he whispers, "I want a girl too. You're right. I have enough room for a lot more."

I nod and lift my head slightly, pressing a kiss to his lips as I feel tears slide down my cheeks. I'm looking forward to sharing that with him.

Three years, one month, six days, twenty-two hours, six minutes, and two seconds later.

"Honey, you need to put her down," I tell Kenton as I walk into the living room.

He's sitting on the couch, wearing a pair of sweats and nothing else. The football game's on the TV, the sound low in the background as our sleeping daughter lies in his arms and our son sits at his side, his head laying against his chest with his eyes closed. Half the time, I wonder if he pretends to be asleep just so he can spy on us. He knows far too much for a three-year-old.

"She just knocked out," he says softly, looking down at her before looking at me again.

I roll my eyes and shake my head, knowing that he's lying. If he's home, the kids are on him. I love seeing him with them, but when he's not home and I have our kids, when I'm alone and they both want to be held all the time, it makes it hard to get stuff done around the house.

"Your mom's on her way over with Viv. They want to look at the backyard and measure to see if they can fit a play set back there."

"She doesn't give up, does she?" he gripes, looking down at Annabelle again.

I know exactly what he's thinking. The minute his mom walks in the door, the kids are no longer ours. They are all Grandma's, and he hates it.

"You have something in common." I smirk.

"Well, seems like she will be useful while she's here after all," he mumbles.

"What does that mean?" I ask, my eyes narrowing as I watch a smirk form on his lips.

"You're gonna find something to do with that smart mouth of yours while Mom takes care of the kids for us for a little while."

I feel a tingle begin and am all of a sudden very anxious for Nancy to show up.

"Strip. Then get on your knees, babe," Kenton grunts, backing me into our bathroom.

As soon as Nancy walked into the house, Kenton handed the kids off to her. I could tell by the twinkle in her eyes that she knew exactly what was going on. Thank God Maz was awake so she couldn't say anything that would have me turning red.

I quickly strip and drop to my knees, watching as Kenton locks the door to the bathroom behind him.

"Finally, she listens," he mumbles.

I ignore that comment and just enjoy watching him walk towards me. His hands go to his sweats, one pushing them down until his cock springs free, the other hand wrapping around himself, stroking as he walks to me.

"Open." His eyes lock on my mouth as I open for him. The second the head of his cock touches my tongue, I moan. "I think you love sucking me off more than I like it, and I like it a whole hell of a lot."

His hand runs down my cheek, his thumb going to my chin. He pulls down on my jaw, making me open more as he slides deeper into my mouth, hitting the back of my throat. His hand lowers, running down my neck then over each nipple, giving them a tug. I moan around him and us one hand to cup his balls before wrapping around the base of his cock, twisting on each thrust, while my other hand goes between my legs.

"Show me how wet you are for me," he demands, and I pull my slick fingers out from between my legs. His hand wraps around my wrist, pulling my fingers to his mouth.

The heat and feel of his tongue on my fingers has me releasing him from my mouth and leaning my head back. Before I can even ask him to fuck me, I'm up and bent over the vanity, his foot kicks my legs farther apart, and I feel the head of his cock touch my entrance. I expect him to enter me slowly, but he surprises me by covering my mouth with his hand as he slams deep in one fast thrust. I scream out, my teeth biting into his palm. His hand pulls my face to the side so he can take my mouth in a deep kiss while he moves rapidly behind me.

"Tilt your ass higher," he says, and I rise up on my tiptoes and put my palms flat down on the vanity, getting more leverage. "Look at us."

My eyes go to his in the mirror and I take us in. His suntanned skin makes mine look creamy white in comparison. His large size behind me makes me look more feminine somehow. My red hair is down, cascading over my shoulders in a wavy mess. We look like we belong on the cover of an old romance novel. His hands move over me before one wraps under my neck, the other holding my breast; the visual alone has my orgasm approaching quickly.

"Come for me. I want to feel it." His words, cock, and hands send me over as I turn my head, pressing my forehead into his neck. I hear and feel him growl his release as his thrusts slow and his hips jerk.

"Love you," I tell him, turning towards the mirror so I can look into his eyes.

"You too, baby," he says, pulling me a little closer to him as I feel his thumb run over the scar on my shoulder.

"Autumn, Anna's diaper needs changing!" we hear Nancy yell, breaking the moment.

I look at Kenton and roll my eyes. Unless the kids are at her house, she doesn't do diapers. She says that she changed enough of them to last a lifetime.

"I'll take care of our girl while you get dressed." He smiles.

"Thanks," I moan as he pulls out.

He turns me in his arms, kissing me deeply before releasing me, grabbing a washcloth, and cleaning us up. After washing his hands, he leaves the bathroom. I stand there for a few minutes looking at myself in the mirror. When I look into my eyes, I see a woman who knows what love is, and that feeling alone has me hurrying to get dressed so I can go be with my family.

"ARE YOU SURE that's him?" I ask, leaning across Kenton, who is sitting in the driver's seat of our truck so I can get a better view out his window.

"I'm sure, baby," he says gently, running a hand down my back.

I look from the young man I'm supposed to be meeting in a few minutes to my husband. "What if he hates me?" I ask. It's the same question I've asked every time we have spoken about this moment.

"No one could ever hate you, and if he does, I'll kick his ass."

"You better be nice," I say firmly. I know him, and he will do just as he says.

"You know I will be. Now, are you ready to go over there?"

"No," I whisper, shaking my head and looking back out the window at the young man.

He's handsome, with dark hair, golden skin, and a long, lean frame that makes me think of his dad. I watch him as he takes a drink of coffee before setting it on the table, lifting his wrist to look at his watch.

"He's waiting for you, baby."

"I'm so scared," I say quietly, sitting back in my seat. My stomach in knots from the anxiety.

"My warrior is never afraid of anything, and if she is, she knows I will be there to fight along with her."

I look into his golden eyes, the same eyes I fell in love with all those years ago, and smile, feeling tears fill my eyes. I have no idea how I got so lucky. I lean forward, this time putting my hand behind his neck and pulling his face forward so I can reach his mouth.

"Thank you," I whisper against his lips.

"Anything for you."

I smile and open the door to the truck, hopping out before he can make it around to my side.

"What did I tell you about waiting for me?" he grumbles, grabbing my hand.

I shake my head but don't reply; we would be arguing for the next hour if I did. We walk across the street, and the second we hit the sidewalk, Dane's head lifts, his eyes lock on mine, and I see for the first time that his eyes are blue.

"Autumn." He says my name, and tears pool in my eyes.

I nod and squeeze Kenton's hand so hard that I'm surprised it doesn't break.

"Kenton." Dane's says, sticks out his hand, and gives it a shake before pulling back. "Can I get a hug?" he asks me, and I feel my body shake but nod anyways.

His arms come around me and I realize how big he is. I would guess his height to be around six two; it's hard to think that he was once growing inside me. Our kids now are still so small being just ten and seven. I start to cry harder and feel myself being transferred from him to Kenton, and as soon as I smell my husband's familiar scent, my anxiety starts to ease and the tears start to lessen. I pull my face out of Kenton's chest and wipe my eyes with the back of my hand.

"Sorry," I whisper, shaking my head.

"It's okay." He smiles, rubbing my shoulder.

Tears sting my nose again as I wonder what his parents must be like to have raised such an amazing man.

"Let's sit down." Kenton says and I feel his hand on my lower back as he leads me to a chair.

"Tell me about you," I say as soon as we're seated.

"Well, I'm in law school and work part time at a firm. I play soccer and run track. Really, I'm kind of boring." He shrugs.

"Do you have a girlfriend?" I ask.

He laughs, running his hand along his jaw. I can't imagine girls his age not falling at his feet.

"What?" I ask when he doesn't reply.

Kenton says, "Babe."

"You sound like my mom," he tells me. Then he looks like he thinks he shouldn't have said that.

"Tell me about your parents," I say softly. I hate that I couldn't raise him, but I hope that the people who adopted him really wanted a child and loved him fiercely.

"Mom's a schoolteacher and Dad's a fireman. They met when my mom's house caught fire and my dad rescued her. They were married not long after they met and started trying to have kids soon after, but it never happened for them, so they gave up and decided to adopt." He shrugs, looking slightly uncomfortable. "Funny thing is, about a week after they brought me home, they found out my mom was pregnant, so I have a younger sister." He smiles, and I can see how much he loves his family. "They're really great parents."

I nod and feel Kenton's hand give my thigh a squeeze. "I'm so happy you had a good childhood."

"Kenton told me a little bit about what happened and why you gave me up for adoption. I want you to know there are no hard feelings or anything." His hand moves to his hair, running through it. "I've had a really great life."

"I'm glad. I just never wanted you to hate me," I tell him quietly.

"I didn't, and I don't. My parents have been upfront with me since I was little, explaining that I was adopted. I was always curious about you, but I have never been upset when I've thought about you."

"Thank you," I whisper, all the fears I've held inside since the day he was taken from me releasing with the words he spoke. I was so worried that he hated me, and I never wanted that.

"Kenton told me you have two kids, a boy and a girl?"

"We do." I smile at him then over at Kenton, who leans in, kissing the side of my head.

"I would love to meet them. And maybe bring my sister with me, if you don't mind."

"I would love that."

"We'll set it up for a weekend when I have time to hang out for a while."

"Okay," I agree with a smile.

He stands and so do I. Then he pulls me in for a hug. I hug him back, memorizing the feeling. He steps back and gives Kenton's hand a shake.

"I'll talk to you soon."

"Talk to you soon," I say as I watch him walk away before facing Kenton.

"Cool tattoo!" I hear yelled from behind me.

I turn around, seeing Dane standing on the other side of the street with his hands in his pockets. I put my finger to the skin behind my ear and bring it to my mouth, kissing it before waving goodbye to him.

We get into Kenton's truck and I lay my head back against the seat before rolling my face in his direction. "Thank you for that."

"Anything for you, babe," he says, and I nod and look out the window as I listen to the truck start up.

I sit forward and put my hand over his on the gearshift. "Anything for you too. You know that, right?"

"You've already given me everything,"

I press my mouth to his and kiss him with every ounce of love I have for him. Then I pull back and get back in my seat. "Let's go home."

"*Home*," he mumbles, squeezing my leg.

I wrap my hand over his and lean my head back, giving a silent thank-you to whoever makes unknown dreams come true.

OBLIGATION

An Underground Kings Novel

Kai's Story

Coming 2015

I feel the sun on my closed eyelids and something sharp poking me in the face. I move my hand, trying to get away from the pain, and whimper when it scrapes against my cheek. I lift my head and run my fingers along the side of my face, feeling something wet. I open my eyes; a light smear of blood is on my fingers. I flip my hand over and see the gaudy ring that is now taking up residence on my ring finger.

"Great." I whisper, closing my eyes and laying my head down again. I prayed earlier when I went to sleep that, when I woke up, the ring I'm wearing now and the man who'd put it there were nothing but a bad dream.

No such luck.

Other books by this Author

Until November

Until Trevor

Until Lilly

Until Nico

Acknowledgements

First, I want to thank God.

Second, I need to thank my fans. You are all amazing! I couldn't ask for any better; You are the reason why I do this.

Next, I need to thank my husband for being my biggest fan and supporter. Your love and encouragement and daily inspiration means the world to me, and without you, I would not have followed my heart and started writing.

To everyone on my team thank you so much.

Mommey and Daddy I love you both.

To each and every blog, reader, and reviewer this wouldn't be anything without you. Thank you for taking a chance on an unknown author. I wish I could name all of you but this would go on forever just know that I love you guys.

To Hot Tree editing. Thank you so much Kayla for all your hard work and pushing through to meet my deadline. I know it was a lot of work but you came though for me. XOXO girl.

To Mickey your so very, very awesome thank you.

To The Rock Stars Of Romance you ladies have been Amazing and I'm so lucky to know and work with you.

To the FBG$ Girls our daily talks and your constant support has made this journey so much better. I don't even remember what it was like before I had you in my life.

To Midian we don't always see eye to eye but I love you woman and I'm thankful for your support daily and thank you so much for helping edit this bad boy.

To Jackie you have made my life so much easier thank you for being such and amazing PA.

To Natasha I heart you hard hookerface I would be lost without your brand of crazy. You make me laugh daily and are always there when I need to talk thank you.

Jessica/ Carrie You girls have been with me from day one and I know in ten years you will still be here I appreciate you both so much.

XOXOXO
Aurora Rose Reynolds

About the Author

Aurora Rose Reynolds is a navy brat whose husband served in the United States Navy. She has lived all over the country but now resides in New York City with her husband and pet fish. She's married to an alpha male that loves her as much as the men in her books love their women. He gives her over the top inspiration every day. In her free time, she reads, writes and enjoys going to the movies with her husband and cookie. She also enjoys taking mini weekend vacations to nowhere, or spends time at home with friends and family. Last but not least, she appreciates every day and admires its beauty.

For more information on books that are in the works or just to say hello, follow me on Facebook:
https://www.facebook.com/pages/Aurora-Rose-Reynolds/474845965932269

Or Goodreads
http://www.goodreads.com/author/show/7215619.Aurora_Rose_Reynolds

Or Twitter
@Auroraroser

Or E-mail Aurora she would love to hear from you
Auroraroser@gmail.com

And don't forget to stop by her website to find out about new releases.

AuroraRoseReynolds.com

ALL AMERICAN ROOT BEER.

8 oz **root beer**

2 oz **Jack Daniel's® Tennessee whiskey**

1 oz **vanilla schnapps**

4-5 **ice cubes**

Garnish with **cherry**

Pour the schnapps, whiskey, and root beer, in that order, over ice. Stir well, and serve with a cherry or two, and for that additional panache, a small American flag pick in the cherries.

Printed in Great Britain
by Amazon